TRENOUTH

Trenouth

Published by The Conrad Press in the United Kingdom 2019

Tel: +44(0)1227 472 874
www.theconradpress.com
info@theconradpress.com

ISBN 978-1-911546-74-0

Typesetting and Cover Design by:
Charlotte Mouncey, www.bookstyle.co.uk

The Conrad Press logo was designed by Maria Priestley.

Printed and bound in Great Britain
by Clays Ltd, Elcograf S.p.A.

TRENOUTH

BEA GREEN

For Emma, my gifted, brave and beautiful girl
and all children suffering from the
autoimmune disease PANS/PANDAS

'Back to her early sea-town home
Scathed, stained after tedious pilgrimages.'

'Dream with Clam-Diggers' by Sylvia Plath

1

The frantic knocking at their front door began at around three o'clock in the morning, in the middle of a Cornish gale force storm.

Elinor had been wide awake anyway. The intense noise, generated by the gusting winds slamming against the crumbling slate cliffs of North Cornwall, made it hard for a city dweller like her to get any sleep.

The seventy-mile-an-hour winds were lashing their small clifftop bungalow. To make matters worse, an external pipe, just outside Elinor's bedroom, had loosened from its fixture and had started to knock irritatingly against the wall. In amongst the shrieking and wailing of the wind, the pipe outside was playing a tappity-tap, tap-tap percussion.

Every so often, as though to mix up the rhythm of the manic orchestra performing outside, the wet spray from the ocean's waves would shatter with a sudden bang against the glass of her bedroom window. Unbelievably, this storm was so fierce the waves were able to reach up and over the steep clifftop at Warren Cove.

Earlier on, when Elinor had looked out of her window at the black November night, she'd seen nothing in the inky darkness but a multitude of white flecks of sea foam, dancing crazily in the wind. On her right hand side she'd spotted a small flashing beacon of white light, flickering bravely in the midst of the opaque night. It had to be the lamp from the old lighthouse at Trevose Head.

Here in North Cornwall, on the edge of the open ocean, the wind was a part of everyday life. Between this home's northern side and the nearest habitation there were thousands of miles of volatile Atlantic water. The ocean led you in a straight line from the small bungalow right across to the North American continent.

Elinor had sat up quickly when she first heard the frenzied thuds at the front door. She wasn't frightened by the wild storm screaming outside her bedroom wall but the fact that someone was out there on a night like this, and thumping on their front door, did scare her.

She felt all her senses sharpen into extreme alertness. Who on earth would be knocking at their door at this time of the night? Given her mental frailty, she could only imagine the worst...

Hidden in the pitch-black darkness of her room she felt her untrustworthy thoughts spiralling out of control, as without any hesitation whatsoever her mind began to fast-forward to horrible scenarios. Within seconds, crazy scenes ran through her head. Ruthless killers were coming out under the cover of darkness to attack them... a deranged rapist was determined to get to her through that front door... or brazen burglars were taking advantage of their isolated location on the Cornish coast.

As the desperate thumping on the door continued, a jolt of burning, red-hot panic made its way down her body. Her heart kick-started into the rapid beat of familiar fear and she could feel droplets of sweat developing on her forehead. She noticed her clenched hands were becoming sticky and clammy as they rested on her thick bedspread. She lifted them up and felt them start to shake and tremble with the adrenaline racing through her veins, just as the rest of her remained rigid and paralysed with terror.

Tense and silent, she stared fixedly at her bedroom door, her eyes widening.

Within the space of what must have been only a couple of minutes, but actually felt much longer to her, she heard the sudden click of a light switch flicking on in the hallway.

For Elinor, who was registering every thumping heartbeat in her chest, time seemed to be extending itself maliciously into an eternity, as if it was slowing down deliberately to prolong the agony of uncertainty and fear in her.

Bright white lines outlined the door into her room, as though the hallway light was reaching out to her, creeping stealthily in through the sharp edges.

And in the midst of the determined hammering on the front door, she heard the steady shuffle of her uncle's slippers, rustling along the corridor's carpet.

Immediately reassured by his comforting presence, she switched her bedside light on and jumped out of bed, scrambling to wrap her thick, leopard print dressing gown around herself and put on her fleece-lined slipper boots.

She quickly yanked open her bedroom door and saw her uncle turning the corner of the corridor as he headed to the front door.

'Leo!'

Her uncle stopped and turned to look back at her.

'Yes, Elinor?'

Bang! Bang! Bang!

The front door was taking a beating.

'You're not going to open the door, are you?'

'Yes, of course I am. Someone's clearly in great distress,' he replied softly, looking steadily at her.

Bang! Bang!

Elinor stared at him in disbelief, trying with difficulty to comprehend why her uncle would think it reasonable to open his front door in the middle of the night to someone unknown and unexpected. Moreover, this was someone who'd evidently decided to appear outside his home in the midst of a gale force storm and at a very unsociable hour.

She knew she shouldn't really have been surprised at her uncle's fearlessness as, according to family hearsay, he'd always been like this. Leo's legendary confidence and courage was possibly one of the reasons that a month ago her mother had decided Elinor should go to Cornwall to stay with her uncle.

These days, Elinor's life was constantly crippled by intense fear. Since Elinor's fiancé had died in a road accident a year ago this fear had somehow managed to take over her life. She wasn't aware initially of its insidious reach but before she'd fully understood the consequences of allowing anxiety to take hold of her mind, it had lost Elinor both her livelihood and her home. She'd had a nervous breakdown and was still, to this day, battling with the debilitating mental health issues associated with extreme anxiety.

A month ago, exasperated at the lack of progress Elinor was making in defeating her demons of fear, her mother had beseeched her to stay with Leo. Elinor's mother had clearly hoped that the distance and the change of scene would bring back the old Elinor. Elinor knew, though, that the old Elinor wasn't coming back. Ever. A large part of her former self had died on the road beside her fiancé.

And now here she was in her uncle's house, on the verge of having a panic attack, and her uncle seemed completely oblivious to her distress.

2

Bang! Bang! Bang!

The frenzied beatings on the door had a renewed sense of urgency, as though whoever was out there sensed their presence, or had overheard them talking.

'Leo, we don't know who is out there,' pleaded Elinor.

Leo smiled at her reassuringly.

'Well, there's only one way to find out, isn't there?' he said calmly. 'I seriously doubt there's any cause for concern.'

To date Elinor had never seen her uncle ruffled or angry. His clear blue eyes looked out on the world with a strange sort of detached placidity. How was it possible one member of the family could be so laid-back and another such a bundle of nerves? It was a complete mystery to Elinor.

Clearly there was a curious mix of genes in their family.

Sometimes she wondered if Leo was so confident and calm because of his imposing physical presence. He was exceptionally tall, broad and strong. As his name implied, he looked like a powerful, if elderly, lion. Elinor, by contrast, was short in stature and had been repeatedly called 'midget' by the boys in her senior school.

Bang! Bang! Bang!

Elinor's erratic mind jumped straight back into the present. As her rambling thoughts dissipated into thin air, she turned her focus once more to the situation at hand.

Leo walked unhurriedly up to the front door and like a frightened mouse Elinor scurried along the corridor in her uncle's wake. When he reached the front door, Leo turned the key firmly in the old rusty lock and pulled open the stiff and ancient wooden door leading into their bungalow.

Elinor peered over the side of her uncle's shoulder.

Six pairs of dark eyes stared back at them.

Standing on the slate steps leading up to their home there were six men with their clothes soaked through with rain or seawater, with no shoes on (for some reason) and looking frightened to death.

'Come in! Come in!' Leo said immediately, inviting them inside, to Elinor's utter horror.

As Leo moved politely back against the wall, Elinor crouched behind the solid figure of her uncle.

The six men didn't move. They just looked back at them in confusion.

After a short moment, Leo waved them in impatiently; the wind was blasting into the house, causing the paintings in the hallway to smack against the wall.

Comprehension flitted across the men's faces, and moving as one close-knit group they walked quickly into the hallway.

Leo shut the door firmly behind the men and turned around to face them.

'Right, what can I do for you young men? By that I mean, what on earth are you doing out there at this time of the night?'

The men didn't reply. They looked blankly at Leo, with absolutely no expression on their faces. They clearly hadn't understood a word he'd said.

3

L eo and Elinor looked at each other in bewilderment.

'I don't think they speak English, Leo,' Elinor said eventually, in a low voice.

Leo looked pensively at the men as they dripped water onto the hallway carpet. Two of them were shivering incessantly. Elinor felt her anxiety slowly ebb away as her heart filled with compassion for them.

'Right, I think we need to get some warm drinks and also some dry clothes. Then I'm going to call the police station and ask them for some assistance,' said Leo decisively.

He turned and walked into the kitchen, filled the kettle quickly and left it to boil.

The men stayed standing, mutely, in the hallway. Despite the fact there was a long wooden bench running along one wall, none of the men had taken advantage of this seating.

Leo glanced at them and then looked speculatively at Elinor, as though unsure of what her response would be to his question.

'Elinor, can you make up some mugs of black coffee? I'm going to fish out some towels and dry clothes for these men.'

Elinor nodded and disappeared into the kitchen, relieved to have something practical to do in this bizarre and surreal situation. She fished out of the cupboard the blue mugs she remembered from her childhood visits to Leo's house.

In those days Leo's wife, her Auntie Lowena, was still alive. Now, ten years after her death, Lowena's everyday feminine touches were missing from the bungalow but Leo had left most things more or less unchanged. These blue mugs had been inscribed with the names of Leo and Lowena's nieces and nephews, as they'd never had their own children.

Elinor put a hefty spoonful of coffee granules in each mug and also a large teaspoon of sugar. Fetching a tray she lined the mugs up and plonked a batch of her uncle's favourite ginger biscuits next to them.

The kettle clicked noisily as it finished boiling and she filled the mugs, making sure she left a space to drop in a dollop of cold water so the hot drink wouldn't scald the men's mouths.

She carried the tray to the dining table. As she walked out of the kitchen and into the corridor she noticed Leo shepherding the men into the bathroom to change their clothes, handing out trousers, shirts and jumpers.

Goodness, thought Elinor, Leo will have nothing left in his wardrobe. She couldn't imagine Leo had a particularly extensive clothing collection. He'd never been personally vain, and working in the fishing industry before he retired hadn't given him cause to be either.

She put the tray on the dining room table and switched the lights on. This room stretched from one side of the bungalow to the other, with windows facing out to the north and south.

The dining room was designed with a dark green and red colour scheme. The sofa, though, was made of worn dark brown leather, with red tapestry cushions scattered on it. The armchairs were all dark green, as was the carpet, but the walls were a lighter snooker table green. The dining chairs were all upholstered in a splash of ruby red fabric. The room had remained untouched from when Auntie Lowena was alive.

A large and unused fireplace, built out of slate, stood against one wall. Next to it was Leo's antique roll-top walnut desk.

Elinor went to the far corner of the room and sat on a dark green velvet armchair, waiting patiently for the others to turn up.

She could hear the men talking amongst themselves in the corridor but, disappointingly, she couldn't identify what language they were communicating in.

Soon she heard the loud rumble of the tumble dryer in the utility room, rotating vigorously as it dried their clothing.

Five minutes later the men followed Leo into the dining room.

4

To Elinor's amusement she found Leo had devised a novel way to communicate with their unexpected guests. He was using silent and overtly theatrical gestures, improvising as he went along.

Leo pulled out a dining chair and signalled with wild gestures that they should sit. The men smiled to themselves but obediently sat down on the chairs surrounding the dining table.

Leo then pulled a chair up to the table and passed around the mugs of coffee and biscuits. Elinor, playing the familiar role of a passive observer, stayed quietly sitting on her armchair at the corner of the room.

She watched the men attentively, noting they all looked to be in their early twenties. Younger than she was, in fact. She'd turned twenty-eight that July.

They were swarthy, clean-shaven men with black cropped hair and they had strong, clearly defined features. Their facial expressions were open and surprisingly calm, given the manner in which they'd appeared.

Elinor looked curiously at them, making those rapid judgements all people make when they meet someone for the first time. She generally found that her intuitive responses whenever she tried to get the measure of someone were strangely accurate.

She was pretty sure her habitual anxiety heightened her

awareness of other people and this in turn made her more perceptive than she'd ever been before. Ironically, this was probably the only positive thing she could take from her debilitating nervousness.

However, these men flummoxed her. Considering the manner of their arrival, she felt no instinctive sense of caution or defensiveness towards the strangers sitting around the table. In fact, she felt strangely relaxed in their presence.

She wondered what language they were speaking in and where their country of origin was. She listened to the guttural sounds of their speech and thought that maybe the men were Middle Eastern, but it was a feeble guess at best.

Leo picked up the house phone, looked up a phone number in his battered copy of the Phone Book and dialled it.

'Hello? Could I speak to the duty officer, please.'

Leo paused impatiently as he listened to the voice on the other end of the phone.

'I need to speak to him now, thank you. I've six men in my house, who don't speak a word of English by the way, and I've no idea where they came from. They arrived at my front door fifteen minutes ago. They were soaked through, with no shoes on, and they need help.'

Another pause.

'We live in a bungalow called Trenouth, at the top of Warren Cove, near Treyarnon Bay.'

Silence.

'OK... They'll be here within the next hour? Right. Thanks.'

Leo hung up and looked across to Elinor.

'They're going to get in touch with the local immigration enforcement officials and get them to come along. I got the impression this isn't the first time they've had to deal with a situation like this.' Leo shrugged his broad shoulders, looking extremely puzzled. 'I've never heard of any problems with illegal immigration here. Never read anything about it either.'

The men, meanwhile, were talking quietly amongst themselves, looking slightly ridiculous in their oversized clothing. There weren't many men around of Leo's shape and build.

'Maybe I should heat up some soup for them? They're clearly hungry,' said Elinor, indicating the empty packet of ginger biscuits.

Leo watched them with pity on his lined face.

'Poor sods. Goodness knows what kind of a life they were living before arriving on our doorstep. I'd guess some soup and bread would be appreciated, Elinor.'

Elinor nodded and walked off into the kitchen.

She pulled out two frozen containers of her chicken soup from the freezer, leaving them to defrost in the microwave. She and Leo didn't have huge appetites, so she tended to freeze portions of her cooked food. While the soup defrosted, she sliced up the remainder of a loaf of bread.

Leo's cooking repertoire, apart from a few seafood dishes, was very limited and it hadn't taken long for Elinor to preside over their meals. She superintended their weekly shopping trips for food at the Tesco in Padstow, and kept their kitchen cupboards amply stocked with supplies. Leo, meanwhile, had accepted her dominance over the kitchen with his usual laid-back sangfroid.

Before long, Elinor was pouring the steaming hot soup into the bowls and putting them up on the serving hatch.

As she looked through the hatch, she saw with hilarity that Leo was still seated at the head of the dining room table, seemingly entirely at ease, even though he couldn't follow a word the men were saying to each other.

The men seemed to be taking this fantastical situation in their stride, unwittingly revealing they'd had plenty of experience coping with the unexpected. They chatted earnestly amongst themselves, cradling their mugs of coffee in their hands.

It was forty minutes before the knocker banged at the front door, announcing the arrival of the immigration enforcement officials.

5

Elinor waited in the dining room with the men, as for the second time that night Leo went to answer the front door. The men had fallen silent as though they had somehow intuitively guessed the presence of British officialdom was about to enter their lives.

A deep, husky voice asked, 'Leo Jago?'

'Yes, that's me, come in please.'

Elinor heard the individuals at the door come into the hallway.

'So you say the men don't speak English?' the husky voice asked in a lowered tone.

'Don't seem to, as far as I can tell.'

'And, just to get our facts right, they arrived soaking wet at your front door?'

'Yes, that's right. I've got their clothes drying in the tumble dryer. Should be nearly done by now.'

'At what time exactly did they arrive here?'

'At ten past three in the morning.'

A pause followed, as though this was all getting scribbled down.

'OK. Would you mind taking us to them?'

All of them walked down the corridor to the dining room.

Leo came in first, as though to reassure the men around the

dining table he was still there. Two individuals, in the distinctive black immigration enforcement uniform, followed him into the dining room. One was a burly man with a beard, who looked to be in his mid-fifties. Next to him stood a petite young lady, with her long blonde hair tied up in a ponytail. In her hand she carried a small notebook.

'This is my niece, Elinor, and these are the gentlemen who arrived unexpectedly, early this morning,' Leo said.

'Hello, Elinor,' said the burly man, nodding at her. 'I'm Steve Maitlin and this is my colleague, Laura Bissell.'

Elinor liked the look of Steve. His warm brown eyes twinkled at her and he had the jovial appearance of someone who was eternally an optimist.

Steve turned to take a better look at the six men around the table and they, in turn, looked back at him apprehensively.

'We'll have to take them to the centre and find a translator for them. Any idea what nationality they are?'

Leo and Elinor shook their heads.

Steve, looking unsurprised, sighed despondently.

'Recently we've been finding more and more young men arriving in small boats,' Laura explained patiently. 'Many of them turn out to be Iranian, strangely enough. We actually think we're only managing to catch a small percentage of them. There are simply not enough of us to patrol the entire UK coastline.'

Steve nodded in agreement.

'There's never been enough of us to fully patrol the main ports, let alone all the isolated bays and harbours around Britain. And at the moment it seems they're going for the quieter entry points,' he said.

'But why on earth would anyone attempt to travel here on a night like this one?' asked Leo, bemused.

'No idea. It's absolute madness...' Steve rubbed his hair in frustration. 'If it hadn't been for the weather, they probably wouldn't have ended up in your house. We suspect most of them have got local contacts to go to, once they arrive here. It's easy enough for illegal immigrants to disappear, once they arrive undetected. The black market is huge in the UK and I'm sure in these parts a few Cornish farmers and fishermen won't be immune from hiring cheap labour, no matter how illegal it is.' Steve shrugged resignedly. 'Everyone's trying to survive, one way or another, including these poor fellows. That's how the cycle goes.'

'It's insane to be out at sea on a night like this. I would even go so far as to say they're lucky to be alive, actually. The ocean beside these cliffs has very strong currents, and it's blowing a gale out there,' said Leo.

Leo looked lost in thought for a minute, while the others glanced involuntarily at the men still sitting at the dining table.

'I wonder where their boat ended up? It could well be smashed into a pulp by now. I'll have a look around the coves once it's daylight,' Leo said. 'I would've thought the south of Cornwall would've been easier for them to reach.'

'Yes, but North Cornwall has had quite a reputation for smuggling in the past, hasn't it?' said Laura quietly. 'You can see why. There are so many hidden coves around the coastline.'

Leo nodded in agreement.

'What'll happen to the men now?' asked Elinor worriedly.

'They'll be fed and given a bed to sleep on,' Steve said calmly. 'We'll have to monitor them until we figure out what their status is. We'll get a translator for them. It'll probably take quite a few weeks to sort out. They don't appear to have any official paperwork on them, which isn't going to make things any easier.'

'They didn't come with any paperwork, as far as I could tell,' said Leo. 'Maybe they left it all on the boat.'

'We'll find out a lot more within a day or two,' said Steve, looking surreptitiously at his watch. 'Right, I think it's time we take these gentlemen off your premises and leave you in peace... You might want to give them their clothes back,' he added, looking at the trousers the men were wearing which, because of their length, were concertinaed up their legs.

Leo went into the corridor and fetched the clothing from the dryer. When he came back through to the dining room, he let the men pick out their garments. One by one, they made their way to the bathroom to change back into their original clothing.

Eventually, all six men stood in a forlorn group by the front door. They waited patiently as the immigration officials said goodbye to Leo and Elinor.

Elinor felt terribly sorry for them. She didn't approve of people trying to enter the country illegally but when confronted with the reality of these young men who'd undertaken a dangerous voyage to this country, all in the hope of securing a better life, she felt incredibly sad.

6

The most striking thing about the following morning was the silence.

The tempest had blown itself out and all was peaceful once more. Even the seagulls were spiralling above the cove silently, almost as if they too were enjoying the calm after the storm.

Elinor didn't wake up until ten and once she ventured out of her bedroom she realised Leo had been up before her. His shoes were gone from the entranceway and his empty porridge bowl was soaking in the sink.

Elinor made herself a strong coffee and wandered through to the dining room so she could look out at the view.

The pale and sickly strands of sun that had made it through the clouds were colouring patches of the sea a bright turquoise green. The rest of the seawater remained a muted grey-blue, reflecting the sky overhead. The clouds weren't moving very quickly because the savage winds from the night before had died down completely.

Elinor sighed to herself as she looked out at the green clifftop. She'd no idea what she would do today.

A middle-aged couple walked past on the other side of the bungalow's Cornish hedge, following the clifftop path, with their spaniel gambolling eagerly ahead of them.

Their Cornish hedge was in actual fact an ancient wall, made of local stone and soil, and with no mortar. But like much of the estimated 30,000 miles of ancient wall in Cornwall it was smothered in vegetation. In the spring, cushions of pink sea thrift covered it, blooming beautifully with a mass of frilly pom-pom flowers.

Elinor stood by the window and watched a large tanker on the horizon. These giant tankers always fascinated her, for no matter how long she stared at them they never seemed to move very far. And yet by the end of the day they'd inevitably vanished over the horizon.

She turned as she heard the key at the front door announcing her uncle's arrival.

Shortly after taking off his boots he wandered to the kitchen. He helped himself to a mug of coffee and came through to the dining room.

'Morning, Elinor! I hope you caught up with your sleep?'

'Yes, I did thanks. I'm just wondering what to do with myself today. What have you been up to?'

'I've been having a little scout around the coves now that the tide's low. I found a small sailing boat wedged against the rocks in Fox Cove. I suspect it's the boat our visitors came in last night. I won't hazard a guess as to whether they owned it or not. The name on the side of it says "La Vague Azur". That suggests it's originally French.'

Leo turned to look out of the window, gazing at the sea in the distance.

'I wonder if the boat travelled all the way from France. It's really very small for such a voyage; it's a pleasure boat if anything. They must've had a competent sailor with them. I can't see how they would've managed it otherwise.'

Elinor assumed that having seen the boat's name, Leo must have descended right to the bottom of Fox Cove. Leo had a head for heights, unlike Elinor.

She'd seen Leo wander up and down the sheer cliffs near his home with the supreme confidence of a mountain goat. Even at the height of the tourist season, very few ventured down into the sheltered coves, because the cliffs were so steep and unstable.

When Leo had been a young boy, his father had taught him all the zigzag cliff paths to follow when descending into the Cornish coves near their house, and to this day Leo still retained this valuable knowledge.

After one futile attempt to climb down the relatively easy descent into Warren Cove, Elinor had given up trying to reach the bottom of any of the cliffs in Cornwall apart from Bedruthan Steps, which, as its name suggested, had a narrow stairwell leading down onto the beach.

In her one failed effort to descend to Warren Cove, she'd looked down at the pebbly beach far below her and she'd predictably panicked. Suddenly, feeling everything spin around her like a merry-go-round, she'd shut her eyes and clung on desperately to the vegetation on the cliff wall. Standing spreadeagled against the cliff face, she'd refused to move.

It had taken her uncle a good twenty minutes, talking to her reassuringly, to calm her down sufficiently to open her eyes again. Eventually, she was able to make her way, carefully, back up to the top of the cliff. It wasn't an experience either of them wanted to repeat.

'Do you think you should let the authorities know about the boat?' asked Elinor, thinking about the stranded vessel.

Leo looked pensive, taking his time to answer, as was his wont. His ponderous and laid-back nature, as always, dictated a reasoned response.

'Yes, I think so. It could help the immigration officials complete the picture. I'll give them a call later on and ask to speak to Steve or Laura. What are you thinking of doing today?'

Elinor shifted uncomfortably under the directness of his gaze.

'I'm not sure. I thought I might go out with the camera and take some photos.'

Leo nodded with approval.

'That's a great idea. I don't think we'll be getting any rain today and the wind has died down. It's a lovely day for some fresh air.'

Elinor smiled at him.

Whether she liked it or not, she was going to have to go out and explore today. Her uncle was a determined man and, like a heavy-duty grass roller, he would patiently squash any resistance out of her.

Given her inherent anxiety, she'd always be reluctant to go out on her own, but as her mother would no doubt have told her, Leo's steady and determined persistence was the best medicine she could get.

With a heavy sigh, she picked up their coffee mugs and went through to the kitchen. Putting them into dishwasher, she then made her way to her room to get changed. The outdoors was summoning her and she had no valid excuses left to make in ignoring its clarion call.

7

Elinor looked across to Treyarnon Bay and fondled the camera in her hands. Her camera was like a security blanket to her because she felt she could hide behind it.

This particular camera was a by-product of her previous vocation when she'd worked as an artist. Two years ago, Elinor had been a successful artist and had used this camera extensively in her work.

It seemed to her a very long time ago.

Unfortunately, since Mark, her fiancé, had died, she hadn't been able to express herself creatively on canvas at all. She hadn't lifted a single paintbrush, despite desperately needing the income, so it was no wonder her mother utterly despaired of her.

She knew countless artists who recreated their emotional traumas on canvas but she wasn't one of them. She didn't want to open the door to what was inside of her head because she was fully aware it was too repugnant and dark to look at. Who would want to buy something born out of the ugliness of despair? Just as they did with conversation, people appreciated the inconsequential and the light-hearted, not the depressed and dreary.

In the days when she'd been actively working as an artist, her Canon camera was her much-valued personal assistant.

Despite how much she liked to draw and paint from life, it was often impossible to capture an entire scene on canvas before the light changed. She often found that within a short time frame, clouds would cover the sun, or the sun would change position, redirecting all the shadows to a different place.

Inevitably, the light changed as the day progressed. A multitude of weather idiosyncrasies could utterly change the landscape in front of her. At times, this could happen, literally, within minutes. By capturing a scene on camera, Elinor found she could finish off a canvas in her studio at her leisure and without losing the essentials of the light on that particular day.

Elinor felt light had affected every part of her paintings. She didn't really see colour, just light and shadow. Brought up in Glasgow, she was used to the lack of sunlight in the winter and the heavy, grey skies, and maybe that was why light was immensely important to her.

She thought it was unsurprising Scotland had produced so many renowned colourist painters: Peploe, Cadell, Fergusson and Hunter. Its harsh climate inevitably created a yearning for colour and light. She remembered how she'd felt during the Scottish winters, when the sun, if it appeared, started to sink rapidly down to the horizon at half past three in the afternoon. The darkness stifled her creativity.

It was then that she relied on her treasured photographs for her artwork. All those images she'd taken in the brighter seasons of spring and summer.

And here in Cornwall she was falling in love with light once more. More than anything she loved the effect of the sky on the seawater. The palette that nature used in the water entranced her. The colours could change radically, depending on the weather and on what lay beneath the surface of the ocean.

On a sunny day, with white sand beneath the ocean, the water turned a bright turquoise blue. If there was seaweed under the water, the sunlight turned the water into a deep blue-green oasis, with tinges of indigo. Cloudy skies could turn it into a range of colours: from a dull slate blue to purple black, from a metallic Prussian blue to a threatening, dark, olive brown.

Sunsets viewed from Leo's little house were also stunning. Then, nature's palette turned to a range of warmer colours to depict the falling sun's demise: from pumpkin orange to coral pink, rose red to buttercup yellow. The clouds would become infused with colour as they captured the sun's dying rays. Elinor would never tire of viewing sunsets from the mound of their Cornish hedge.

Today, as she looked across to Treyarnon Bay, she saw there were a few surfers attempting to make use of the waves curling towards the shoreline. Surfers here fascinated her too and she wasn't quite sure why. Maybe it was the reckless abandon with which they seemed to harness themselves to the thundering waves. The surfers she'd watched so far seemed to have no fear and she envied that.

She decided to walk across Treyarnon Bay, making her way to the rocks straddling Treyarnon Bay and Constantine Bay. From there she'd be able to watch the surfers more closely.

8

There were five surfers in the water vying for the very few surfable waves. The wind wasn't blowing hard, let alone offshore, so the waves weren't so impressive today.

Elinor lifted up her camera, looking at the surfers through her viewfinder, trying to trace their rapid movements as they balanced on a wave. It didn't take long for the waves to peter out, and she felt the frustration of the surfers out there as they desperately tried to get a good run on the feeble rollers coming in.

Ten minutes later, one of the surfers made his way out of the seawater and walked briskly onto the beach, passing close by her without even flicking her a glance of recognition or acknowledgement. She didn't like the look of him. He was heavy set and was scowling fiercely as he stomped past her.

Elinor moved her legs towards her chest protectively as she sat with bent knees on her rock, invariably observing closely everything around her.

The others didn't take much longer to follow the first surfer. One by one they slowly gave up and walked out of the ocean.

One surfer drew her attention because of his colourful surfboard. It looked as though he'd coloured it himself. In awkward, wacky letters, it seemed that the name 'Doc Dude' had been scrawled across it with spray paint.

Elinor wasn't sure she'd read the name correctly, and was so intent on watching the surfboard she hadn't noticed its owner walk right up to her.

She looked up in surprise as his shadow fell over her.

'Hello,' said the surfer quickly, noting the sudden alarm in Elinor's eyes.

Elinor relaxed.

'Hello.'

'I don't think I've ever seen anyone trying to take photographs of us at this time of year,' the surfer said curiously.

Elinor studied him. He had a shock of bleach blonde hair and a face pink and roughened by the icy cold of the seawater. His eyes were a warm shade of brown and his smile seemed to be genuine.

'I'm visiting my uncle and I've enjoyed watching the surfers on the beaches around here. I was just keen to watch you all close-up today.'

'With a camera?'

Elinor smiled knowingly.

'Why, yes! It's a very good camera actually, with a fantastic zoom. It's not the fastest in the world, but it's actually the preferred choice for many renowned photographers.'

The surfer looked at the camera with interest.

'So you're a photographer?' he asked at last.

Elinor paused for a moment.

'No, actually I'm an artist.'

'That's a cool profession. We've loads of artists here in Cornwall. Every village seems to have one. Have you met Barbara Bligh?'

Elinor shook her head.

'She's a well-known artist and she lives locally in St Merryn. Next time you're stopping in St Merryn, you should look her up. She's always happy to welcome fellow artists.'

'OK, will do. I hope you don't mind me asking, but I'm intrigued by the artistic doodle on your surfboard. What does it say?'

The surfer looked at his surfboard and laughed out loud.

'A friend did that for me. It says "Doc Dude", which is what the other surfers call me, because I work three days a week as a GP over in Wadebridge. They like to have me with them out in the water, as it's handy if any of them comes to grief on the waves. By the way, my name's Tony Reece,' he said, reaching out a hand.

'I'm Elinor Campbell.'

As she shook Tony's hand, Elinor felt the icy chill of the sea in his fingers.

Tony shivered suddenly, as though suddenly aware of how cold he was.

'Right, I'd best get going. I've got some warm soup and a cup of tea waiting for me at home. Nice to meet you, Elinor.'

He smiled, nodded at her, and walked quickly to the path leading out of the beach.

Soon it was just Elinor and a few seagulls paddling in the shallow water. She surveyed the landscape around her. The beach was empty and, Elinor realised, surprisingly bleak without the surfers to liven it up.

9

As Elinor walked up the road from Treyarnon Bay to her uncle's bungalow, she saw his garage door was open. Before going into the house she wandered over there, wondering what her uncle was up to now.

She had fond memories of this garage.

In the centre of it was a roughly made wooden table. She remembered it from her childhood. On balmy summer days, her uncle used to drag the table to the sheltered side of the house and they'd eat their meals outdoors. As they ate lunch in the garden they would revel in the luscious sunshine and the oxygenated air of the coast, complacently ignoring the interested stares of the walkers on the clifftop.

Leo had made the table out of driftwood, hand picked from the coves near his house. The garage was filled with an interesting collection of objects from his foraging: small bowls filled with colourful bits of glass, softened and polished by the sea, a worn red and white safety ring float and a lobster pot with frayed rope at one end, amongst other things.

As a child, Elinor used to hope avidly that the lobsters that had been caught in this lobster pot had managed to break free by slicing at the rope with their claws. She'd hated the sight of captive lobsters in the holding tanks at Padstow, with their majestic claws tied up in garish elastic bands.

Those miniature titans of the sea had been captured and were ignominiously waiting to end up as someone's dinner. The thought of them being boiled alive was utterly repugnant to Elinor. More so now that she felt she was herself a miserable prisoner to her fears and insecurities.

She remembered as a child delving into a deep pool of seawater within a cave at Bedruthan Steps, and watching the dark shapes of the lobsters moving across the sandy floor as they tried to escape the blinding light from the torches.

Her mother had scolded Leo for taking them into the cave because by the time they'd made their way out the tide had risen and they'd had to wade their way across to the steps leading up the cliff face. Many people had been caught out by the fast-rising tide at Bedruthan Steps. It was a deceptively beautiful beach with dangerous currents.

Elinor looked at the back of the garage where some old wooden surfboards were stored. They were stacked vertically against one wall and covered in cobwebs. They clearly harked back to a different era. Intrigued with them for the first time, she walked up to the surfboards and traced her fingers down their roughened surface, feeling the texture of the wood under her fingertips.

Elinor smiled as she imagined what the reaction of the other surfers would be if she turned up on the beach with one of these. She couldn't quite believe how much the antique surfboards differed from the ones she'd seen that morning in Treyarnon Bay.

Leo was nowhere to be seen in the garage. As she turned to leave, Elinor glanced briefly at a small collection of objects on the wooden table.

A dark green-brown purse-shaped object was resting on the table. It was a cat shark's egg case, with long tendrils at each corner to anchor it to the sea floor. Elinor had seen a few of them washed up on the beach at Treyarnon Bay.

Next to it was a plastic bucket filled with mussels, giving her hope they'd be having them for dinner later on. Her uncle, having worked with fish for most of his life, was very handy at cooking seafood. The last time he'd picked mussels, he'd astounded her with the way he'd cooked them with garlic, white wine and cream. It had been a meal to remember.

Naturally curvy, Elinor had always watched what she ate, but after living for a year in the private hell of extreme anxiety she'd realised her body shape concerns were petty and futile. Strangely, her anxiety had brought her complete release from hating herself and worrying about her looks.

And now living here, far away from home and by the Cornish coast, she felt freed of all the expectations she'd placed on herself.

10

Elinor left the garage as she found it and went into the bungalow, hoping Leo was home. She felt in need of some company.

Seeing his boots by the front door, she went through to the kitchen and put the kettle on. She wandered into the adjoining dining room and found Leo sitting at his desk, looking through what seemed like a pile of photographs.

'What are you up to, Leo?' she asked interestedly, peering over his shoulder and looking at the large pile of black and white photos.

Her uncle turned and looked up at her.

'Are you back already? That was quick.'

'I've been out for a good hour and a half!' protested Elinor indignantly.

Leo looked at his watch.

'My goodness, yes, time has got away with me today. It's lunchtime.'

'Stay where you are, I'll bring you a cold plate of food. You look like you're busy.'

'Yes, I've been digging up some old photos and diaries. Our chat with those immigration officials got me thinking about the past. Our family members have lived on this spot for hundreds of years, as you know, and they were here when smuggling was at its height in the 18th century. I'm doing my own little bit of research today.'

'Are you suggesting our family was involved in smuggling back then, too?'

'But of course they were,' said Leo impatiently, as though talking to an obtuse child.

Elinor smiled to herself. Sometimes her uncle seemed to forget she was nearly thirty years old.

'The majority of people here in Cornwall, in those days, were dirt-poor miners or fishermen, struggling to make a living. Smuggling was sometimes the only way they could survive,' Leo explained, enthusiastically sifting through the pile of photos. He seemed to have separated many of them into individual piles. One pile seemed to consist solely of various sea caves.

'Quite a few miners were enlisted to build tunnels to the coves, so contraband goods could be moved to shore unseen and avoid the taxman. I'm sure there was one such tunnel built near here... I'm trying to remember what my grandfather told me about it.'

Leo picked a photo out of the pile and lifted it up to show Elinor.

'See, here's a photo of Pepper Cove, just to the right of our bungalow. You can see its long entrance and steep, sheer cliffs. It was the perfect cover for bringing in goods and avoiding the customs officials. Of course, that's why it's called Pepper Cove. Spices were taxed in those days too.'

Elinor gave the photo a cursory glance. She walked past Pepper Cove just about every day and knew it well.

'And we also have Wine Cove, of course, next to Pepper Cove.'

'Now that one must've been a difficult one to negotiate,' said

Elinor. 'It has a great big rock sticking out of the sea, right at the entrance.'

'True,' admitted Leo. 'Although who knows what the coastline looked like back then. These cliffs are constantly crumbling. On the other side of our wall, there used to be a good ten metres of land before the edge of the cliff. Now today, thanks to rock falls, there's probably two metres left, at best. One day, erosion will take this house away with it too.'

Elinor was speechless for a moment, unwilling to entertain the thought for even a minute. A clear vision of their bungalow collapsing through the roof of the cave beneath it was already developing in her head. Realistically, Warren Cove's cave was not yet deep enough for that, but there was no doubt the day would come.

'There's a good chance nothing will happen for another hundred years, though,' Leo added hastily, seeing the look of apprehension on Elinor's face.

'Is it true that the Cornish people in those days used to cause shipwrecks deliberately, by luring vessels into dangerous waters with lights?' Elinor asked, trying to change the subject.

Leo chuckled.

'There's always been myths about wreckers. But that's all it ever was. A myth. For a start, it would have to be one heck of a light to attract the attention of a ship. Ships would be avoiding bright lights anyway, taking them as a warning. Also, back in those days, the last thing you'd want to do is attract the attention of the authorities, which you would do if you walked about the cliffs with bright lanterns.'

Leo pulled out a black and white photo of a tanker caught between the rocks, looking as helpless as the beached carcass of a whale. He passed it to Elinor to look at.

'That shipwreck happened in Fox Cove, in 1969. You can still see the metal skeleton of it these days at low tide. Although it's now covered in seaweed and crustaceans, of course.'

He paused for a minute, as he pondered Elinor's question about the wreckers.

'What's true of shipwrecks in Cornwall back in the 18th century, Elinor, is that the locals, trapped by poverty, were scavengers. As soon as they heard news of a shipwreck, they would race to it, often ignoring the plight of its crew, in order to salvage some of the goods for themselves. They were as avaricious as vultures, fighting amongst themselves and often attacking any customs officials that arrived, with stones or any other weapon that came to hand.'

Leo chewed his lip as he thought about it.

'In those days the authorities didn't have enough customs officials to deal with the problem.' He sighed despondently. 'The officials who tried to intervene, and catch the thieves, were in an unenviable position. Although I'm sure the locals just saw them as fair game.'

Elinor smiled. Leo was a law-abiding citizen. He didn't fit the image of a descendent of crooked and ruthless smugglers. Elinor wondered what kind of smuggling their family had been involved in: brandy, gin, spices or tea? Tea Cove had a nice ring to it, she thought...

Her stomach had started to rumble, so she gave her uncle a pat on the shoulder and went into the kitchen to rustle up some lunch.

11

'So, did you take any useful photos this morning?' asked Leo, as they sat at the dining table, munching their lunch.

Elinor wondered what he meant by 'useful'. She looked suspiciously at her uncle, wondering for a crazy moment if her mother had been on the phone to him, egging him on to get her painting again.

'I mostly sat and watched the surfers who were in Treyarnon Bay,' she said at last, slightly defiantly.

Leo didn't rise to the bait. He calmly took another bite of his ham and tomato sandwich. He had a bad habit of talking through a mouthful of food.

'Ah, yes. Surfing's become extremely popular in Cornwall. The real surfers only surf here in winter, when the tourist crowds are gone and the waves are bigger. However, it can't have been a good day for surfing today. The wind's died down completely.'

Elinor giggled.

'Yes, they weren't at it for long before they gave up. I spoke to one of them. He had a spray-painted surfboard that intrigued me. He said his name was Tony, I think, and that he works in Wadebridge as a GP.'

Leo looked blankly at her, so he'd clearly never met the man before.

'He also said there's an artist called Barbara Bligh living in

St Merryn,' added Elinor, hoping Leo would know who this was. Leo's eyes lit up.

'Barbara Bligh? Yes, I know her. A wonderful lady and a very talented artist.'

Elinor resolutely ignored the twinge of jealousy she felt on hearing him praise Barbara's art. She had to accept her own career as an artist was long gone. She looked down at her hands, holding a half-eaten sandwich, and noted how healthy they were looking these days now that they weren't dried out with white spirit and paint.

'Barbara doesn't exactly live in St Merryn,' continued Leo. 'She has a steading about ten minutes' walk from there. It's buried behind the barns at Blackheath Farm.'

Leo took another bite of his sandwich.

'She had a studio built in the garden four years ago, which caused no end of complaints from the farmer,' he added, once he'd swallowed his mouthful.

Elinor looked at Leo, remembering something he'd told her previously.

'The same farmer you told me to steer clear of? Richard Glynn?'

Leo nodded, pleased she'd remembered.

'Yes, there's always been bad feeling between our family and his. Although now that I think about it, he's at loggerheads with quite a few people around here. He's always resented his family selling off farmland and letting these houses get built on the coast. In those days it was worth nothing, but now any plot by the sea can fetch a small fortune.'

'But that doesn't explain why he should feel badly towards you. It's not your fault your ancestors built this house.'

'I know it's ridiculous. But he's a hot-tempered young man.'

Elinor didn't say anything, hoping the silence would encourage Leo to explain things further.

'There's also the added complication that he's solely responsible for dealing with the rubbish from the caravan park across the road, as well as our bins,' said Leo with a trace of grim amusement in his voice. 'The council doesn't take our rubbish away; he does, and he resents it. He can't do anything about it, as technically it's in the deeds. He owns the field next to our house and the access road. He's been mighty unpleasant when he's come across me dropping off rubbish at the entrance.'

'The surfer said Barbara Bligh likes welcoming people to her home and he gave the impression people drop in on her all the time. Surely that wouldn't be the case if the farmer was a problem?'

'Blackheath Farm is a huge farm. They have wheat crops, cows and the caravan parks in the summer. You'd be unlikely to bump into him. He's a busy man. Besides, her steading's just off the main road out of St Merryn. I can take you there if you like.'

'That would be nice,' Elinor said, smiling at her uncle. 'I might as well get to familiarise myself with the local arts and crafts scene.'

Leo looked pleased.

'Let's schedule that in for tomorrow, then. Today I want to finish having a look through those diaries, and then I'm having a pint at The Farmer's Arms with a few friends. You're welcome to join us,' he invited, as he'd done ever since she'd arrived a month ago.

She shook her head silently. She couldn't stand pubs at the moment. She didn't like watching people getting drunk.

Her fiancé Mark had died at the hands of a drunken driver.

He'd been walking home after work, as he usually did, when he'd been hit. One minute he was walking along the pavement and the next, a car, which had spun out of control, slammed into him. The car had run right over him and knocked down the two-metre high garden wall of a house. The driver was found to have been four times over the legal limit.

And just like that a precious life was snuffed out and, in a domino effect, the other lives connected to it were irrevocably changed.

12

At eleven o'clock the next morning, after doing some grocery shopping, they ambled along a country path to Barbara Bligh's home. Leo knew all the paths within ten square miles of his home. Elinor had realised shortly after arriving in Cornwall that living in one place all your life had its advantages.

She wasn't keen to walk across a field full of cows, but to Leo this was second nature. He made his way nimbly over the tussocks, walking through a wooden gate into the field of cows without a backward glance.

The ground was squelchy and gloopy after the storm, so Elinor was glad she'd put on her wellington boots. The Cornish hedge encircling the field was covered in long grass and plants, which hung limply in the dank air.

Their breath left little puffs of condensation as they walked.

This wasn't the Cornwall Elinor was used to seeing. She'd always visited as a child in the spring and summer months, when the countryside was covered in flowers and the ground baked by the sun until it was hard as a stone.

Today, a wet mist seemed to have descended, coating everything in transparent water beads. Little droplets hung loosely on their hair, their jackets and trousers. The stalks of grass all around them were covered in miniature silver beading, as were the delicate cobwebs stretched across patches of grass.

Even the cows looked miserable. Huddled together at one end of the field, they lifted their noses with interest when Leo and Elinor walked past, their curious, warm brown eyes following their every move. But they didn't seem to have the energy to investigate further on such a gloomy day, much to Elinor's relief.

Within a short space of time, after walking up a narrow gravel driveway, they reached an old stone building, all on one floor, with a tidy garden at the front of it. There didn't appear to be any lights on.

Leo rang the doorbell and waited patiently for a minute or two. Then he tried again.

It didn't seem Barbara Bligh was at home.

Elinor groaned inwardly. She'd been hoping for a hot cup of tea before they set off again back through the mist.

'She must be in the studio,' Leo muttered, making his way round to the side of the house.

Elinor followed docilely behind him.

They walked along a narrow path lined with holly bushes, which Elinor thought was pretty inconvenient for people visiting. She felt the prickly leaves dig into her arms and legs as she walked past, the little barbed stings as unwelcoming as you could get.

At the bottom of the garden, they discovered a curiously constructed building. It was almost oval in shape. The walls were seemingly made of sandstone but there was no roof to it, just a cone created by fitting together triangular pieces of glass. It looked not unlike a glasshouse, but it was so oddly shaped it certainly caught one's attention.

Elinor started to feel a little more sympathetic towards the farmer who'd complained about the structure. It didn't remotely blend in with the surrounding landscape. This studio was garish and eye-catching. Maybe that was the point... Either way, Barbara Bligh must be quite a character, she thought.

Leo knocked with his fist on the door.

'Come in!' said a croaky voice.

They opened the door and walked into the studio.

The first thing that caught Elinor's eye was a three-bar heater attached to a socket in the wall. However, it seemed particularly futile. The temperature in the studio wasn't much warmer than outside.

A tall lady with a mass of curly hair, whom Elinor assumed must be Barbara, was standing before an easel with a couple of paintbrushes in her mouth.

Elinor inhaled deeply. The smell of white spirit and turpentine was awakening a long forgotten yearning in her.

She remembered how, not so long ago, her hands were red and raw because of the strength of the white spirit she used when painting. She began to recall how she often used her fingers to smudge and blend when painting, loosening the oil paint on her canvas with a mixture of turpentine and white spirit.

Elinor looked across at Barbara, suddenly realising that while she'd been reminiscing Barbara had been studying her with interest.

Barbara slowly removed the paintbrushes from her mouth and put them down.

She came forward to politely shake hands with Leo and Elinor, leaving little dabs of yellow oil paint on their hands.

Barbara was dressed in what looked to be a bright purple

overall, but it was hard to tell given the sheer volume of colourful oil paint stains on it.

Thinking back to the past again, Elinor recalled how, often when cleaning up after working on a painting, she'd find paint stains in the most unlikely of places. Sometimes there'd be oil paint smudged across her eyelids, where she'd unconsciously rubbed her eyes. Other times, she'd discover flecks of paint stuck to her hair, or her legs and shoes.

Back then, nothing she owned seemed to be safe, or immune, from the oil paint's insidious reach. Even to this day, her watch-strap still carried vivid paint marks on it. Mark used to tease her about her clothing expenditure, convinced she was unable to paint without destroying her wardrobe at the same time...

Elinor shook off the sharp pain of her memories and smiled engagingly at the eccentric woman in front of her.

Barbara had pink streaks scattered throughout her white hair, in what looked to be a professionally done, expensive hairstyle. Elinor couldn't pinpoint her age. She seemed to have one of those faces that never gets older, with only very fine lines etched around the eyes.

'Hello, and welcome to my studio,' Barbara said with a flour-ish, bowing like an elderly courtier from the 17th century. 'I take it this is your niece, Leo?'

'Yes, indeed. This is Elinor and she's visiting from Glasgow.'

'Glasgow? My, that's a long way away. From what I've heard, they've a great art scene in Glasgow, and the art college there has a fantastic reputation too. It's so sad the building's been decimated twice.'

Elinor nodded politely but didn't comment. To have a famous, iconic building destroyed by fire twice was devastating to most people in Glasgow.

'And Leo says you paint.'

Elinor looked pleadingly at Leo who was, annoyingly, avoiding looking at her.

'Well, not any more really. I used to,' she said reluctantly.

Barbara looked confused.

'What do you mean "you used to"? I think if you're an artist once, you're always an artist. It's in your bones, surely?'

Elinor felt taken aback by her bluntness.

'I've lost interest in doing it these days, I guess.'

Barbara looked utterly shocked, as though Elinor had just spoken a profanity or done something sacrilegious.

Elinor turned to look at the canvases stacked against the wall.

'Are those your paintings? I'd love to see them,' she said, trying to move the conversation to less sensitive subjects.

'Yes, yes. Let me show you them. Some are still barely sketches in oil, as I like to work on more than one project at once.'

Elinor nodded in wholehearted agreement with her statement, because she could see this energetic woman would thrive by flitting from one painting to the next.

Elinor herself had tended to work slowly on just one painting at a time, waiting for each layer of oil to dry out before moulding it into the picture she wanted. Her landscape paintings had been different. She needed to work quickly then, and with more spontaneity, polishing them off later in her studio.

She wasn't sure which subject matter she preferred more: landscape or still life. She'd been master of both. Art critics had described Elinor's artwork as 'versatile' and 'innovative' due to the variety of both her subject matter and brushwork.

Now, though, since her fiancé's death, she felt as though her artwork had happened in a different life or in another world. These days, she seemed to see everything through a panel of glass, strangely emotionally detached and divorced from her surroundings, whereas before she'd been fully immersed in her subject matter.

13

Later on that afternoon, Elinor was given an opportunity to scrutinise Barbara's kitchen. After Barbara had happily shown them her paintings, she'd invited them into her house for a cup of tea. Elinor was thankful for the hospitable offer, as, after spending an hour in the cold studio, her toes were feeling decidedly numb.

Barbara's kitchen was as brightly coloured as her artwork. The paintings in the studio were mostly still life renditions, although some were also folkloric, depicting characters from old Cornish fairy tales. Barbara compensated for the stark realism of her still life paintings by using an unusual palette of bright colours, often blending them into abstract forms in the background.

Her folkloric paintings, meanwhile, were surreal depictions and nightmarish in quality. Elinor felt you definitely needed an acquired taste to appreciate these unusual paintings.

Barbara's kitchen was as unusual as she was herself. The thick walls had been coated with bright yellow paint. The kitchen units and dining table were very modern but the dresser belonged in an old farmhouse. Hanging on the hooks, and leaning on the shelves, there were ceramic plates and mugs that had clearly been hand-painted in a warmer climate. Each was different from its neighbour; it looked as though Barbara had bought them all at random, on her travels.

The floor was made up of old terracotta tiles, worn with age.

Elinor shivered. Clearly Barbara was accustomed to the cold. The temperature in the kitchen wasn't much different to that of the studio outside. Barbara, noting her shivers, stood up and threw two pieces of wood into the wood burner in the kitchen. She then lit the crumpled newspaper underneath the wood with a match.

'It won't take long to warm up the room,' Barbara reassured her.

Elinor could sense Leo silently mocking her for being a city girl. Of course, he'd always see her as someone who was softened by having every available comfort at her disposal. His attitude made sense when you realised he'd spent his entire life living right next to the Atlantic Ocean.

She hugged her mug of tea to her body, in a hopeless effort to keep warm, and tried to focus her mind on the conversation taking place between Leo and Barbara. Leo was telling Barbara about their unexpected visitors from two nights ago.

Barbara had bent forward, eagerly listening to Leo, seemingly both intrigued and concerned in equal measure. She pulled her bright pink glasses down from her head and put them on as if she wanted to observe Leo a little more closely. After Leo had finished talking, Barbara put down her mug of tea.

'I've heard an interesting story from a neighbour of yours, Leo. She lives in a cottage right next to Treyarnon Bay, at the bottom of the road. What's she called again?'

Barbara put her hand to her forehead, in dismay at her forgetfulness. Leo and Elinor waited patiently for her to continue.

'Sheila Burns... That's right! Anyway, Sheila says she was

woken up one night with the noise of a dirty white van parking next to the wheat field. She doesn't sleep well and she's heard, and seen, this same van arriving late at night, maybe four or five times since the summer. She says she's overheard people speaking a foreign language too, the nights when the van's been there.'

Elinor and Leo stared blankly at her for a moment, struggling to comprehend what Barbara was trying to imply. Was she suggesting there was a people-smuggling operation taking place at the bottom of their road? Leo rubbed his eyes as if all this conversation was wearing him out.

'I don't understand, Barbara. Are you assuming there's a connection between those young men arriving on our doorstep and this white van?' asked Leo caustically. 'I have to say, it sounds like a fantastic "fake news", right-wing conspiracy theory to me. From what I can make out, the boats these young men are using aren't equipped to travel far. Most of them seem to be aiming for Kent.'

Barbara didn't say anything in response to Leo's scathing rebuttal of what she'd told him. She looked slightly abashed at having propounded such a wacky assumption. Elinor couldn't help reluctantly agreeing with Leo, even though she didn't want to disparage Barbara's theory as Leo seemed to have done without a second thought.

'Barbara, are you originally from Cornwall?' Elinor asked at last, breaking the uncomfortable silence.

'Yes, I am. Although I did spend five years travelling around the south of Spain in a camper van. In the interests of my art, of course,' she said, smiling wryly. 'I was in my early twenties when I did that. I'm too old for that kind of caper now. My mother left me this steading and I've been here ever since. Not very adventurous, maybe, but I escape to other places, mentally, with my art.'

'I just wondered where you got these gorgeous plates and mugs.'

Barbara stretched her neck back so she could look up at her dresser.

'Oh, those... I do still go on short holidays to Italy, Spain or Portugal. Usually with friends. I've got into the habit of bringing back anything that catches my eye. I've built up quite a collection over the years. There are worse vices one could have, I guess.'

Barbara shrugged and turned her piercing black eyes back to Elinor.

'What about you? Where did you train to be an artist?'

'Me?' asked Elinor, taken aback.

Leo and Barbara laughed raucously at the inanity of her question. Elinor watched the pair of them as they sat smitten with laughter, and thought they reminded her of Tweedledum and Tweedledee in the *Alice in Wonderland* stories. If they carried on like this they'd soon be finishing off each other's sentences.

'Well, let me see. I did a foundation course at Manchester and then I studied Fine Art at Edinburgh College of Art.'

'What made you choose Manchester?' asked Barbara, going straight for the jugular in her questioning.

'A boyfriend.'

'Seriously?'

'Yes. I used to be a hopeless romantic, I'm afraid.'

'But not any more?' pressed Barbara, clearly fascinated with the thought of someone allowing romantic feelings to dictate their future career path.

There was suddenly an uncomfortable pause in the conversation. Barbara, catching sight of the look Elinor gave Leo, groaned.

'I'm sorry, Elinor. I'm always putting my size eight boots into every conversation. I'm lucky I've any friends left at all. Please, don't take my questions personally. I'm genuinely interested in people and I don't mean to cross the line.'

Elinor smiled ruefully at Barbara and put a reassuring hand on her arm.

'It's not your fault, Barbara, really it isn't. I appreciate your interest in me. I'm just carrying a lot of baggage. But I need to get over it all. That's partly why I'm here now, staying with Leo.'

Barbara nodded, with understanding and compassion in her eyes.

'Then I hope you won't mind me suggesting something?' asked Barbara tentatively.

Elinor shook her head cautiously.

Barbara was like a firecracker; you never knew where, or when, she was going to go off on one. She's absolutely irrepressible, thought Elinor, waiting to hear what she had to say next.

Barbara looked down and started to smooth down the sleeve of her cherry red blouse, letting her fingers slowly follow its creases.

'I've no idea what you've been through, or what the problem is, obviously...' Barbara said, cautiously feeling her way forward. 'But art? That's a fundamental form of human expression. It's what elevates us from the animal to the human. And it's a totally freeing, spiritual exercise. Why don't you at least drop by, just once a week maybe, and try dabbling with some paint?

You'd provide me with some much-needed company at the same time.'

Elinor thought back to the cravings that had surged in her when she'd smelt the mix of oil paint, turpentine and white spirit.

She nodded.

'Sure. I'll be delighted to comply with that.'

'Fantastic,' said Barbara, beaming at her with pleasure.

Elinor looked across to Leo, and caught a singularly foolish smile on his face. She could read him like a book. That smile confirmed he felt progress was being made.

14

Elinor stood in the shallows at Constantine Bay snapping the surfers with her camera. She kept a close eye on the seawater lapping around her wellington boots, watching carefully as the water ebbed and flowed.

She felt the icy tingle of sea spray, and the rain pelting her face mercilessly.

Apart from the surfers the beach was, unsurprisingly, deserted. A strong offshore wind had ensured perfect surfing conditions.

Elinor had spent the night wide awake, wondering what subject she could paint when she went back to Barbara's studio.

All she could think of were the adrenaline-fuelled surfers, riding the waves with reckless abandon. She decided they should be her subject matter. That's what she wanted to feel, free and reckless. Not trapped in an endless, tiring cycle of anxiety and stress.

She was already starting to understand the natural rhythm of surfing, and was able to quickly pick out the more skilful surfers. She was also learning to read the waves as they formed.

To Elinor, watching surfers was like watching a fight at the Colosseum. The sound of the waves was like that of a lion's deep roar, the white plumes on the waves looked like fiery manes racing to the shore. Watching the surfers risk damage to their bodies, as they tried to harness the power of the waves, left her breathless with excitement.

As she put down her camera after taking a shot, she was suddenly electrified with fear. An accident was unfolding out at sea. She could feel the thudding of her quickened pulse echoing loudly in her ears. Her hands, in a now familiar routine, started to shake with adrenaline.

A surfer had jumped a wave too late. He'd tried to catch a wave that had all of a sudden become steep, like a wall, and it had also started to crest in the direction his surfboard clearly wanted to go in. Within seconds, the board had flicked up into the air, and he'd disappeared under the weight of a collapsing breaker.

Some of the other surfers, who'd been in front of him and were paddling back out to sea, had seen him disappear. They quickly moved across to where they thought he was.

Nothing but crashing waves and swirling foam appeared on the spot for a good couple of minutes. But, after what seemed to be an eternity, a head popped out, gasping for air. Soon he was surrounded by three other surfers, all of them checking he was still intact.

'He'll be fine. He's swimming to shore now. Although he'll feel like a rag doll that's been put through the washing machine,' said a deep voice at her side.

Elinor came back to earth with a jump.

She realised she'd pushed back her hood in order to see better and the rain had soaked her hair and crawled under her collar. It was now dripping unpleasantly down her back. She pulled her hood up and turned to face the man beside her.

It was the surfer she'd spoken to before on Treyarnon Bay.

He was obviously making his way into the water for the first time that day, as his wetsuit seemed to be relatively dry.

'Hi. I'm sorry, what was your name again?'

The surfer grinned, not in the slightest bit offended.

'My name's Tony Reece. I remember your name... Let me see, Elinor, isn't it?'

Elinor laughed.

'Yes, it is. I'm sorry for being so rude. I've never been very good at remembering names.'

'Don't worry about it. So you're still photographing surfers? Even in the rain?'

Elinor blushed. It did look like a bit of an obsession. After all, how many others would be out in weather like this?

'Surfing fascinates me.' She pointed out to water. 'They look so free.'

'As free as the sea allows them to be, I guess, but I get your meaning. Have you tried surfing yourself?'

Elinor chuckled at the thought.

'No, never. The waves would make mincemeat out of me.'

'Not necessarily. Everyone has to start somewhere. Most people learn the craft and then put it into practice.'

Elinor shook her head.

'I've never been sporty. I'm not sure I'd be capable of learning how to do it.'

'You only need to have a reasonable amount of balance and core strength. The rest is instinct. You either have it or you don't. Only one way to find out.' Tony turned to look at her with the enthused eyes of an addicted surfer. 'There's a beginner's surf school at Porthcothan Beach every Saturday morning, as long as the weather's reasonable. I'm usually helping out at it. The guy that's in charge, Mick, is a friend of mine. You should give it a try.'

'Maybe,' said Elinor, shrugging her shoulders casually and nodding.

'You're not going to even try, are you?' asked Tony, laughing at her knowingly.

Elinor bristled. What was it with the Cornish? She wasn't used to dealing with sledgehammer tactics, yet ever since she'd moved here they seemed to be coming at her from all sides.

'I might,' she said audaciously, staring him down.

Tony's laughter subsided. He looked down at her meekly.

'OK, then. Well, maybe see you there. I'd best head off and catch some waves before the wind changes.'

'Sure, see you later,' Elinor called out gruffly, above the roar of the ocean.

She watched him wade confidently into the water, as she stood in one spot, with her arms folded protectively around her.

Was it really that obvious she'd no desire to get out of her comfort zone? Certainly Tony seemed to imply it. And Leo, despite his laid-back attitude, seemed to see the need to prod her continually, to get her to try things out. Well, maybe, just for once, she'd surprise them both...

15

'Leo, do you need the car this morning?'

Leo looked up from his usual weekend breakfast of fried kippers.

'No, why?'

'I was thinking I might try out the surf school in Porthcothan.'

Leo looked thoroughly taken aback.

'Surf school in Porthcothan?' he repeated, his mouth full of kippers.

'Yes,' said Elinor, trying to sound as though this was the most normal thing in the world to be doing. 'They've apparently got a beginner's class. I thought I might give it a go.'

Leo nodded placidly. He'd noticed her recent interest in the surfers but Elinor had appreciated that he hadn't commented on it. She didn't need to feel supervised.

'Do you need any money for it?' mumbled Leo, after taking another mouthful.

'No, thank you. Mum's given me plenty to get by on,' Elinor said quietly, very shamefacedly. Nothing could be more humiliating and demeaning than being a twenty-eight year old who still needed to scrounge off her mother. Still, there was no getting around it now.

Leo looked at her with understanding in his eyes but didn't say anything. There was no need for explanations. They both knew how far Elinor had fallen.

'Why don't you walk there? No need to take the car.'

Elinor flinched at the notion of walking all the way to an hour-long surf lesson and back again. Her fitness levels hadn't quite reached those of Leo.

'I'll think about it for another time… I mean, maybe I'll do that later on, if I stick out the course. What are you planning on doing this morning?' asked Elinor brightly, trying to get a measure of revenge on Leo's attempts to keep her active.

'I'm going to try and explore a couple of caves near here, once it's low tide. I've been waiting for the lowest tide of the month, which will be today.'

'Any reason why you're wanting to go cave hunting all of a sudden?'

'Well, I've been delving into the past, as you've seen, and also looking back at our family's history here on the coast. As I've already told you, those young men have got me thinking about our smuggling ancestry. And I remember my grandad told me about a tunnel which the miners dug near here at the height of the smuggling craze. It stretched from the back of a local cave and ended up exiting further inland. Quite simply, I want to find it. I know my grandfather found it.'

Elinor wanted to ask Leo to take care of himself. Walking into slippery, dark caves didn't seem the kind of occupation for someone of his age. But she sensed Leo had a will as unstoppable as the ocean itself. Once he'd decided on a course of action he was going to follow it through, no matter what anyone said to him.

'Just leave me a note and tell me which cove you're in, in case we need to come and find you.'

'I'll text you,' said Leo, smiling at her concern. 'My mobile's waterproof.'

'Yes, but you might not have a signal down there.'

'I will outside the cave, and I'll text you from there,' said Leo, firmly, brooking no argument.

'OK!' said Elinor resignedly, getting up from the dining room table and reaching across to pick up Leo's empty plate.

Before long, she was in the old Volvo, following the blind twists and turns of the road to Porthcothan.

Steep Cornish hedges were on either side, making it nearly impossible to see any oncoming drivers. They hemmed in the road. No doubt they were used to corral cows in a different age but they were thoroughly inconvenient for the modern-day car driver, thought Elinor, tooting her horn vigorously at the blind corners.

One way or another, history was etched into every nook and cranny in Cornwall.

16

Ten minutes later, she parked the car on a road lined with houses, spying Porthcothan Beach at a close distance.

She looked at her watch. It was 9.35 so she still had a good twenty-five minutes before the class started.

Porthcothan Beach was a very long, sheltered beach and she could see why they would have a beginner's surf school here. The waves would never be as mighty and powerful here as they were on beaches that were fully exposed to the open ocean and its winds.

Before long she was walking across the soft sand to a stand with 'Dolphin Surf School' on it in big red letters. Next to the stand sat a gangly young man in a wetsuit.

Elinor assumed he must be the man in charge. She cleared her throat loudly.

'Hello. I'm here to sign up for surfing lessons.'

The man, who'd been busy looking at his phone, jerked his head up and swivelled round to look at her.

'Great! My name's Mick. Welcome to the club. What's your name?' said Mick, holding out his hand and shaking Elinor's.

'Elinor Campbell.'

'OK, Elinor,' said Mick, bending down and rustling around in his rucksack. He eventually brought out a handful of papers.

'You've to fill this in and sign it,' he said, passing her a form and pen. 'Today's a free lesson for you, but if you sign up after it then I'll need the ten weeks paid for, upfront. Account details are on the info sheet.' He handed her another slightly crumpled piece of paper. 'If you don't have your own wetsuit, you can get yourself one from the trailer, back there,' he said, pointing to an open trailer that was at the edge of the beach. 'You can change in the cubicles next to it.'

Elinor nodded and bent down to lean the form against her thigh so she could fill it in. Predictably, Mick was back on his phone again.

Once she'd filled in the form (ticking the box for experienced swimmer) and handed it to Mick, she made her way to the trailer. She had her swimsuit on under her clothes, but for someone who'd been as body conscious as she'd been, to put on a wetsuit was going to require a great deal of courage. She knew she was visiting Cornwall and was unlikely to bump into anyone she knew, but this was still going to require what her grandmother would call 'gumption'.

She looked into the trailer, piled high with wetsuits, and smelt the heady scent of rubber and sea. She started to sift through the wetsuits, trying to estimate which one of them was closest to her size. To her horror, most of them were coated in sand.

Eventually, she picked one out and went to get changed in the cubicle. Pulling on the wetsuit with a grimace of distaste, she felt the previous wearer's sand and grime sticking to her skin. She pulled at the rubbery fabric, yanking it up her legs and over her hips, finally wrestling like a maniac to get the arms on. At the end of it she was panting and felt like she couldn't move. She then had to reach to her rear, in what was practically a yoga stretch, to pull the zip up her back.

She put her clothes neatly into her shopping bag, and left the bag on the floor of the cubicle.

She waddled out onto the beach, trying to get used to the feel of the wetsuit. With a gasp of dismay, she saw there were four boys, who looked to be about eleven years old, lined up in front of Mick.

She was tempted to hurry back into the cubicle, but Mick had caught sight of her and waved her over. With her head bent low in embarrassment, she went and lined up with the boys.

'Right, guys, welcome to your first surf lesson. You might think it's all about rushing into the sea and having a go, but I'm afraid it's not. At least, not at the start. I'm here to cover the basic safety training, and to explain to you how to paddle out and pop up. Got me?'

All five of them nodded their heads, as though someone, somewhere, was yanking on a chain attached to their necks.

'Great. Today's first half hour will be about basic procedures, the second half hour you'll get a chance to go in the water. Firstly, you need a board,' Mick said, as he turned to a pile of boards piled up next to his chair.

He started handing them out like they were candy. Elinor ruefully noticed they were all getting the same size of surfboard. Which made sense, as the young boys were almost the same height as her.

'OK, one thing surfers routinely practise is holding their breath. Why do you think that is?'

'So you can swim underwater when the waves are coming at you?' asked a cocky boy with a thatch of red hair.

'Not quite... It's because when a powerful wave hits you, it can hold you under the water for quite a while. So you've to steer clear of any large waves until you can easily manage the smaller ones,' said Mick blandly. 'These waves you see here are small waves.'

He pointed to the water and they all turned obediently to look.

'You can get six-foot waves on Constantine Bay. The bigger waves might look like more fun, but when you fall off a big wave and get hit by it, it's like being hit by a sledgehammer. A big wave will drag you under, shake you around and hold you down there for quite a while. If you're down really deep, your ears will start to ache with the pressure.'

Bloody fantastic, thought Elinor, wondering why she was doing this.

Mick stared closely at them all to make sure they were taking in his teaching.

'The most important thing is to remember to try and stay relaxed when under the wave, because if you panic you'll find it a lot harder to hold your breath. As soon as you start panicking, your body will become rigid, too, which could cause more damage to your limbs.'

They all stood there silently, listening avidly to Mick. Elinor looked at him with disbelief. This was supposed to be fun, wasn't it? It didn't look as if surfing was worth it. She decided to bow out gracefully after that day's lesson.

'OK. Let me see... There are five basic rules you have to stick to when surfing. One: follow the advice of the lifeguards, at all times. Two: wear your leash so you don't lose your surfboard. Surfboards can keep you afloat in an emergency and make you easier to find. Three: check your equipment for damage before use,' said Mick, talking so quickly Elinor was finding herself struggling to keep up with him.

Mick paused for a minute as if trying to remember what he'd just said. He'd obviously given the same speech so many times that he'd managed to lose track of where he was in his talk.

He coughed apologetically. Then his face cleared, as he remembered where he'd left off. It was like a light bulb getting switched back on, thought Elinor amusedly.

'Make sure your surfboard is in good shape, in other words. Four: you can bodyboard between the red and yellow flags, but you can only surf between the white and black flags on any beach. Got it? Five: the most important one in my view, is that you have to learn what's called surfer etiquette.'

Mick waved his finger vigorously in the air, as if to emphasise his point.

'That is, you've got to know when it's your wave or your turn, or else you'll become extremely unpopular. Don't get in the way of other surfers. You don't want a lot of irate surfers after you, believe me.'

He bent down and picked up a pile of leaflets and started to hand them out.

'Here are the basic guidelines for surfing manners summarised, along with the safety procedures. This leaflet explains how you must communicate when you take a wave, shouting "left" or "right" to let others know what direction you're going in. Also, whoever is closest to the peak of the wave has the priority. It's important to remember that.'

Mick picked up a surfboard and showed it to them.

'Right, these are beginners' surfboards. They are foam soft tops, *not* like the standard epoxy and hand-shaped boards favoured by the pros. The reason we use these to start with is that they're light and there are fewer risks in the water with them. Have any of you ever been hit by a surfboard?'

They all shook their heads.

'Well, I can tell you from experience it bloody hurts. You want to avoid the pain, believe me. These boards are also more buoyant so you can catch more waves and learn faster. They don't manoeuvre as easily as the pro boards, but they're a stable ride for wobbly beginners. So it's a win/win situation, don't you think?'

Mick didn't wait to hear their answer. He put the board down on the ground and began to walk behind the group. They all stretched round to try and see what Mick was doing, but before she had time to think, Elinor felt a heavy thump on her back, pushing her forward.

She had to put out her right foot to stop herself falling forward onto the sand.

'Cool! So Elinor's what we would call a Regular, meaning her right foot's the one that's strongest,' said Mick. 'So that one has to be at the back of the surfboard. The left should be forward.'

Mick then went on to push the others forward. By the end, four of them were considered to be Regulars, and only one was what Mick called a 'Goofy Surfer'. In other words, left-footed.

He then went on to explain about the 'stringer', the imaginary line running down the centre of the surfboard, and how their foot arches had to be positioned, equally, on either side of the stringer.

Finally, he got them to stand up on the boards.

While he was checking their positions on their surfboards, asking for feet to be a shoulder width apart and knees pointed into each other, Elinor spotted Tony Reece arriving with another group of young boys.

Seeing them, she started to wonder if she'd finally lost the plot completely. Was she going to be the only girl out here? And was she the only one above the age of fifteen? It certainly looked that way. She sighed...

17

Elinor shrieked loudly as felt herself falling with a resounding smack onto the water. Bitter, salty seawater entered her mouth and nose. She rose up to the surface, choking and spluttering and pushing back her hair. She quickly flung her two arms over the surfboard and lay there exhausted and immobile, letting the water rock her.

She noticed all the lads surreptitiously trying, but failing, not to stare at her.

She had no dignity left. The other four boys had all managed, by now, to stand up on their boards. She hadn't managed to get her balance on the board once. Let alone allow a wave to carry her towards shore. Mick had done his best, holding her board for her so she could 'pop up' onto it, but she still couldn't get her balance right.

Despondently, she'd decided by the end of her lesson that surfing was not for her. Her swimsuit had ridden up uncomfortably into the crack between her buttocks, her ribs were sore from banging on the board as she launched herself onto it and paddled out to the ocean. Astonishingly, her toes were also killing her. She hadn't realised how much they'd be used as she tried to 'pop up' onto the board.

'OK, guys, good work. That's it for today. Remember to keep practising your surfboard position at home, so it becomes second nature. Well done, all of you,' shouted Mick.

Elinor had laid her head on her arms and didn't feel like moving. But it was the end of the lesson. The others were all making their way onto the beach, to dump their surfboards before heading for home.

She started to kick her legs in the water, manoeuvring herself towards the shoreline.

Tony Reece was making his way towards the water with his troop of young surfers. From a distance, they looked like little ducklings following their leader. The Dolphin Surf School was definitely running a conveyor belt of apprentices today.

By the time Elinor was wading tiredly through the surf at the shoreline, Tony Reece was encouraging his group into the water.

'Hi Elinor. How did you get on?'

Elinor looked at him crossly.

'Surely you must have heard me? I haven't managed to keep my balance once during the lesson. The other little tikes who were in there with me have all managed to get on their boards. I'm afraid I don't think this surfing malarkey is for me.'

'Hold on, Elinor! You can't give up that easily.'

'Give up that easily? Are you having a laugh? I'm going to be black and blue with bruises tomorrow. I can't even feel my toes any more, they've been wrenched that much. I'll be lucky if I'm able to walk in the morning. Believe me, I've tried.'

She could see Tony was trying not to laugh. She was now feeling worn out but she could feel a bubble of hysteria forming in her too. She sternly repressed it. This was all Tony's fault, after all. He was the one who'd challenged her to learn.

'Look Elinor, there are exercises that you can do at home

to improve your balance. All it takes is a little practice. If you can wait for half an hour, while I finish with this lot, I can show you.'

Elinor paused for a moment. She was unsure if she still wanted to be sucked into the crazy world of addicted surfers. She saw Tony looking anxiously at his group, waiting patiently for him in the shallows.

'Oh, OK then. It's probably going to take me half an hour to get myself out of this wetsuit, anyway. I'll wait until you're finished,' she conceded.

'Great. See you then,' said Tony, already making his way out to join his class.

Elinor stretched back her shoulders and walked across to the surfing stand, dumping her surfboard next to the others.

'Thanks, Mick.'

Mick looked up from his phone and smiled.

'No worries. I look forward to seeing you next week.'

'I don't know about that, Mick. I mean, I couldn't even get up on the board today.'

'You'll do it, Elinor, you really will. I mean it. It takes us oldies a bit longer to learn, but we all get there in the end. I tell you, once you've ridden your first wave you'll be hooked,' said Mick, with what Elinor was beginning to recognise was the look of a surfer fanatic.

'OK. I'll definitely think about coming back. Thanks anyway,' said Elinor, not feeling strong enough to commit herself to any more surfing torture.

She walked quickly off to the changing cubicle. Taking off her wetsuit was such a painful procedure that she started to wonder if she'd done more than bruise her ribcage. She sat down for a moment to allow the pain to ebb.

It was a relief to feel the soft, dry layers of her clothing touch her body but her jeans felt tight and uncomfortable. She made a mental note to bring her joggers with her next time. If there was a next time...

Ten minutes later, she wandered out onto the beach to watch Tony as he taught his young students to balance on their surf-boards. She wondered why he bothered doing this. After all, working as a GP he must make a tidy sum. What could possibly be the appeal in teaching people to balance correctly on a surfboard? She didn't get it. Tony Reece was a mystery to her.

Before long, Tony's surf lesson finished and Tony walked up to her, signing for her to follow him. She walked behind him as he made his way determinedly up the beach. He stopped for a moment by the surfing stand, to pick up a tennis ball, and then carried on walking.

Elinor, stoically ploughing through the sand in his wake, started to wonder where they were going. They walked on until they reached the edge of the road. Once they were on the road itself, Tony turned around to face her.

'Right. There are two exercises you can work on to improve your balance. Stand, feet hip-width apart, and distribute your weight evenly between both legs. Like that. Now, shift your weight to the right and lift your left foot off the floor.'

Elinor tried to hold her left foot up, but within seconds she found she was tumbling forward. Tony quickly caught her arms and propped her upright again.

'OK? Got the balance again?'

Elinor nodded, unable to speak as her leg wobbled with the strain of holding her upright.

'OK. You hold that for thirty seconds and then you do the same with the other side. You keep repeating the exercise, every day, until you feel fairly confident.'

Elinor put her foot down again and breathed a sigh of relief.

'That's it? That's what you do to get better balance?'

'Well, I'm afraid that's not all you're supposed to do. The next stage for this exercise is that while you're balancing on one leg, you throw a tennis ball up in the air and catch it. Like this,' Tony said, demonstrating by balancing on one leg and tossing the tennis ball up and down.

'You know, there's no need to show off. I've already had my face rubbed into it,' said Elinor with a sniff.

Tony grinned at her and stopped.

'Finally, you need to build up your core strength for surfing. It'll make a huge difference to your ability. That means wide press-ups, diamond press-ups, staggered press-ups, tricep press-ups and, of course, sit-ups.'

'You've got to be kidding me! What on earth are diamond press-ups?'

Without another word, Tony threw himself on the ground and demonstrated how to do a diamond press-up.

Elinor rolled her eyes up to the heavens. She looked humorously at Tony as he stood up again.

'I'm going to have to write all this down. It's clear you surfers have quite a repertoire of exercises to do. How on earth do you find time for it all?'

'You just fit it into your daily schedule,' said Tony, taking it all completely seriously. 'If you send me a text, I can send you a return text later on, with a link that explains all those exercises.'

Elinor took her phone out of the bag and saved to her address book the mobile number Tony reeled off to her. Not so much because she had any serious intentions of following through with his advice, but because he was a good-looking man and she wasn't about to turn down the opportunity to take note of his contact details.

18

The next morning Elinor groaned as she moved. Every muscle was screaming in pain. She rolled herself off the bed so she wouldn't have to use her stomach muscles. Her ribs were still killing her. Suddenly she began to feel anxiety creep up on her. What if she'd actually managed to break her ribs?

As she sat on the edge of the bed, she started to shake with fear. Her mind started taking her places she didn't want to go. She shut her eyes, and tried the relaxation breathing she'd been advised to do when she felt like this. But breathing deeply in and out only heightened the pain under the ribs and made her think about it more.

She reached out and grabbed her phone, an idea having occurred to her. She panned down the numbers and found Tony Reece's. He was a doctor, wasn't he? Without a moment's hesitation, she dialled his number.

'Hello?'

His voice was groggy, heavy with sleep.

Elinor suddenly realised it was five o'clock on a Sunday morning. Oops. She felt the urge to hang up the phone before she got herself into a whole load of trouble, but the worry about her ribs was gnawing away at her. Her anxiety won the battle.

'Tony, I'm so sorry to disturb you this early. It's Elinor.'

'Elinor?'

'Yes, me.'

'Are you OK?'

'Not really... You see, I'm worried I might have broken my ribs.'

'Sorry, repeat that again?'

'I'm worried I might have broken my ribs!' repeated Elinor an octave higher, starting to feel exasperated.

'Why, have you fallen somewhere?'

'No! It's from surfing yesterday.'

'Elinor,' said Tony, a note of anger creeping into his voice. 'There's literally no chance you could have broken your ribs at Porthcothan Beach yesterday. There were barely any waves, and even if you'd landed hard on your surfboard the water would've cushioned you.'

'But it really, really hurts...'

'Yeah, well, it will do if you're out of shape.'

'I'm sorry? What did you just say?' spluttered Elinor, feeling her hackles rise.

'I'm saying, Elinor, you're unfit. You struggled to stand on one leg for even a few seconds yesterday. You're out of shape. If you've not been exercising properly for some time, your muscles will be sore after a surfing lesson. Now, can I go back to sleep, please?'

'OK. Sorry. Bye.'

Elinor hung up quickly, feeling like a five-star idiot. Part of her wished she could prove Tony wrong, but she had a horrible feeling he was right. She was unfit and out of shape.

She sat up straighter.

That's it, she thought, I'm going to prove them all wrong about me. I'm not unfit. I just need to try and do a few more stretches in the mornings. She looked down at her mobile and tapped on the link Tony had sent her, the one with all the different press-ups on it.

She sighed as she watched the video clip. And then she got on all fours to start practising, shutting her mind to her screaming muscles, which were pleading with her to stop.

Twenty minutes into her exercises, she heard a knock on the door.

'Come in!' she yelled.

Her door opened and Leo stuck his head in.

'Elinor, are you OK?'

'Yeah, why?'

'I couldn't figure out why you were yelling so much. I thought you might be having one of your nightmares.'

Elinor sat up.

'No, Leo. I'm fine.'

She started to giggle.

'I'm trying out these surfer exercises and I'm still in agony from yesterday's lesson. It's so bloody painful, you wouldn't believe it.'

Leo burst out laughing.

'From what I've heard coming from your room, I would. Good grief, Elinor, are you sure you're not overdoing it?'

'No. I've got to get fitter. All those boys managed to get up on their boards and I just couldn't. And now Tony Reece is saying I'm out of shape and unfit.'

'So what's this, now? You're trying to compete with some eleven-year-old boys to prove this surfer wrong?'

'Exactly.'

Leo looked at her in amusement, shaking his head in

mock disapproval.

'Fancy a cup of tea?' he asked after a moment.

'That would be lovely, thanks. I won't be too much longer. I've only got the tricep presses to do next...'

Leo left to go to the kitchen, and shortly afterwards Elinor heard the kettle boiling from a distance.

Five minutes later she hobbled gingerly down the corridor, making her way slowly towards the kitchen. She was walking like John Wayne, with her legs bowed and wide apart. The insides of her thighs were red raw, as a result of rubbing against the sandy fabric of the wetsuit she'd worn the day before.

Leo watched her as she walked into the kitchen and perched on a stool, wincing as she did so.

He shook his head.

'Just look at the state of you, Elinor. I'm not sure this surfing is such a good idea. I'm supposed to send you back to Scotland in better shape than you arrived. Not looking as though you've been beaten up on a dark night. Your mother's going to kill me.'

'I'm going to get into good shape,' insisted Elinor, lifting up her cup of tea and taking a grateful gulp.

'You're a stubborn girl, no doubt about it. You shouldn't let those surfers wind you up. They're not worth it.'

'Oh, I know that. It's just that I'm so sick and tired of being pitied. I had enough of that in Glasgow after Mark died. And I think those boys looking at me like I was a lost cause yesterday was just the last straw.'

Elinor looked across the kitchen table at Leo, pleading for his understanding. She wasn't sure why, but Leo's support in this was important to her.

'It's set something off in me,' she continued, trying to explain. 'And I don't appreciate Tony and Mick treating me like a baby, either. I want to figure this out for myself. For once, I want to prove to myself I can do it.'

'Well, as long as you're doing it for yourself, that's fine,' said Leo, nodding placidly.

'I woke Tony up at five this morning,' added Elinor, looking sideways at Leo to gauge his reaction. She took a blasé mouthful of tea, trying to diminish the impact of her words.

Leo stared at her, as though she'd finally confirmed his worst fears. The look on his face clearly stated that he thought she'd gone completely mad.

'Why would you do that?'

'I felt really bad about it afterwards,' admitted Elinor. 'My ribs were killing me and I started to panic about them. You know how it is with me. And Tony's a doctor, so I thought I'd give him a call and ask him if he thought I could've broken something. Only I didn't realise until he answered that it was so early. Now I feel awful about it.'

'Oh, I see. Well, it isn't such a big deal, after all. Why would you feel bad about it?'

'For waking him up so early, of course, and also for using him like that. I mean, that's the reason doctors don't give out their phone numbers, isn't it? So they don't get deranged patients calling them at all hours.'

Leo shrugged nonchalantly, laid-back as always.

'Don't start worrying about that kind of thing. After all, he was the one who gave you his phone number in the first place.'

Leo chuckled suddenly.

'It'll teach him not to hand out his number to strange women. They could be dangerous lunatics like you. A *Fatal Attraction* kind of thing...'

Elinor flung the tea towel at him.

19

'Leo, did you find the tunnel you were looking for?'

Elinor was sitting by the window, reading her book, while Leo sat at his desk and worked through the paperwork piled up on it.

'No, I didn't. One cave at Pepper Cove came to an end within ten metres. The other, after what I'd say must've been fifteen metres or so. It was very disappointing.'

'Don't you think a rock fall could've blocked off this old tunnel?'

'Possibly, but that's unlikely. Even when there's a rock fall, it's rare for access to a cave to be completely blocked off,' said Leo pensively. 'And you've to remember the tunnel was built by Cornish miners. They knew how to build good tunnels; their lives depended on it. I'd be very surprised if the tunnel itself had collapsed.'

Leo looked thoroughly despondent.

'I know there's a tunnel near here, because my grandfather saw it,' he reiterated. 'I'll just have to put my thinking cap on, again, and figure it out.'

Elinor sincerely hoped he'd lose interest. Searching for an underground tunnel, along this volatile coast, didn't seem to her a very safe occupation. He seemed almost as obsessed with this tunnel as she was with surfing. Maybe it was a family trait, in their Cornish DNA, to be as persistent and unyielding as the surrounding cliffs. It was obvious neither of them liked the taste of defeat...

Leo leaned back on his desk chair and swivelled round to look at Elinor.

'By the way, there's a book fair on this afternoon at St Merryn Church, in aid of roof repairs. Would you like to go and have a browse?'

Elinor put her cheap thriller on the coffee table.

'I'm not very discerning as far as books go, but yes, that would be a nice thing to do.'

She stretched out her sore arms and yawned, thinking she could do with a hot bath to ease the pain.

'I love that old church. It reeks of so much history. I can almost feel the spiritual presence of the generations of Cornish men and women that have attended it over the centuries,' she added enthusiastically.

'Yes, it's very old,' said Leo prosaically. He wasn't really interested in anything that didn't have to do with the sea. Leo, at heart, was a fisherman through and through.

Later that afternoon, they wandered onto the grass outside the church where covered stalls were laid out. All were positioned between the tall tower of the church and the front entrance. Scattered at a distance were old gravestones, some of them tilted at an awkward angle.

The canvas coverings of the stalls were flapping vigorously in the wind. Elinor hoped it wouldn't blow any harder because the stalls didn't look terribly robust.

St Merryn Church was in Treveglos, which was about a quarter of a mile outside the village of St Merryn. The distance, though, hadn't stopped people turning up for the second-hand book sale.

A coated and scarfed crowd, like a flock of grazing sheep, were surrounding the stalls. It was busy. Trust a book sale in the middle of a Cornish winter to be a big event, thought Elinor.

She wasn't terribly keen on crowds and tended to avoid them if she could, so she hung back and watched from a distance. Leo, of course, had been greeted within minutes of arriving, and was busy talking to some of his cronies.

'Hello. You're Leo's niece, aren't you?' said a lady standing next to her.

Elinor turned and peered at the woman, who looked to be in her early fifties, and whose raven black hair was shaped in a neat 1920s bob. She was wearing a stylish bright-red thick duffle coat and a pair of knee-high brown leather boots.

'Yes, I am,' said Elinor, wrinkling her forehead in confusion. 'Should I know you?'

'No, no, of course you wouldn't know me. Everyone in St Merryn, though, knows Leo and we all knew he had a niece visiting. He's not been seen around the village as much as usual. You're obviously keeping him busy!'

'Actually, Leo does his own thing. He's always been a bit of a loner, in that respect. But it's been really lovely staying with him. I'm grateful to him for letting me.'

The lady stuck out her hand to shake Elinor's.

'I'm Jane Fairfax, the vicar of this church.'

'Oh! Wow,' said Elinor inanely, shaking hands with her. 'You do the services at this church?'

'Yes. Even though, sometimes, there's only fifteen of the congregation attending. Which can make singing the hymns a bit of a challenge, to be honest with you. It's a very small parish, especially in the winter. But there's lots to love about this old church.'

'I know. I love it. It has such a nice atmosphere to it.'

'I can show you around just now if you like, and tell you some of its history. It's open today.'

'Thanks, I'd like that... I'll just tell Leo where I am.'

Elinor had a quick word with Leo, and then walked to the front entrance of the church with Jane.

Before they went in Jane pointed to the church tower.

'Of course, back in Norman times, our tower was what one chronicler described as "short and stumpy",' said Jane. 'They subsequently made the tower bigger, in an effort to make it look more grandiose. In the 15th century, I think it was. Personally, I think they overdid it, because it looks far too big next to the original church. A simple case, I think, of men overcompensating for other things...'

Elinor giggled. She'd never met a feminist vicar before, but there was a first time for everything.

'You might think it odd that the church isn't actually in St Merryn, but in the Middle Ages the community around here was totally farm-based. All the ancient pathways, and rights of way, centre on the church. I'm sure Leo would agree with me on that point. He seems to know most of the pathways around here.'

'Yes, he does. He's like a walking map.'

They strolled up the aisle of the church, Jane's boots clipping briskly on the hard floor.

'The most beautiful part of this church, in my view, is the seven pillars and these gorgeous Gothic arches. They're made of Cataclews Stone, quarried from Trevose Head. You can see Trevose Head from your house, can't you?'

Elinor nodded.

'And the font is beautiful too. It's made from the same stone. You can see the twelve apostles on it,' said Jane, walking up to it and touching it fondly. 'Most people praise the carved roof of the church. It's called a wagon roof, for obvious reasons. But for me, the ancient stone they've used for the arches, pillars and font is what makes this church special. This stone will last longer than any other part of the church.'

'Are you fundraising for the ceiling of the church?' asked Elinor, bending her neck back to look up at it.

'No, thankfully, the wood inside the church is still in good condition. We need the money to repair the exterior roof. A lot of the slates are starting to crumble and disintegrate. Unfortunately, the Church of England has more important priorities, and we're having to rely on the good faith of the people who value this church to help us raise the money needed.'

'Wasn't it a bit risky, holding a book sale outdoors at this time of year?'

Jane laughed.

'If the weather had been rotten, they would've set up their stalls in our church hall. However, at the moment the church hall is set up for the Christmas pantomime rehearsals. So it would've been inconvenient, to say the least, to move everything out of the way. God's blessed us in that respect,' Jane said, smiling.

Elinor didn't say anything. She hadn't seen much sign of God's blessings in this last year of her life, and was inclined to feel bitter towards people who claimed they were real.

20

'You wouldn't believe, would you, that this insignificant little Cornish church would've had connections with Greece and the Eastern Mediterranean, but it does. Incredible as it sounds, there's evidence North Cornwall traded with what was then called Byzantium, many hundreds of years ago.'

'That's utterly weird. It would've been such a long journey for them to make. You have to wonder why they bothered to come here.'

'Tin. The Byzantines wanted Cornish tin. Apparently, after the Romans left Britain, the Anglo-Saxons dominated the South East of Britain. They were considered barbarians,' said Jane humorously. 'But the Byzantines still had a healthy trading relationship with the Kingdom of Dumnonia.'

'Dumnonia?'

'Dumnonia, basically, was Cornwall, Devon and a part of Somerset and Dorset, all put together into one kingdom. It was the kingdom the legendary King Arthur belonged to.'

'Well, everyone's heard of King Arthur. But Dumnonia? What a bizarre name. I've never heard of it before,' said Elinor, fascinated.

'I know, it's a really odd name,' agreed Jane.

Jane and Elinor looked silently up to the stained glass window. It was strangely peaceful inside the church, even though you could hear the rumble of the book fair outside.

They had both sat down on a pew. Jane had her long legs stretched out in front of her, with her ankles crossed. She didn't remotely look like a vicar. Elinor had even begun to wonder, for a moment, if she'd been taken in.

'This church is called St Merryn, some think, after the Byzantine saint, St Marina,' added Jane, after a moment. She obviously felt she'd drifted away from her original mandate of explaining the church to Elinor. 'She was a young girl, who was executed for her faith in Jesus, in the city of Antioch. Around about 300 AD.'

She took out a tissue and wiped her nose, which was dripping in the chilly air of the church.

'And they think St Ives was named after a young girl called Ia, who was another Byzantine martyr,' she continued. 'So basically this church and the town of St Ives were named after two girls from what is Turkey today but was actually Greece back in those times. Two feisty, rebellious young girls who became saints. No doubt about it, they must've been as bloody-minded as my fifteen-year-old daughter is today.'

Jane sighed sadly, and looked down at her wedding ring, as though reminding herself of her family. Elinor was curious to find out more about Jane's cryptic references to her daughter, but she felt it would be rude to ask.

'I sometimes think they knew how to honour and respect women better in those days,' continued Jane, after a moment. 'Especially when I think of how long it's taken for the Church of England to accept women as vicars.'

'I agree with you. It's taken far too long,' concurred Elinor, again surprised at Jane's candour.

Elinor thought for an instant about the curious historical links between North Cornwall and the Byzantines.

'So you're saying the Byzantines influenced the people of Dumnonia, to the extent they named two places in Cornwall after two of their saints? Doesn't that sound a bit improbable?'

'Not really. The Byzantines seem to have had a good relationship with the people of Dumnonia. They've found archaeological evidence, in Devon, of their beach parties.'

Elinor chuckled at the bizarre notion of these two ancient civilisations having a beach party together.

'It's true!' laughed Jane, anxious to prove her point. 'Apparently, there were great celebrations when the Byzantines arrived. Not surprising, really, when you consider they were bringing Byzantine wine with them.'

'Byzantine wine?'

'Yes, they traded Cornish tin for Byzantine wine. It's hilarious to think that's how much our ancestors prized their wine.'

21

Jane and Elinor walked back out into the sunshine. Most people had moved away from the stalls and were gathered around the tea trolley, which was serving refreshments near the church hall. Several people were holding hot mugs of tea and coffee, or were finishing up crumbs of scone and jam.

'Next time you're walking near Constantine Bay, you should have a look for the ruined church and holy well of St Constantine,' Jane said, as they stood at the door of the church. 'It's worth a visit. You'll find them on the edges of Trevose Golf and Country Club.'

'That's odd. Leo's never mentioned it.'

'Most locals probably take it for granted. But it's very picturesque. Supposedly, as legend has it, Constantine, a Cornish landowner or king in the 5th century, was stopped from killing a stag by a man called Petroc. When he tried to kill Petroc he was paralysed – until Petroc prayed for him. Subsequently, so the story goes, Constantine converted to Christianity and built the church and well.'

'There are so many myths and legends around here. It's very confusing,' complained Elinor, her mind boggling with all the historical facts.

'But of course. There'll always be legends here! You're in the land of Tintagel, after all. The home of King Arthur, Merlin and the Round Table. The Celts have always loved myths and storytelling... Are you going to come and have some coffee?'

'Actually, now it's quiet I'm going to have a browse through what's left in the bookstalls. Thank you so much for telling me all about the church.'

'Not at all. It's been lovely to meet you, Elinor. No doubt we'll meet again,' said Jane, with a smile.

Jane turned and headed towards the refreshments. Several parishioners caught sight of her and moved forward to speak to her. Elinor was suddenly glad Jane had had a bit of breathing space with her in the church. It couldn't be easy to be at the constant beck and call of her churchgoing flock.

She walked to the bookstall and started sifting through the boxes.

To her surprise, quite a few of the books were very salacious. Elinor started to wonder what kind of a double life some of these pious churchgoers were leading.

Under a mound of rather tatty paperbacks she found a very small hardback book of Jane Austen's *Sense and Sensibility*. She didn't have much patience for reading the classics but this book attracted her. Its pages were edged in gilt, and the book itself was bound in beautifully preserved red fabric. She put it to one side and continued her search with renewed enthusiasm, hoping there'd be other treasures to be found.

She'd gone through three more boxes before she finally came across a book she'd read. Elinor had what she herself would call popular taste, liking books that were enjoyable but which didn't challenge her too much intellectually. She found an old copy of *Circus*, an Alistair MacLean book. A bit dated but still a good read. Today's equivalent would probably be a Jack

Reacher thriller.

Elinor was already getting a feel for the generation of book readers in this church. She had still to find a book written in the last five years in one of the boxes...

She was starting to weary of browsing. She looked up to see if she could spot Leo anywhere. From the start, he seemed to have vanished into the St Merryn community gathered there. After looking around for five minutes, she finally spotted him carrying dirty mugs into the church hall to be washed.

'We'll be wrapping it up soon, love. Book sale finishes in twenty minutes,' said an old woman, who'd been shuffling backwards and forwards on the same spot, trying to keep warm.

Elinor nodded, rather relieved. There was nothing like a prolonged browse in a yard sale to wear you out. But she already had a bargain hunter's adrenaline rushing through her veins, so she wasn't prepared to stop. Not until she had to, that is.

Reinvigorated by the narrow margin of time left to her, she buried herself in the remaining boxes.

Finally, when she came to the last box she saw at the bottom of it a fairly large, and old, leather-bound book. It was in a battered state, the ring binding barely holding on by a few threads. But the book itself was bound in an attractive, camel-coloured leather binding with gilt lettering.

Elinor inspected it carefully. It was a copy of *Frankenstein* by Mary Shelley. She looked inside it and saw the first couple of pages had been torn out, but the story itself was intact.

Inside the front cover of the book, a short poem was scrawled in black ink. In neat, sloping writing was written:

'To see a World in a Grain of Sand,
And a Heaven in a Wild Flower,

Hold Infinity in the Palm of your Hand,
And Eternity in an Hour.'

Elinor was enchanted by the poem's words. She was completely absorbed in the poetic inscription and only realised where she was when she heard someone impatiently clearing their voice and saying loudly, 'Are you wanting to buy the book, Miss? We've got to pack up now.'

She looked up from the book and saw a rotund gentleman, in a tweed cap, standing in front of her waiting for a response. She glanced back down at the book she was holding in her hands. On the first page, it had the sum of ten pounds written in pencil. Which she felt was a bit steep. But should she be haggling at a book sale in aid of raising funds for the church roof? Probably not...

She knew *Frankenstein* was a book she'd never want to read. She didn't like horror of any kind, and had enough trouble coping with anxiety as it was. But the beautiful, handwritten inscription had a magnetic charm for her. She didn't want to let it go.

'Yes, please. I'll take this book, thank you,' she said, recklessly, throwing away any cautious thoughts. She handed over the money and put the three books she'd purchased carefully into her handbag.

Later that afternoon she showed Leo her book purchases. He was very interested in the old leather-bound version of *Frankenstein,* holding it with surprising gentleness in his gnarled hands and turning its pages with great care.

He had a bookcase full of old books he'd collected over a lifetime from an antiquarian book dealer in Wadebridge. Needless to say, most of his collection had something to do with the sea: old biographies of people like Admiral Nelson, Francis Drake, Christopher Columbus. Books on the *Spanish Armada*, the *Mary Rose* and a pirate ship called the *Queen Anne's Revenge* were squeezed in amongst more modern books on Cornish shipwrecks and other nautical subjects.

He offered to take Elinor's book to the book dealer he knew to get it properly repaired, so Elinor gratefully handed it over to him and promptly put it out of her mind.

22

Elinor watched as her tear drops landed on the mounds of oil paint and balanced there, in little self-contained bubbles, before quickly disintegrating into oblivion. It had always seemed strange to her how it took so much heartache and emotional pain to produce tears, but how quickly the tears abandoned you without taking the pain away with them.

Barbara was absorbed in her painting and was totally unaware of the acute emotions attacking Elinor as she worked on her first painting since Mark had died.

In the background two people on Coast FM were blethering about the winners in the latest Cornish Sustainability Awards.

Elinor tried to focus, through her blurred vision, on her painting. It had all gone so well up to this point. She'd had her photographs of the surfers developed the week before and she'd picked out a photo where the sun was shining brightly on the ocean, highlighting the ripples of water and the edges of the surfer's surfboard.

Initially, she'd mixed blue with a little green and a little white to create the right shade of blue for the water. Once she had the blue tones just right on the hard board, she'd then added little touches of red so as to lend a purplish tint to some of the shadows.

Afterwards she'd quickly moved on to using her favourite

combination of dark blue and brown, to create the impression of depth and darkness looming in the ocean. Her plan was to wait until the paint had dried and then to add dramatic touches of white and light yellow, to highlight the reflections of the sun against the moving water.

It was when she'd started to work on the figure of the surfer that she'd felt herself slowly unravel. She knew her subconscious was dredging up memories she would rather have kept buried.

She used to paint Mark all the time. Of course, there'd been no easier subject to draw or paint because they lived together. She'd moulded landscapes and buildings around him.

Mark had been her muse. He was the solitary male figure in her paintings, standing with his back to the viewer, just like the solitary figures in the Romantic paintings of Caspar David Friedrich.

Now she was painting a stranger on a surfboard and she was struggling to connect with her subject matter. And the loneliness was overwhelming her.

'Elinor, are you all right, my love?' asked Barbara, with concern in her voice.

Elinor looked up from her painting. As soon as Barbara saw her ravaged face, she dropped her paintbrushes and walked purposefully across to where Elinor was seated.

Without demanding a word of explanation, she wrapped her arms around Elinor and at that point the floodgates opened. Elinor sobbed uninhibitedly into the comforting arms holding her. Barbara helpfully said nothing, but kept a firm grasp on Elinor's shaking shoulders.

'I'm so sorry, Barbara, I thought I was ready for this. But I'm not. It's too painful,' whispered Elinor, after a while.

She reached across and grabbed the paper towel she'd been using for her painting. Oblivious to the paint marks on it, she blew her nose and wiped her sticky face. She'd no idea how much time had passed since she'd started crying.

'Don't be ridiculous, Elinor. This is precisely why you should be doing this. You're never going to heal if you continue burying things, or running away from them. Avoiding the pain doesn't heal you. You need this.'

There was a silence as they sat there, next to each other on the bench, with their arms wrapped around each other. Barbara looked at the painting Elinor had been working on.

'Darling, you've got phenomenal talent. I guessed that already from what Leo told me, but still... That's going to be a beautiful painting. All the more so because of the pain you've had to slay in order to do it.'

Elinor tried to assess the painting impartially. It was shaping itself nicely. As always when she inspected a painting, her fingers itched to amend and change little flaws she alone could identify. She didn't just work from the photographs but also from the image she would fix in her mind at the start of a painting. That image always stayed with her throughout her art projects, dictating her brushstrokes.

Elinor sighed and looked at her watch. It was nearly six o'clock.

'I'd best get going or Leo's going to start worrying about me.'

Barbara laughed.

'It'll take a Category 5 typhoon to get that man worried. Stay and have some dinner with me before you go. Let's leave things on a high note. I'll text Leo.'

Elinor nodded submissively. Her tears had left her spent and drained.

Twenty-five minutes later she was tucking into a beautiful sirloin steak. Barbara had a healthy appetite and expensive taste in food and drink. They drank liberally from a bottle of Camel Valley wine, apparently from an award-winning Cornish vineyard in Bodmin.

Barbara's Siamese cat made an appearance, by which Barbara informed Elinor she should be greatly honoured. Apparently, Brindle didn't make himself known to people unless he felt comfortable about it.

'I'm sure Leo would've scared the living daylights out of poor Brindle. He's got such a very deep voice,' Barbara said, as she stroked the purring cat.

'Doesn't he try to jump onto the table?' asked Elinor, thinking about her remaining piece of steak.

'No, he's been well brought up. He knows I'll always offer him leftovers. Plus, with what he catches outside, I suspect he's full enough.'

'Are there any other members of the household I haven't met?' wondered Elinor, looking around surreptitiously to see if there were any photographs (always a clear giveaway) in the kitchen.

'No, I'm afraid it's just Brindle and me. You must know that I really do sympathise with your feeling of desolation, Elinor. I haven't always lived here on my own. My partner, Glenn, died six and a half years ago, from bowel cancer. It still feels like yesterday. Sometimes, I wake up at night and instinctively reach over to touch him and then, suddenly, realise he's not there any more.'

Elinor looked at Barbara compassionately. She was always so caught up in her own troubles, she'd lost sight of the fact that there were people everywhere going through their own individual traumas.

'I haven't managed my pain very well, to be honest with you. How did you keep your sanity?' asked Elinor, quietly.

'I'm a bit of a hermit, so alone time works wonders for me when I'm under pressure. My painting saved me I guess, in that respect. My sister, too. She lives in Penzance, and I'm in daily contact with her.'

Elinor nodded and drank some more wine. She'd already decided she was going to get a taxi home. Not only was she now over the limit for driving, she could also feel herself getting steadily more lightheaded. Even if she'd tried walking home she'd have become utterly lost within a short space of time.

It had been such a long, long time since she'd had an alcoholic drink. Mark had died at the hands of a drunk driver and in her rage she'd refused to drink any alcohol since then, but now she was feeling liberated and unrestrained. The shackles of the past had dropped away from her, at least for a brief moment in time. She was going to freely drown her sorrows in some Cornish wine tonight.

Barbara seemed to be matching her glass by glass, so clearly the pair of them were setting themselves up for a rough ride in the morning.

It was only later on in the evening that she suddenly remembered the medication she was on and wondered what impact the alcohol would have on it. As far as she could remember, when he'd prescribed her medication the doctor hadn't warned her about drinking. She decided not to worry about it. Which was an exhilaratingly unusual stance for a hypochondriac like her.

By this point she was in a taxi and on her way home. She was replete with wine and good food, and feeling she'd made a new friend in Barbara. As the taxi crawled its way around the twisting and narrow corners of the hedged roads, she looked out at the drab winter landscape and decided Cornwall was proving to be her place of healing.

She smiled to herself. Her mother was going to get a shock when she saw her again.

23

At eight thirty the next morning, as the light was beginning to dawn, Elinor was woken up unexpectedly by the loud sound of rotor blades turning.

For a moment, she wondered if she was hallucinating. Her head was heavy from the wine she'd imbibed the night before with Barbara, and her mouth was dry. Her eyes were sore, too, no doubt also craving some moisture.

After a minute listening to the peculiar noise, she jumped out of bed and pulled back the curtains.

She gasped.

In front of her was a helicopter, hovering right above Warren Cove. On the edge of the cliff, at a safe distance from the helicopter, she could see the bulky figure of her uncle.

She scrambled over to her chest of drawers and pulled on the first items of clothing she came across. She bundled her hair into a woolly hat, fully aware that the draft from the helicopter's blades was going to be turbulent. She wanted to see what was going on and didn't want to get blinded by her long hair slapping her in the face.

She ran out into the chill morning air and circled the house, making her way to the Cornish hedge. She leapt and scrambled up the uneven side of it. Soon she was sitting up on the wall's grass-padded top. Securely on her perch, she looked up at the machine thundering above her.

Outside, without the cushioning of the double-glazed windows, the noise of the helicopter was deafening.

The helicopter appeared to be winching up a red padded sleeping bag on its rope. Inside the bag there was, very clearly, a human body.

Leo was coming along the cliff towards her. The expression on his face was harshly rigid. She could see that even from a distance. She wondered what was going on.

She turned and continued to watch the helicopter.

Slowly and painstakingly, the sleeping bag reached the helicopter's open door, and then suddenly it disappeared into its cavernous stomach. The helicopter continued to hover above the cove and it was evident it was communicating with someone down below. Shortly afterwards a rope, with a harness attached, was dropped down from the helicopter into the cove again.

Elinor was surprised. She'd expected to see the helicopter fly straight off to hospital with its injured casualty. She was struggling to figure out what was going on. Surely if someone was injured they'd be off by now?

Instead the helicopter winched up another man from the cove. He was latched into a secure harness and was hanging and turning in the air like a curious mobile. This man had on a bright orange jumpsuit and a helmet, so he was obviously one of the rescue workers.

Once he'd been carefully winched up into the helicopter, it tilted at an angle and flew rapidly away into the horizon.

Elinor watched it until it was just a minuscule black dot in the sky and then turned to Leo, who was standing on the other side of the wall.

'What the hell was that all about?'

'That was a neighbour, apparently. I didn't know him. He lived down at that house,' Leo said grimly, pointing with his finger at a two-storey, grey stone house, a little further down the slope, and a little nearer to Pepper Cove and Treyarnon Bay than they were.

'Was? Are you saying he's died?'

'Unfortunately, yes. He'd been battling terminal cancer for some time. He couldn't take it any more and, so they tell me, he decided to take matters into his own hands last night.'

Elinor looked at him in horror.

'Do you mean he took his own life?'

'Yes, I'm afraid so. He threw himself over the cliff edge, with his dog too, apparently. That's what the police said earlier this morning. At least it's been early enough not to attract any rubberneckers. Apart from the two of us, that is.'

Stunned and shaken, Elinor stared fixedly at the cliff edge, as though by doing so she'd get more answers. But all there was now, in the empty space above Warren Cove, was a solitary seagull floating on a buoyant cushion of air rising up from the cove below.

Her mind, wayward as ever, refused to focus on the reality of the situation. All she could do was to wonder, irrationally, why this neighbour hadn't chosen a cove nearer his own house. Why right outside their home? And why did he take his poor dog with him? The whole situation was hideous.

Leo stood next to her, standing as still and immobile as a heron. With his thick grey muffler wrapped around his neck and his grey wool coat, he didn't look unlike one, either.

'The government really has to start to listen to people suffering from terminal illnesses. It should introduce changes to the laws in this country,' commented Leo, eventually. 'People should have the right to choose how to die when they face terminal illnesses and a high degree of physical discomfort.'

Elinor didn't say anything. Mark's life had been snuffed out in an instant. It seemed to cheapen the value of one's life to go that quickly, so she was inclined to think life must be worth fighting for.

She shuffled around so she was no longer facing the cliff. She felt strangely empty and hollow. She was stunned to think someone would have had the resolution to jump off a cliff edge like this one. What kind of pain must he have been carrying inside?

Leo had his back to the cliff too and was looking pensively down at the grey house, which seemed peaceful and ordinary enough at this early morning hour.

The field in front of their house was covered in a silver sheen of dewdrops. The cows had their heads down to the grass, oblivious to the dramatic scene that had unfolded a few metres away. Elinor wondered if they'd had a fright when the helicopter appeared. If so, they now seemed remarkably composed.

'No one should ever feel that they have to take matters into their own hands. There are better ways to die than throwing yourself off a cliff. We treat animals with more compassion, in that respect, than humans. If they're suffering we put them down...' muttered Leo angrily to himself.

'You seem to have very strong opinions on the matter, Leo,' commented Elinor, surprised to see her normally placid uncle so worked up.

'Yes, I do, I'm afraid. My grandfather, that's your great-grandfather, had motor neurone disease. Basically, you end up suffocating to death. He would've liked a say on how his life ended but he had no choice. And I know I don't want anyone keeping me alive, at any cost, when my time comes.'

Elinor pondered this for a while and in the end decided she agreed, for the most part, with her uncle.

She felt humans craved control over their lives and so often didn't have it. No one expects to be diagnosed with a terminal illness, but once they are, giving people a measure of control and choice over their demise was bound to give some relief from the agony of uncertainty.

So many were ready to let go, but were waiting at the whim of their physical bodies. Nursing homes were bunged full of residents, living a limited, imprisoned life, and kept going with a cocktail of medication and medical care that preserved life when there was no longer any quality to it.

Leo started to stamp his feet vigorously, as though suddenly realising how cold he was.

'I'm sorry for being so morose, Elinor. Let's go inside and get the kettle on. We could do with some coffee and warm toast. Things like this take time, and reflection, to recover from.'

'I totally agree with you on that one. I'm not going to forget this in a hurry, if ever,' said Elinor, jumping down from the wall and wincing at the excruciating pain erupting in her head when she hit the ground. 'Actually, I could do with a full cooked breakfast this morning, Leo. Would you fancy some? I've got a raging hangover.'

Leo looked at her in surprise, but tactfully didn't say anything. It wasn't clear if he approved or not, but, as ever,

he avoided interfering. Which is exactly what Elinor loved
about him.

24

Later on that morning, Elinor stood on the slate steps outside Trenouth for a moment, before bending down and tying the shoelaces on her trainers a little bit tighter. She knew she was procrastinating, as she always did before a jog. Even though she'd become a lot fitter recently, she still found it a challenge to motivate herself to go out running.

She'd resolved this dilemma by sticking an unattractive photo of herself in a swimsuit on her bedroom mirror. Looking at it usually did the job.

On her first run along the coast, she'd only managed ten minutes before she was wheezing like an asthmatic. Ignoring the concerned looks of other walkers on the clifftop, she'd carried on running, determined to break the barriers her lungs and heart were putting up. She was sure at some point her protesting heart was going to give up on her, but fortunately it didn't.

It wasn't many days before she was finding, to her surprise, she'd reached a level of endurance she didn't know she was capable of.

After the horrible start to the morning when they'd been witness to a lifeless body being uplifted from their cove, both Leo and Elinor had gulped down a hearty amount of food for breakfast. They'd savoured each mouthful, each silently recognising that their deceased neighbour would no longer have the pleasure of doing so.

But once she'd eaten the enormous cooked breakfast and drunk several glasses of water, she could feel the edible fuel lodged in her stomach and knew she had to run some of it off.

Besides, a heavy lump of sadness had also settled at the pit of her stomach and she wanted to shake it off. There was going to be no better cure for her acute emotional pain than pushing her body to the limit. The physical exhaustion of her run would ease the mental tiredness she always felt when she was in low spirits.

She briskly zipped up her velour running top and set off. Once over their wall, she raced ahead down along the cliff path to Treyarnon Bay. As she jogged along the edges of the bay, she noticed some surfers were out in the ocean.

Ignoring them she ran on, following the path along to Constantine Bay. She made her way to the edges of Trevose Golf Course, trying to keep an eye out for the ancient Constantine chapel and well.

Soon, she could see from a distance the pyramid shape of the well's roof.

In amongst the carefully groomed grass there was a modern stone structure with a slate roof – all its sides open to the elements – and inside were the old remains of the well. Elinor ran up to it and rested beside it for a moment to get her breath back.

She looked down at the clear water.

Of course, people had superstitiously thrown in numerous coins of various denominations, as people have done with wells or fountains for centuries. Some of the coins had landed around the edges of the well and Elinor wondered if the greenkeepers ever profited from this unexpected largesse. She doubted this ancient well would reach the profitability of Rome's Trevi Fountain, where supposedly up to 3,000 euros were thrown in every single day.

Close by were the remains of the old chapel, buried underneath heavy gorse bushes. A couple of greenkeepers were busily employed cutting down the undergrowth from around the chapel's archway.

Elinor politely said hello to them and then turned to head back towards the coastal path.

She didn't like loitering for too long on the golf course because it was busy and popular. Sometimes the golfers tended to get annoyed when she jogged across the fairway, and she'd hear them yelling at her from afar. But living down here in Cornwall she was fast developing a thick skin, and would just give them a rude gesture before carrying on. She was sure one day some pompous twat was going to corner her with a golf club official, but so far she'd escaped any reprimand.

She ran along the coastal path that skirted the edges of Booby's Bay, the beach nearest to Trevose Head, feeling the soft grass cushioning her heavy tread.

From a distance, Trevose Head looked like a slumbering green lizard, with its head sticking out and dipped into the ocean's water. Its physical presence was strangely docile and benign, even though it charismatically dominated the horizon.

Trevose Head was the focal point for any clifftop within a five-mile radius and the protruding land mass drew your eye, like a coquetting young lady craving attention. You could clearly see Trevose Head even when you looked out from Leo's house.

It was only on foggy days that Trevose Head disappeared from sight. When the land mass was shrouded sadly in thick mist, the mournful tones of a foghorn would echo across the water as a warning.

Elinor was sure she'd be fit enough to run to the tip of Trevose Head one day, but that wasn't her goal for today. Looking at her watch she saw she'd already been running for forty minutes, which was her target time. Once she reached the end of Booby's Bay she turned and resolutely headed back to Constantine Bay.

When she reached the edges of Constantine Bay she ran to the top of a sand dune and then let gravity pull her down the steep slope, her legs giving way to the slipping sand. As she stumbled downwards she felt the sand pouring into the cracks in her shoes and socks.

Unexpectedly, her ankle twisted in the loose sand and with a shriek she found herself falling and rolling down the precipitous, and unstable, mound.

She landed shortly afterwards on a soft patch of sand at the bottom and lay there, gasping and laughing dementedly at herself, as she turned her face upwards to the sky. It was strangely comfortable lying on a bed of sand and after her vigorous run she felt no inclination to get up again.

'Elinor, are you OK?'

Elinor brushed the hair off her face and looked up into the concerned face bent over her. Two dark brown eyes, creased at the corners, stared down at her, surrounded by a freckled pink-tinged face, a flat nose and a broad mouth. It was Tony Reece.

'Yes, I'm fine. Why?' she asked perplexed.

Tony grinned.

'First I hear a shriek, and then the next minute I see this figure tumbling down the sandy slope. Then once you landed, you didn't move, so I assumed you must be injured.'

Elinor sat up, conscious of all the sand that must be stuck to her hair and to the parts of her body that were soaked in sweat.

'So you decided to come to the rescue. That's sweet of you.'

'Not quite. I was just checking you were still alive, really.'

'Why can't you just accept you were coming to my rescue?' asked Elinor, unreasonably irate.

Tony looked embarrassed.

'Sorry. If that's what you want to see it as, then OK. Sure. Do you want some help to get yourself up?' he asked, stretching down a hand.

Elinor grabbed it and pulled herself up.

'Well, I wasn't planning on falling down the dune. But it was kind of fun,' she said, dusting herself down.

Tony looked up at the sand dune.

'Yeah, I used to like rolling down it too when I was young boy.'

'Come on then, Tony. Why don't you do it now? Life's short. You shouldn't resist the impulse to have fun...'

Tony smiled with real merriment. It seemed to take a supreme amount of effort to get a smile out of him, Elinor thought, but when it came it was well worth the labour.

'It's OK. I'll pass, thanks,' Tony said. 'I get my thrills from the surf now. I was going to say to you, I think you're doing fantastically well at the surf school. I'm glad you didn't give up.'

Elinor felt pleased he'd noticed her improvement. She was

now managing the smaller waves relatively easily. For the last couple of weeks, though, they'd only exchanged brief greetings as they'd passed each other in the water.

'I could hardly have done worse than that first day. Anything's bound to be an improvement on that.'

Tony looked at her jogging outfit, as though suddenly noticing it for the first time. Elinor suddenly felt self-conscious, aware of her skin-tight jogging bottoms, her waist bulging over the top, and her hefty sports bra. Annoyingly, she could feel herself blushing.

'Is this part of a new fitness regime, then?' asked Tony. 'With rolling down the dune as part of the circuit?'

'You know what they say, "a healthy body means a healthy mind",' she said, airily quoting the old cliché.

Tony nodded.

'You're absolutely right. Well done you,' he said, serious again.

Elinor felt a mild irritation at his prudish tone and started to wonder if he ever felt the inclination to crack a joke. After a dismal start to the day she felt in need of some levity. She preferred it when he smiled, but she wasn't about to go and roll down the dune again.

She shivered as a cold breeze started gusting, pulling yet more strands of hair out of her long ponytail.

'OK, then. I'm going to head back and get changed. I'm due at Barbara's this afternoon.'

'Barbara's?'

'Barbara Bligh. I've just started working on a painting at her studio.'

Enlightened, Tony looked pleasantly surprised. More than that, he looked pleased for some unexplained reason. Elinor couldn't understand why, but refrained from questioning him about it.

She zipped up her top and looked around for the start of the path leading to Treyarnon Bay.

'Hold on a minute, Elinor. As you're a newcomer around here, I wondered if you'd fancy joining us for a drink at The Farmer's Arms on Friday night?'

Elinor pondered this. Having declined so often Leo's invitations to The Farmer's Arms, she felt it would be a little churlish to then turn up at Tony's behest. But then again, she didn't have many acquaintances in Cornwall and she did miss having people to socialise with.

'Who's "us"?' she asked curiously.

'Mostly the surfer crowd. It's never too late a night as most of us like to catch the waves early in the morning, before heading off to do other things at the weekend. Like surf school.'

'What time do you all meet?'

'Most of us are there by half past eight.'

'Thanks for the invitation, Tony. I'll think about it... I might see you there. My uncle tends to go on a Friday night, too, so I could always accompany him. Anyway, I'm really going to have to go. I've totally cooled down now and I'm keeping you from your surfing, too.'

Tony clearly agreed, so they walked companionably along the beach together until Elinor saw Tony's surfboard tossed down on the sand a short distance away. After a quick farewell, Tony then began to jog towards the sea and Elinor started the long walk home in eager anticipation of a hot shower and a cup of coffee.

25

'Barbara, do you know Tony Reece?' asked Elinor as the pair of them got stuck into their paintings at the studio.

'Yes, I do. I've known him for a long time. Why?'

'He was behaving a bit oddly this morning. When I said I was going to be in the studio with you this afternoon, he seemed almost overly pleased. It was a bit weird.'

Barbara chuckled to herself.

Elinor stopped what she was doing and looked across at Barbara, trying in vain to comprehend why Barbara would find Tony's odd behaviour so funny.

Barbara caught her eye and smiled.

'Tony's such a sweetheart. He's as transparent as they come. He's like a glass, you can see straight through him. He has no filter or guile. Which is the nicest thing about him. However, I keep telling him his lack of reserve is bound to get him into trouble one of these days.'

'I see,' responded Elinor untruthfully, accepting Barbara's glowing report on Tony but not really understanding how this would make him pleased to hear that Elinor was visiting Barbara. She felt faintly dissatisfied with Barbara's nebulous response to her query.

She shrugged petulantly and picked up her brush again, resolving to get lost in her painting once more.

The CD player in the corner was belting out 'Take On Me' by A-ha. Barbara clearly liked to stick to the old classics but Elinor didn't mind. She was quite often so absorbed in her painting she didn't notice the music.

Elinor started to mix up the different coloured paints on her palette, trying to match up the colour to the exact tint she had in mind for the surfboard in her painting.

'Tony was friendly with my partner Glenn,' volunteered Barbara unexpectedly, a little while later, after they'd been painting in silence for a while.

She put down her brush and swung round on her stool to face Elinor. Realising that Barbara had decided to explain things a bit more, Elinor stopped painting and listened politely to what she had to say.

'They used to go fishing together. In the beginning, I never liked it when they brought back freshly caught fish. I started having nightmares after trying to gut the first fish Glenn caught. A sea bass it was. I still remember it to this day. After that Glenn made sure he gutted and filleted the fish before he came back home. I'm pretty sure he probably gutted the fish on the rocks before arriving here with it.'

'Gross.'

'Yes, although there's truly nothing like the taste of freshly caught fish.'

Barbara loudly smacked her lips together and gestured expressively like an Italian. Barbara was a true foodie. Elinor smiled at her briefly and turned back to her painting as Barbara continued to talk.

'It's such a sublime experience eating fresh fish. You can taste the nourishment and the richness of the sea so much better.

So much more so than in a fish that's been sitting in the sunny window of a fishmonger's all day.'

Elinor mumbled an assent. She was now engrossed in working the lines of the surfboard in her painting with one paintbrush and, with yet another paintbrush, trying hard to portray the white surf of the wave splashing against it.

'He still brings me fresh fish on occasion,' mumbled Barbara in a provocative voice, casting a sly look in Elinor's direction.

'Sorry, Barbara, could you repeat that again? Who brings you fish? Tony Reece?' asked Elinor crossly, reluctantly detaching herself mentally from her all-encompassing, self-absorbed focus on her painting.

For an insane moment Elinor wondered if Barbara was trying to make her jealous. Wondering why she should wish to do so left her feeling perplexed and vaguely suspicious. She quickly dismissed that idea from her mind.

Frustratingly, she wasn't finding it easy to pick up on the cryptic messages Barbara was trying to send her, with her covert little glances and teasingly random comments.

Elinor's concentration on her painting was such that every verbal distraction seemed to her as irritating as a buzzing fly. A fly that seemed to be attracted by the smell of her sweet perfume and was refusing to leave her in peace.

She reluctantly put down her paintbrushes and strived to engage in the conversation once more, looking enquiringly at Barbara.

'I was just saying Tony Reece brings me freshly caught fish occasionally. It's lovely. I'll have to invite you round next time he does that,' repeated Barbara patiently.

'That's nice of him. It does make you wonder how he finds

the time to be a GP, to teach surfing, to go surfing himself and also to go fishing.'

'He only works three days a week.'

'Still.'

'He's a man of many talents,' giggled Barbara naughtily.

Elinor looked at her thoughtfully.

'I'm sorry, am I missing something here, Barbara? Is there something going on between the two of you?' she asked, suddenly wondering if Barbara and Tony were an item. That would explain a lot.

'No, not at all!' said Barbara, sobering up straight away and looking alarmed. 'I'm just messing with you, that's all, darling. There's really not much to say. Tony and I are old friends and Tony would've been glad to know that you come here, solely because it's company for me. Does that answer satisfy you?'

Elinor didn't reply because she felt slightly ashamed at her unaccustomed persistence. She couldn't explain why she'd so wanted an answer to her question in the first place.

'He often feels compelled to drop by and see me since I've been on my own. I guess it'll make him feel better to know you're keeping me company now,' said Barbara, lifting up her glasses and tiredly rubbing her eyes.

Barbara, with her bright pink glasses sitting on top of her head, was back to looking as innocent as a small child again. The pale pink stripes in her hair glistened in the sunlight beaming down from the strange cupola above her.

Elinor paused for a long moment before turning to the picture in front of her once more. She couldn't help thinking that Tony and Barbara were in cahoots about something, and she began to wonder if they'd been talking about her behind her back. Possibly she was just being her usual paranoid self, she thought, shrugging her shoulders again.

In a fairly harmless and frivolous way, Barbara seemed to be enjoying teasing Elinor with the obliqueness of her comments about Tony Reece but Elinor was finding Barbara's mischievousness intensely annoying, especially when all she wanted to do at the moment was paint.

It was time to change the topic of conversation, decided Elinor, hoping that by doing so she'd be able to concentrate on her painting once more.

'It sounds to me, from what everyone around here says, that you're never short of company,' Elinor observed.

'It's true that in the summer months I'm mobbed with visitors but in the dreary winter months things get very quiet, as you'll have noticed. It gets quite depressing,' commented Barbara, finally turning her attention back to her painting once more, much to Elinor's relief.

Elinor hadn't told Barbara about the dramatic clifftop suicide that had occurred outside Trenouth that morning, which might have changed Barbara's perspective somewhat on the lack of excitement in Cornwall during the long winter months. But today Elinor didn't feel in the mood to talk about it. She was doing her usual trick of burying tragedy underneath layers of self-preservation.

'Yes, I did notice the other week that a book fair is considered the most exciting event to happen at this time of year,' muttered Elinor, mixing up some oil paints on her palette.

'I know. It's a little tragic isn't it? I'm very grateful for your company. I like having people around but Cornwall's a wasteland over the winter months.'

Barbara put her brush down and stretched sleepily. She started sifting through her brushes to locate the right-sized brush for her next bit of painting.

'Half the homes here are holiday homes,' she continued, looking at her canvas once more with half-closed eyes. 'It's a real problem because it makes it hard for villages and towns to be a community, when people are only here for short-term holidays. Let alone the fact that these wealthy people who own the holiday homes price out the locals. At least the local councils are slowly starting to address the issue, only allowing new housing to be available to people buying a first home or a main residence.'

'Are homes here that expensive?' asked Elinor curiously.

'Any home on the coast, with a view of the sea, would expect to be in the million pound bracket.'

'Wow. So that means Leo's sitting on a gold mine.'

Barbara laughed.

'Leo doesn't need money to make him content. He'd have been just as happy if his house was worth nothing. He's a rare breed who's actually happy with his life and what he has.'

Elinor pondered this for a few moments in silence. It was true that Leo's innate ability to be fulfilled was a treasure in itself. Painting did the same for her. It fulfilled something deep within her soul that nothing else could.

Conversation in Barbara's studio came to a halt as the pair of them allowed their imaginations to be transported magically into the images developing on their canvases, and in what seemed to be no time at all the dusk had settled outside, reminding them it was time to stop painting and get some rest.

26

Elinor drove back to Trenouth after her painting session with a pleasurable feeling of deep satisfaction. Her picture was going well and it was a relief to realise she hadn't lost the ability to paint during the sabbatical she'd given herself over the last year.

She put the radio on at full blast and sang back at the tunes belting out of the speakers. She drove past the field of cows and up the driveway to Leo's house.

Oddly, given it was already dusk, there were no lights on in the bungalow. Elinor frowned to herself. It wasn't like Leo not to be in at this time of day. She felt her spirits sink as she wondered if Leo had been searching for that wretched smuggler's tunnel again. Still, the only way to find out was to see if he was in the house.

Elinor switched off the engine, pulled the handbrake on and gathered up her bulky shoulder bag that contained, amongst other things, her preliminary sketches and photographs. She sighed and went up to the front door, fumbling with the heavy key in the lock and cursing as always the stiffness of the old door.

As soon as she was inside the front door she switched the lights on. She dumped her heavy bag onto the bench in the hallway and made her way through to the dining room.

Elinor found Leo sitting on one of the dark green armchairs and in semi-darkness. He was looking out of the window and sitting so still he could've been carved in stone.

Elinor switched on one of the lamps.

'Leo?' asked Elinor, worried. 'Are you OK?'

Leo stirred and slowly turned to look at her. Elinor walked up and plonked herself on the sofa next to him.

'I found the tunnel.'

'Really? You found it? Well, that's fantastic. You always said you knew there was one.'

'Yes,' said Leo, not looking particularly pleased with his discovery.

Elinor studied his face, trying to figure out what was going on inside his head.

'You don't sound terribly excited about finding it,' said Elinor finally, in a gross understatement. 'What's the problem?'

'I think I might just have opened Pandora's box, to be honest with you, Elinor. It's a discovery that's shaken me. What I saw at the mouth of the tunnel has me troubled and I'm really not sure what to do about it now.'

'I don't understand. What did you see at the entrance? And where is the tunnel anyway?'

'I went into one of the caves at Wine Cove. It's not easily accessible. I had to put on my waterproof fishing gear and wade through a metre-deep rock pool inside of the cave. Right at the back of the cave, about three metres above the cave floor, there's a square hole cut into the rock face. It's clearly man-made. I looked into the opening and it's definitely a tunnel, and as far as I can see the tunnel heads upwards.' Leo started to chew his upper lip. It was a habit of his when he felt flummoxed by a difficult conundrum and it mostly happened when he was working on the *Sunday Times* crossword.

'I didn't go into it myself, obviously, but what surprised me most of all was that the tunnel still seems to be in use.'

'Don't be ridiculous. Who'd want to go up a disused and dirty tunnel these days?' scoffed Elinor, refusing to believe people would want to explore what was bound to be a wet, smelly tunnel.

'Well somebody clearly does,' retorted Leo. 'There's a waterproof canvas bag tied to a hook next to the tunnel entrance and in it there's five waterproof torches. Why would that be there if the tunnel wasn't in use?'

'Maybe there's a crazy thrill-seeker that's getting his kicks from exploring a secret tunnel.'

'With five torches? Come on, Elinor. There's also a hook clearly meant to be used to tie a dinghy or a small boat to.'

'So? It's probably a thrill-seeker with a small boat. What's the big deal?'

Leo shook his head stubbornly.

'I don't agree. I haven't got a good feeling about it. It's too well prepared and organised to be a one-time thing. Something dodgy is going on with that tunnel.'

Elinor looked into her uncle's eyes and saw he wasn't about to change his mind. Those clear blue eyes were filled with resolution and determination. Leo was a man who'd built a close spiritual bond with nature over a lifetime and he wasn't about to ignore any instinct lurking in the pit of his belly. He possessed finely tuned antennae for anything that didn't compute with his sense of right and wrong.

'So what are you planning to do about it?' asked Elinor,

resigned to the fact Leo wasn't going to let his suspicions rest.

'I'm not sure. There's nothing illegal about having five torches tied to the entrance of an old smuggling tunnel. I need to gather more information. I've started wondering if Barbara's story might not be so crazy after all.'

'What story?'

'Surely you remember when she told us about the neighbour at the bottom of our road? The one who was getting woken up in the middle of the night by a white van? I think I might go and have a word with her.'

'Oh yes! I seem to remember you shot Barbara's suspicions down in flames at the time. Are you saying you think it might all be true now? You owe Barbara an apology, if that's the case, Leo. You really weren't very nice to her about it.'

Leo nodded in silent agreement.

Elinor looked at him, intrigued by his sudden acceptance of Barbara's outlandish ideas and the possibility that the tunnel he had found might have a secretive, even sinister, use.

'If you're planning on interviewing Sheila Burns, can I come with you?' she asked suddenly, her interest kindled.

'Of course you can. We can head down there in the early morning tomorrow. I don't want to frighten her by turning up in the dark, when she's not expecting us.'

Elinor smiled ironically, remembering how, not so long ago, six young men had turned up in the middle of the night at Trenouth. Leo had then shown a great deal less regard to her fears than to Sheila Burns'.

Elinor got up and headed to the kitchen to rustle up some dinner.

Later that night she slept better than she had done for a

long time. She slept deeply and no eerie dreams disturbed her sleep for once. Painting was working its magic on her and she was able to drift away pondering the alterations she wanted to make next time she was up at Barbara's studio. Everything else in her life was fading into the background: her surfing, Leo's tunnel and Tony Reece were all things that suddenly didn't seem to matter so much...

27

Leo woke Elinor up at what she considered to be an utterly hideous time of the morning. Elinor had a tendency to be a night owl so she did not appreciate Leo opening her door and yelling 'Good morning!' at the top of his voice when it had just turned eight o'clock.

Leo, as was his habit, had been up at six, and after two hours he was like a caged animal, ready to go out adventuring. He was giving up his daily constitutional walk along the cliffs this morning, all for the sake of some investigative research into the smuggler's tunnel, and his impatience to get going was palpable.

Elinor, cursing her stupidity in asking to accompany Leo on his visit to Sheila Burns' house, sat up and stared blearily at him.

'You're not planning to visit her now, are you?'

'Yes, of course. Strike while the iron's hot is what I say.'

'OK, OK. Can you give me half an hour?'

Elinor watched with amusement as Leo strived to conceal the impatience he was feeling.

'Yes, that's fine. There'll be a coffee waiting for you in the kitchen.'

'Thanks, Leo.'

Once Leo had left, Elinor threw herself back onto the soft

pillows of her bed. All she wanted to do was fall asleep again but her curiosity was nagging away at her. She wanted to see how Sheila Burns would react to Leo's questions. She had no idea what assumptions Leo was making about the tunnel, but he was clearly following the scent like a dog in search of a bone.

With a sigh she threw off her covers and made her way to the bathroom.

After a cold shower she felt her mind sharpen and start to engage with the day, the sleepy mists of her deep slumber grudgingly giving way to alertness once more.

She managed to make it to the kitchen within twenty minutes.

She knew all she needed was a coffee and she'd then be able to keep up with Leo's energetic search for answers. Leo was waiting for her and silently handed her a hot mug of coffee when she made an appearance, which was gratefully received. As she sipped it she looked out of the window at the gentle cows, which were all gathered calmly in a small group right next to the barbed wire adjoining Trenouth's garden. Their large brown eyes stared right back at her.

What did cows think about, she wondered? They were certainly curious enough, but did they ever yearn to roam free as their ancestors must have done at some point in time?

Elinor's uncle Rory, on her Scottish father's side, had been a sheep farmer in Aberdeenshire and they'd spent many weekends visiting his farm. To her surprise, her uncle told her that sheep were actually not stupid at all, contradicting the well-known myth that they are helpless and clueless bundles of wool.

Apparently sheep were capable of a whole range of complex emotions and had impressive memory and recognition skills, as proven by a study in 2001 that suggested sheep could remember up to fifty faces for two years. More than most people could do...

Elinor wondered if these cows had similar unknown talents. If she stayed here much longer, she thought, she was going to end up a vegetarian.

Leo cleared his throat.

'Eh, Elinor? Are you ready to go yet?'

Elinor jumped back into the present and quickly dropped her mug into the sink that was full of soapy washing-up water.

'Yes, sorry, I was daydreaming. I'll just grab a cereal bar and eat it on the way.'

She quickly picked up a couple of cereal bars from the kitchen cupboard and followed Leo out of the house, stuffing the bars into the pockets of her tracksuit top. She couldn't cope without breakfast. She'd tried numerous dieting techniques in the days of her drastic yo-yo dieting but the one thing she found she couldn't go without was breakfast. She'd been quite happy to starve for the rest of the day, but only as long as she had some breakfast in her.

She followed Leo's quick pace as he strode down the road ahead of her, surreptitiously stuffing her mouth full of moist muesli and raisin cereal bar as she walked.

At the end of the road encircling the field outside Trenouth there was a junction. Leo turned left, following the road down towards Treyarnon Bay. As they walked down the road there was a Cornish hedge on their left hand side. Behind the hedge was a large wheat field. It was fully sown now it was winter, full of delicate grass like green stems, stems that would turn golden yellow by early spring.

At the bottom of the road Leo turned right down a short

dead-end road, full of potholes and broken tarmac, that had four houses on either side. He started searching the house names on the right hand side. He soon spotted a small cottage called 'Chi An Treth'.

'This is it. "Chi An Treth". That's basically Cornish for "Beach House". Not a very original name,' grumbled Leo, with all the arrogance of someone who considered his own home the most desirable property within ten square miles.

He walked up a paved garden path towards Chi An Treth. The garden was well tended and it was obvious it would be full of beautiful blossoms when spring came. This house was sheltered from the worst of the wind, unlike the cliff-edge homes, and so could afford to grow a large variety of flowers that would not survive in the more exposed parts of the coast.

The house itself was slightly unusual in that the walls were coloured a cornflower blue and the windows were painted brilliant white. Elinor smiled to see the colours of the Scottish flag plastered over the house, although in truth the cottage had more of a Scandinavian air. Elinor could picture in her mind the pine wood floors and furniture inside it.

Leo pushed the bell button by the front door. It didn't take long for the door to open, and an old lady holding a mug of tea peered out at them, looking very surprised.

'Oh! I thought you were the milkman. He's always saying I don't leave the right change for the milk. How can I help you?'

Leo had positioned himself behind Elinor, clearly thinking she should do the introductions.

'Hi, I'm Elinor Campbell and this is my uncle Leo Jago. We live just up the road, in the house opposite Warren Cove, and we're friends of Barbara Bligh. We wondered if we could have a chat with you. She told us you'd seen some strange goings-on late at night? We're interested to hear what you have to say about it.'

'You're nothing to do with the police, are you?' asked the old lady suspiciously.

'No, not at all. My uncle's just trying to find some answers to some questions he's got. He saw something unusual when he was down at Wine Cove and wondered if it was in any way connected to what you've seen.'

The old lady beamed at Leo, obviously delighted to find a fellow conspirator, and she quickly waved them into her tiny hallway.

'Come through to the kitchen and I'll make you a cup of tea,' she said, as she walked to the back of the house.

Elinor noted the back wall of the cottage had been extended at some point and the kitchen was now a large room with a wide glass window overlooking an ample garden. No doubt an avaricious developer would look to make use of all the garden space and would have built a larger house, or even flats, but there was something uniquely quaint and fetching about this dainty little cottage.

The decor wasn't remotely Scandinavian; it was all walnut and oak furniture that looked to be at least two hundred years old. The floral wallpaper in the kitchen looked like a Laura Ashley product from a decade ago.

'Take a seat,' said the old lady, indicating the dining table.

Leo and Elinor sat down on a couple of chairs, with their backs to the garden so they could watch Sheila pottering about in the kitchen.

'I'm Sheila Burns, as Barbara must've told you already. I see

Barbara when I go to the day care centre at Truro. She volunteers there on Thursdays and does some art with us. She's a special lady, that one. She has a heart of gold. She's organising an art exhibition with our work at the end of January. Her classes really keep me going, so they do,' said Sheila, talking rapidly and without pause as she filled a teapot with tea and boiling water.

She took an old-fashioned glass bottle of milk from the fridge and put it on the table, along with three mugs. She then began pouring the tea, talking all the while. For someone who'd been worried they might be the police she suddenly seemed remarkably outspoken. Maybe their connection to Barbara Bligh was the magic talisman to gaining Sheila's instant trust.

Leo and Elinor listened politely while Sheila talked incessantly about the local guild and then went on to moan about cost of food shopping. Eventually, once she'd sat down at the table with them, she petered out and looked at them expectantly.

'What do you want to know?'

'I just wondered if you could tell us what you saw when the van woke you up late at night. Was the van on this street?' asked Leo.

Sheila shook her head.

'No, it wasn't on our street or others would have noticed it, I'm sure. It was out on the main road running next to the wheat field.'

'Can you see the main road from here?' asked Leo, twisting round to look out of the window.

'Yes, I can see it from my upstairs bedroom. Do you want to have a look?'

'If you don't mind, that would be helpful,' said Leo.

Sheila nodded and without any more preamble led them to the top floor.

They went into the main bedroom, and pushing the chintz curtains aside they all peered out through the window. Sure enough, they had clear sight of the road Leo and Elinor had just walked down, as well as a good view of the field, with its neat, green rows of swaying wheat heads stretching into the distance.

'That's where I saw it,' said Sheila, pointing to the bit of the road that connected with the corner of the wheat field.

'Was it in the same place every time you saw it?'

'Funny you should ask that. Yes, it was, actually.'

'That's interesting. Why would it always stop there, I wonder? Did you see anyone with the van?'

'Most of the time it seemed the van was parked there for a good hour or two, as if waiting for something or someone... I don't know. I didn't always stay up for very long. I'm getting old. The driver was a young man, didn't look much older than you,' Sheila said pointing to Elinor.

'Would you be able to identify him?'

'It wouldn't be easy. It was dark and he had a hooded jacket on. But I did take the number plate of the van. Here it is.'

Sheila went to her bedside table and opened a drawer. She pulled out a piece of paper and handed it to Leo. Leo took out his mobile phone from his trouser pocket and photographed the piece of paper before handing it back to Sheila.

'Thank you. You've been very helpful.'

Sheila looked intently at Leo, holding tightly to the paper with the number plate on it, her bird-like head turned to one side as she observed him.

'So what do you think's going on? Have you any idea?' she

asked impatiently.

'Not really, Sheila,' said Leo ruefully. 'I'm afraid I'm stumbling around in the dark. I'm as confused as you are. However, I'm not going to let this go because my instinct's telling me something's going on that's not right. Whatever it is that's happening, I'm determined to get to the bottom of it. We'll stay in touch. Would you like my phone number in case anything else suspicious grabs your attention?'

Sheila nodded eagerly and passed Leo a piece of paper and pen. While Leo wrote down his mobile number, Elinor stared out of the window, looking up at the road beside the wheat field.

It all looked thoroughly mundane and peaceful, a million miles from any illicit activity. However, looks could be deceiving and even here, in such a quiet part of Cornwall, the most extraordinary things could happen, as had been proven the last few weeks.

28

The next day, at around three in the afternoon, Elinor was walking down to Treyarnon Bay with her camera when she saw Leo climbing over the Cornish hedge next to the wheat field. Greeting Elinor sheepishly, he clambered laboriously down onto the road.

'Leo, for goodness' sake, what are you up to now?'

'I was just having a closer look at the wheat field.'

'But why wouldn't you go in by the gate, as usual?' asked Elinor, genuinely astonished to see her uncle appearing so furtive.

'Well, I saw Richard Glynn approaching with a tractor and I thought the sooner I removed myself, the better.'

Elinor chuckled.

'It's not like you to run scared, Leo.'

Leo grinned at her.

'I'm not scared of that tosser. I just don't want to make him suspicious of me. I'm not entirely sure that he isn't involved with what's going on down here.'

'That's a bit fanciful, I would've thought. After all, he's been a farmer here for years and his family for decades before him. I would've thought he wouldn't want to put all he has at risk for something dodgy or illegal.'

Leo shrugged.

'We'll see,' he said non-committally. He eyed Elinor's camera. 'Are you heading off to take some more snapshots of the surfers?'

'Yes, I've nearly finished my first painting and I want to get another photograph lined up for a second painting. After that, who knows? I might need new subject matter... By the way, Leo, are you heading to The Farmer's Arms tonight?'

'Yes, I am. Why? Are you thinking you might join me for once?'

'Well, yes I was, actually. A couple of days ago Tony Reece invited me to join his group of friends, who seem to be all surfers, for a drink. Apparently they meet around 8.30 on Friday nights.'

'I see,' said Leo, quietly amused, an annoyingly knowing look in his eyes.

'I know what you're thinking,' said Elinor hurriedly. 'I've not got the hots for Tony Reece, if that's what you're assuming. It'll just be good to get to know some other people who live around here.'

'Absolutely. I wouldn't have dreamt of you wanting to do anything else but that,' said Leo placidly, but Elinor could tell he was blatantly and unabashedly lying. 'I'll be leaving around seven. If you're OK walking on country lanes in the dark, with a torch, I'll be delighted for you to join me. If not, you can always take a taxi. It's up to you.'

'I'd rather go with you. I won't know anyone there apart from you and Tony Reece, and there's no guarantee Tony will be there anyway.'

'Oh, I'm sure he'll be there if you let him know you're coming,' Leo replied cheekily, striding away up the road before she could answer back and leaving Elinor staring indignantly after him.

She turned and walked purposefully down to the beach. She was not going to demean herself by texting Tony to let him know she was going to the pub tonight. She wasn't that desperate...

She jumped down the smooth rocks on the edge of the sandy beach, and then stepped through the cloying sand in her heavy wellington boots, scrunching up her eyes to see if she could see the surfers from a distance. There were several black dots in the midst of the swirling mass of moving water on the right hand side of the beach.

She walked diagonally up to the edge of the seawater and started to snap photos with her camera, knowing she would delete at least half of them by the end of the day.

It was so hard to capture a good picture of a surfer. They moved so quickly and often she thought she'd taken the perfect picture only to find that the photo was hopeless, more often than not depicting a figure with flailing legs and arms, or a surfboard that seemed totally disconnected to its rider.

In her photos she wanted to show a surfer riding confidently on a wave, the master of the curling rollers, not a graceless, awkward figure on the verge of tumbling into the ocean. She was determined to depict the beauty and grace of the sport in her paintings and she knew that deep down, in the most secret part of her heart, she also wanted to be one of them.

An hour later, with sixty-seven photos stored in her camera, she gave up and made her way back to Trenouth, this time avoiding the wheat field that seemed to be of so much interest to Leo and heading home up along the coastal path.

Alexander plants intermittently lined the path Elinor was walking on and she bent down to break a stem off one of them. These plants were dotted up and down the cliffs near their home. She sniffed like an addict at the strong lemony scent emanating from the broken end and, as always, she was amazed that such a small stem was capable of producing such a pungent smell.

Leo had told her once that these plants had been brought over by the Romans and, oddly, unlike many other more native plants they seemed to thrive in the salty air by the ocean.

The tiny yellow flowers of Common Bird's Foot Trefoil and the softer yellow woolly heads of Kidney Vetch dotted the clumps of tough coastal grass, alongside the closed heads of thrift that were waiting until early spring to bloom. In the distance the dense stems of heather congregated by a wooden gate, also waiting until the right time of year to display their pink glory.

Elinor continued to sniff at her Alexander stem and watched the seagulls to the right of her showing off their acrobatic skills on the wind currents drifting up from the coves underneath them.

Looking down into Pepper Cove she suddenly caught sight of a dark grey seal's head popping out of the water and staring up at her curiously. The ocean water was bubbling and churning angrily around it, humming loudly like a hostile swarm of hornets. Like the Cheshire Cat in *Alice in Wonderland*, the seal head seemed to be both immovable and impregnable against the volatile water surrounding it.

Elinor watched it for a minute or two and then walked on.

As she moved away from the cove she looked back and saw that, just like the Cheshire Cat, the seal's head had vanished into the water once more.

She scrambled up to the top of the Cornish hedge bordering Trenouth's garden and jumped down onto the soft grass on the other side.

The garden was liberally covered with miniature hills where moles were clearly hard at work. A careful gardener would have been irritated by the unsightly bumps but Leo wasn't bothered in the slightest. However, thought Elinor, once spring came and the need to cut the grass became more acute Leo might well have to do something to encourage the little miners to dig elsewhere.

She skipped up the slate steps at the front door and let herself into the house.

She made herself a cup of tea in the kitchen to warm herself up, and then sat down on her bed to go through her images. She was so absorbed in her photographs, weighing up carefully the ones that were worth keeping and ruthlessly deleting the ones she would never use, that she lost track of time.

Leo knocked gently on her door at half past six, asking if she wanted some soup for dinner, abruptly making her aware of the late hour. Having agreed to some soup, she hastily started pulling clothes out of her chest of drawers, trying to think what she should wear for an evening at the pub.

She ended up going for the conventional option: a black polo-necked jumper, black leather jacket, black jeans and black boots. Nothing very imaginative but it was a safe choice for a first night out in Cornwall. She wouldn't look much different to how she looked in her wetsuit, she thought woefully to herself...

And so an hour later she found herself clinging desperately to Leo's arm as they walked along the uneven dark country paths to The Farmer's Arms.

There were no street lights near the fields they walked across. The full moon was out that night, so at least there was a ghostly white mantle on the surrounding countryside, but even with the dim shimmer of the moon and the blinding light of Leo's torch, it was still very hard to see anything clearly. Elinor was deeply regretting her decision to accompany Leo to the pub.

Eerie shadows laced their way across the hedges and trees on both sides of them. Little white rabbit tails bobbed in the darkness, the call of an owl swept across the quiet night and Elinor could sense, more than see, the other creatures of the night padding silently around them: foxes, field mice, weasels and badgers. Little, hidden eyes, no doubt gazing at them in amazement as they walked past. Shiny, wet noses would be turned upwards, sniffing at their unfamiliar scent.

Elinor struggled to understand how Leo could be so comfortable with the darkness. Where she grew up, in the West End of Glasgow, there was light 24/7. All of it was artificial, of course, but also strangely reassuring. Street lights, tenement lights, car lights, shop lights. All signs that one wasn't alone, that other people were out there going about their business with familiar monotony.

She started to shiver with fear, not cold, and began to count the long minutes until they arrived at the bright lights and warmth of the pub.

29

The exterior of the pub was like a typical Cornish house: solid stone walls painted white on the outside, with a grey slate tiled roof. As soon as Elinor opened the door and stepped in, she felt the sudden blast of heat from the central heating system hitting her hard. Small beads of sweat started to form under her thick jacket.

As she hastily removed her leather jacket she glanced around the room. It took her eyes a few minutes to adjust to the dingy surroundings after the bright lights outside.

On the exterior of the building, lights were scattered plentifully, shining down on the outdoor wooden tables and chairs and on the pub sign. Inside, chocolate-brown tables and chairs, wooden beams and a black tiled floor merged with the dim interior lighting to make it feel like underground lair.

Leo was hailed by a small group of older men who were huddled tightly in a corner of the room. Leo put his hand on Elinor's elbow and guided her across the room to his cronies, introducing her as his niece. The men politely made room for her and one of them got up to get Leo and Elinor a beer from the bar.

Elinor cast small covert glances across the room to see if she could spot Tony and his friends. The room was surprisingly full of people for a cold, dark evening and it took her a while to let her eyes roam around the crowded room. Eventually she caught sight of Mick's distinctive frizzy long hair at the other end of the pub. He was part of a big group of people gathered around three large tables.

Eyeing the youthful party avidly, Elinor could make out Tony's stocky shape and his thick thatch of fair hair. He was deep in conversation with two others, one of them a slim girl who had straight blonde hair reaching down to her waist and was wearing one of the shortest dresses Elinor had ever seen, which seemed all the shorter because the girl's long legs stretched under the table with her canvas shoes peeking out at the other side.

Seeing that Tony was totally engrossed in chatting with his two friends, she decided she'd better not approach him until an opportunity presented itself later on.

Elinor turned her attention to Leo's friends who, to be fair to them, were all interested in talking to her and asking her about herself. If they hadn't all been so much older, she would have been flattered by their attention. It was obvious it had been a while since many of them had had the chance to chat to someone so much younger than themselves, and a girl at that. Gratefully sipping the beer that had been plonked in front of her, she chatted away to Leo's friends, some of whom she'd already met during her excursions to St Merryn and Padstow.

It must have been about twenty minutes later when Elinor heard her name called out amidst the babble of voices surrounding her. She turned around and saw that Tony was waving at her from the bar, a delighted smile on his face. She excused herself from the table and, ignoring the knowing looks Leo and his friends were exchanging with each other, walked over to where Tony was standing.

She was suddenly very conscious of her flushed face and the strands of sweaty hair sticking to her forehead. It hadn't been such a good idea to wear her thick black polo-necked jumper after all.

'Elinor! I wasn't expecting to see you here. When did you arrive?'

'About three-quarters of an hour ago. We came by my uncle's preferred mode of travel, torchlight.'

Tony looked at her, confused.

'I don't understand. Are you saying you walked all of the way here in the dark?'

'Yes, that's exactly what I'm saying. We walked here by torchlight, through country fields. Some of them even had cows in them.'

Tony laughed.

'Well, I'm on the non-alcoholic beer tonight and I've got my car with me. So I'd be happy to give both of you a lift back home if you like.'

'It's OK. Leo's friend has to stay off the booze because of his diabetes and he usually drops Leo back home on a Friday night. But thanks for the offer.'

Tony nodded abstractedly. The barman had come up to him to take his drink order and was waiting impatiently for it.

'Would you like a drink, Elinor?'

'I'll have a beer, thanks,' said Elinor remembering she'd emptied her half pint a while ago.

Tony turned and gave a substantial drinks order to the barman who began to pour out the drinks.

'Why don't you come and join us?' asked Tony, indicating his corner of the room. 'We don't bite, and if you can cope with listening to some surf speak you might enjoy yourself.'

He looked speculatively at Leo's table.

'Plus we're at least two decades younger than your table,' he added, as though this had to be an enticement.

Elinor could feel herself blushing. She didn't think it would be cool to admit it but she actually enjoyed Leo's company and that of his friends. By the time you reached their age you had nothing to prove and very little to lose, so communication tended to be honest and straightforward. She liked that because you knew where you stood.

Elinor turned and looked at Tony's group doubtfully.

'Are you all surfers?'

'Yes, why, is that a problem?' asked Tony, looking defensive.

'No, not at all,' said Elinor, picking up her drink and waiting for him to lead the way across to his table.

30

Tony introduced Elinor to the table and rapidly reeled off the names of the seventeen people sitting there. They passed over Elinor's head in a blur – she'd never been very good at remembering names anyway – but one name caught her attention.

Richard Glynn.

Looking across the table she realised that Richard Glynn was the scowling young man who'd stomped past her a few weeks ago when she'd been photographing the surfers at Treyarnon Bay for the first time.

Tonight he was dressed smartly in a shirt and tie, his black hair combed back and glistening with some kind of hair gel. His harsh features weren't scowling tonight. In fact, the deep bark of his laughter was repeatedly booming across the table.

Richard Glynn...

The grumpy farmer Leo had warned her about. And clearly a surfer too.

Assimilating this interesting bit of information, Elinor sat down in a bit of a daze next to Tony, wedged in tightly between him and the blonde girl he'd been talking to earlier. She drank her beer absent-mindedly, listening to the chat around her and gradually realising, belatedly, that they might as well have been talking in Mandarin for all the sense she could make out of the conversation.

'Yeah, Michael's a Benny,' said the girl next to her dismissively.

'And a complete Barney,' agreed Mick. 'He's totally clucked. I really don't know why he keeps turning up. He's a frube and I don't see that changing any time soon. He's been out there for five days now and nothing's happening.'

'Have you had your board fixed yet, Mick?' asked Tony, noticing Elinor's complete bewilderment and changing the subject.

'No I haven't fixed the crease yet... I was hit by a total bomb in the impact zone the other day,' Mick said, turning to the others briefly. 'It was so grim. I was totally worked. I'll get the board down to Jim's shop in Newquay on Monday. By the way, Elinor, I wanted to say to you that I think you're ready to join us in Constantine Bay. In fact, I really think you should give it a try.'

The girl next to Elinor turned to her in surprise.

'You're a dude?' she asked.

Elinor gazed back at her confusedly, not understanding her question. She noticed that the girl's face was bare of make-up but that she was still a very striking young woman, with large, dark blue eyes and a quirky pattern of dark freckles on her tanned skin. She looked to be in her early twenties.

'I haven't seen you out there before,' said the girl, perplexed.

'She's a grom, Jennifer. She's still on the ankle busters in Porthcothan at the moment,' elaborated Mick helpfully.

'Oh right! A quimby,' said Jennifer, losing interest. Elinor felt her hackles rise.

One of the other men laughed.

'Don't bother with Jennifer, Elinor. She's a radical surfer, always charging the waves. She's only stoked when she meets her match.'

'Oh shut up, Ed,' said Jennifer impatiently. 'Don't you listen to him, Elinor. He's just a junkyard dog.'

'Hey, that's out of order!' protested Ed, after the others near them laughed.

Elinor couldn't help but feel their banter was incredibly juvenile, even though she couldn't follow half of what they were saying. Despite her incredibly short skirt, Elinor could tell that Jennifer was a thorough tomboy and would have little respect for someone like her who was always beset by her fears and anxieties.

She felt extremely out of place amongst these experienced and knowledgeable surfers and, despite her fascination with them as a group, she was longing to be elsewhere.

Jennifer, having lost interest in Elinor, was now talking to someone on the other side of the table, leaving Elinor to look down miserably at her empty pint glass.

She felt a warm hand place itself over hers and squeeze it reassuringly. She looked up to find Tony looking at her apologetically.

'I'm sorry, Elinor,' he said kindly, bending down and talking into her ear. 'I can totally see how it's a bit overwhelming listening to these idiots. I'm sorry for bringing you into the group. They really don't mean any harm but we've all become a bit cliquey, I'm afraid. We spend most of the winter together, which isn't necessarily a healthy thing. Come on, let's get up and get another drink at the bar. It's the least I can do to make up for it all.'

They both stood up and made their way to the bar unnoticed by the others who were now all arguing vociferously about something, with none of them showing any willingness to listen but instead shouting over one another with practised ease.

Tony and Elinor climbed on to the tall bar stools and waited for the barman to attend to them.

'Do your friends talk like that all the time?' asked Elinor after a moment.

'I guess they must do. I'm so used to the way they speak I don't really notice it.'

'It's really confusing. Like they belong to some elite club or something.'

'That's utterly ridiculous! For one, surfers aren't an elite club. We're morons really, if you think about it. Who else would risk their life and limbs surfing on the waves?'

'It seems to me to be more of an adrenaline addiction than an act of stupidity. I mean, I totally get it. I really do. I'd like to be able to do the same but the more time I spend around surfers the more I realise I'll never get there. I'm too different and I'll never be good enough.'

Tony gave her a puzzled look and waited patiently while Elinor asked the barman for a gin and tonic. He ordered another non-alcoholic beer.

'Why aren't you having anything to drink? Are you a teeto-taller?' asked Elinor, curiously.

'No, I'm not teetotal actually. I just have to be careful on a Friday night because I'm on dawn patrol.'

Elinor stared at him.

'Dawn patrol?'

'Sorry. That's surf speak again. I'm going surfing first thing in the morning, so I need a clear head. Look, what you just said about not being good enough is complete and utter rubbish. You heard Mick. He thinks you're ready to try the waves at Constantine.'

'I know, it was nice of him. But in reality I'm so clueless and fearful. I'll just have them all mocking me, like they were mocking that other guy tonight.'

'So? Why should you care what they think?'

Elinor gave Tony a steely look.

'It's easy for you to say that when you surf as well as any of them.'

'We all started as newbies. All of us.'

'They certainly don't behave like it,' said Elinor, indicating their table with her thumb.

'You know, one of the things you need to be able to surf well is balls. If you're going to join us, you're going to have to forget about your fear and what people think of you, and just go for it.'

'That's just it. You don't understand,' said Elinor, sensing herself getting lightheaded and looser in tongue with every passing minute but somehow unable to stop herself. 'I'm afraid of everything. Every single little thing... I'm on the highest dose of Sertraline you can be on, all because I'm afraid of everything. I'm a total coward, in fact.'

Tony watched her avidly, as though she was a rare species of bird that had suddenly landed in his back garden.

'Don't you get it?' said Elinor, annoyed by his silence, and talking louder and louder in her vehement effort to be understood. 'That's why I'm so fascinated with surfing and with you surfers. I envy you all that freedom and fearlessness. I've been

149

a prisoner to my anxiety for over a year now. It feels like it'll never leave me. And with all the encouragement your friends give to people who aren't as good as them, what chance have I got? I'll always be a nervous wreck no matter what I try and do.'

Tony cleared his throat.

'Despite what you're saying, I still think you should keep at it, Elinor. You've put so much work into surfing.' He glanced at her glass, with a look that said he was starting to guess she was getting tipsy. 'Tell you what, why don't you do a dawn patrol with me in a week's time? Weather permitting, of course. There's rarely anybody else there at the crack of dawn on a Saturday.'

While Tony calmly polished off the remains of his beer Elinor thought about his suggestion, moving her fingers up and down her glass meditatively. Out of the corner of her eye she caught sight of Leo making his way towards her, torch in hand.

She smiled to herself. Only Leo would think it normal to turn up at a pub with a torch. When she saw Tony peering at Leo's torch with a bemused eye she started to giggle.

'Elinor, how are you doing? Alastair's ready to go now and take us home. Are you coming with us?' asked Leo jovially.

'Leo, this is Tony Reece.'

'I gathered that,' said Leo complacently, shaking hands with Tony. 'She's told me a lot about you.'

To Elinor's annoyance she felt herself begin to blush.

'All good, I hope!' joked Tony, looking amused and flattered at the same time.

'Oh yes! Absolutely,' said Leo, wilfully ignoring Elinor's frantic and pointed glare. 'She has a thing for surfers, as I'm sure you've noticed.'

'Leo, please don't let me hold you back. I've still got a drink to finish. I'll catch a taxi and meet you back at the house,' said Elinor, talking rapidly, striving desperately to find a way to shut her outspoken uncle up.

'Don't worry, we can wait for you to finish your drink,' said Leo obstinately, clearly reluctant to let Elinor come home on her own.

'Leo, I'm very happy to drop Elinor off,' offered Tony, intervening in what was becoming a fraught conversation between the two of them. 'I'll be going soon anyway and it's not far out of my way. I know the roads around here like the back of my hand. It's the least I can do after subjecting Elinor to my friends tonight.'

'Well that sounds like an offer we can't refuse, doesn't it?' replied Leo, with what Elinor thought was a crass wink. 'OK, I'll leave you two to it, then. See you back at the house, Elinor.'

Leo turned and walked back to his table where his friends were all unabashedly staring with interest at Tony and Elinor.

31

'That's the problem with a small provincial place like this. Every little thing becomes of interest,' muttered Tony as he turned to face the bar again.

He called across to the barman for a packet of crisps, and when they were given to him offered some to Elinor. Elinor grabbed a handful, glad to have some stodge to soak up some of the alcohol swilling about inside of her. She crunched her way through her little pile of crisps, thinking regretfully she was going to have to go for a run in the morning.

'He's very embarrassing,' said Elinor after a minute, feeling she was simply stating the obvious.

'I wouldn't say that. He's blunt, certainly,' replied Tony, not pretending he didn't know who she was talking about.

'Yes, well, he likes to wind me up. He's got a mischievous soul, my uncle does. I don't think he's ever grown up, really.' Elinor popped another crisp in her mouth and continued to talk with her mouth full. She'd given up caring about the way she looked. 'He's obsessed with finding hidden tunnels near our house, and then when he does find one he can't let it go. He's convinced there are some shenanigans going on with it. It's like living with a character out of *Treasure Island*.'

'Barbara speaks very highly of him,' said Tony, as if this was all there was to be said.

'Yes, and what is it with you and Barbara?'

'Me and Barbara?' repeated Tony, looking thoroughly surprised.

'Yes, you and Barbara,' persisted Elinor, latching on to the topic that had been bugging her for a few days. 'She seems to know everything about you. Like you're lifelong friends or something. And I got the impression you've both been talking about me?'

Tony started to look embarrassed, giving credence to Elinor's suspicions.

'I've known Barbara for a long time. She's probably already told you but I was friends with her partner,' said Tony quietly, adroitly circumventing Elinor's question. He started to fidget with a couple of beer mats, balancing them on top of his empty glass.

'Yes but why would you talk to her about me?'

Tony looked at her exasperatedly.

'Why do you think, Elinor? I'd told her a while back that I'd suggested you look her up and then I found out later on you were painting with her in the studio. Barbara's very picky. She doesn't let just anyone paint with her. So yes, we were chatting about you. There's no crime in that.'

'I know that. But Barbara's almost as bad as Leo at teasing me and I'm getting fed up with it all to be honest with you.'

'She's teasing you about me?'

'Yes, she is. The last time I was there she was saying she was going to invite me round the next time you brought her some fresh fish.'

Tony chuckled.

'Those two should set up a dating website. That would keep

the pair of them gleefully occupied. They're an absolute hoot.'

Elinor, slightly miffed, didn't say anything. She was suddenly starting to feel extremely tired and her bed was becoming an attractive prospect. She looked at her watch and saw it was close to eleven o' clock.

She wondered if Tony would be willing to leave soon. If he was going to get up for the 'dawn patrol' tomorrow he'd have to go home before long.

She was lucky. Tony, who didn't seem to miss much, had seen her looking at her watch and got off his stool, suggesting they head home. Fifteen minutes later she waved Tony off from the doorstep at Trenouth and then disappeared inside the house, calling out to Leo to let him know she was home at last.

32

It was a bright sunny morning in Wadebridge. As they'd crossed over the bridge spanning the River Camel, the river had been shining in the sunlight with a mass of silver points, looking like the reflective scales of an enormous blue fish curling away into the distance.

Elinor was intrigued as to why a Cornish river would be called Camel but Leo had explained to her that the Cornish name for the river was Dowr Kammel, meaning crooked river. So there was no association with camels of any sort, much to Elinor's disappointment.

Leo told her that Wadebridge used to be called Wade because people and livestock used to cross the river at low tide. There used to be a chapel on either side of the river, the King's Chapel on the north side and St Michael's on the south side. People would pray for a safe crossing at one chapel and then when they had safely waded through to the other side of the river they would give thanks at the other chapel.

In the end a bridge was built because a vicar, distressed by the number of animals and people who died trying to cross the river, planned and raised the funds for its construction. From then on Wade became Wadebridge.

Elinor and Leo were making their way to Molesworth Street to collect Elinor's *Frankenstein* book from the antiquarian bookseller. Leo had dropped off the book for repair on one of his many visits to the shop and Mr Ashcroft had phoned Leo a week ago to say it was ready for collection. Intriguingly, Mr Ashcroft had apparently been very eager for them to drop by early, before the shop became busy. He didn't mention why.

Leo stopped at an old, peeling, pale blue door on Molesworth Street. It looked a little incongruous amongst the smart, well-tended shop fronts. He pushed it open and walked down a narrow, dark alleyway to a little square courtyard at the far end. There was an unobtrusive shop on the right hand side of the courtyard, with 'Back Lane Rare Books' written at the top of it, in gilt letters against a dark blue shop front.

The shop had one of the strangest windows Elinor had ever seen. The front window was made of mottled glass except for the centre where there was a small square of clear glass. Behind this clear glass there was a solitary book perched on a miniature shelf with a light shining on it from above.

Elinor stood up close to the window and looked at the book, interested to find out its title. It was *The Adventures of a Treasure Hunter* by Charles P. Everitt.

'He has a sense of humour, Stephen does,' commented Leo, waiting patiently by the shop door as he noticed Elinor inspecting the book in the window. 'That book is a memoir of a lifetime in the rare book trade between the late 1800s and 1940s. It's apparently full of humorous insights into the history, practices and mindset of book dealers from an earlier age. Full of history and gossip, apparently. Not my taste, though.'

Leo pushed open the shop door, setting the bell above it to clang loudly. Elinor, who was following Leo into the shop, wondered if Mr Ashcroft was a little deaf. She would hate to have to work with that thunderous bell ringing out all day.

The inside of the bookshop initially looked to be completely deserted. Its ceiling was preposterously high. It was evident someone had knocked through the flat above the shop to create extraordinarily tall shelving. Hundreds of books were stacked neatly on wooden shelves stretching up to the ceiling.

Elinor caught sight of a ladder on the right hand side of the shop and, stretching her head back, saw an elderly man with a mop of unruly white hair slowly climbing down its precarious rungs. Not wanting to startle or distract the old man on his perilous descent, Leo and Elinor said nothing as he made his way down the ladder, taking his time.

Finally, after a few minutes, the old gentleman reached the ground and approached them with a welcoming smile on his face.

'Hello, Leo! I'm so glad you came. I was going to call you again to remind you to pop in. Is this your niece Elinor?'

As Leo nodded, the old gentleman shook her hand enthusiastically. He had a surprisingly youthful face with black button eyes and a large patrician Roman nose. A pair of half-moon glasses were perched midway down his nose.

'I'm Stephen Ashcroft. I'm honoured to meet you. Come into my back office, both of you, and I'll show you what I've discovered about the book you left with me. It's very interesting.'

Mr Ashcroft went to the shop door and locked it shut, putting the closed sign up on the outside before he did so.

He then led them to the back of the shop and pushed against what looked to be a wall of bookshelves, but which in actual fact turned out to be a false door with wooden books and shelves carved into it.

Elinor shook her head in disbelief. This was taking eccentricity to a whole new level.

33

Mr Ashcroft led them down a short corridor into a small office. While Leo and Elinor sat themselves down he disappeared out of the room with a kettle to make them a cup of tea.

Elinor looked around curiously.

Mr Ashcroft's office also had shelves on all three walls but they weren't as full of books as the shop had been. Large empty gaps, like missing teeth, appeared between collections of books. Unusual granite bookends, in the shape of gargoyle-like mammals and birds, kept the books upright.

Little coloured papers attached to the shelves seemed to be linked to whatever work was associated with the books above them. On the papers were written bizarre instructions: 'Alkaline buffer', 'Backing', 'Complex paper tears', 'Heat-set tissue', 'Hinging in', 'Rebacking'.

One of the shelves behind the desk had a miscellaneous collection of items: pens, paperweights, diaries, what looked to be an antique red glass decanter and a large circular pottery bowl. With a start, Elinor realised there was fur protruding from the top of the ceramic bowl.

Standing up slightly from her chair Elinor took a closer look and saw there was a large ginger cat curled up inside the bowl, seemingly fast asleep.

Mr Ashcroft burst into the office, carrying three mugs of tea. Once he'd given Elinor and Leo their mugs and put his down on the desk, he reached up to the shelf that said 'Rebacking' and carefully pulled Elinor's *Frankenstein* book out of its section.

He then sat down behind his large kneehole desk, pushing his glasses up his nose.

'Right, then,' said Mr Ashcroft, his black eyes seeming to shine with interest as he looked down at the book in front of him. 'This book you've brought to me for mending is very intriguing, Leo. Fascinating, in fact. Firstly, do you have any idea where the poetic lines written in the front of it are from?'

Leo and Elinor, in synchronisation, shook their heads.

'"To see a World in a Grain of Sand, And a Heaven in a Wild Flower, Hold Infinity in the Palm of your Hand, And Eternity in an Hour." Those are words from William Blake's *Auguries of Innocence*. A very famous poem of his.'

Mr Ashcroft placed a proprietary hand on the book, considering his next words carefully.

'I'd better give you both some background to this book. Mary Shelley, the author, was the daughter of Mary Wollstonecraft. Mary Wollstonecraft is nowadays considered the founding member of the feminist movement. A very able writer in her own right too, of course, but she's not remembered so much for that.'

Leo and Elinor listened politely, wondering where all this was leading them. Elinor struggled to believe Mr Ashcroft would have the leisure or time to discuss every book in depth with all his customers. He was clearly going somewhere with this, though what Mary Shelley's mother had to do with anything was a bit of an enigma.

Mr Ashcroft cleared his throat.

'Mary Wollstonecraft, Mary Shelley's mother, knew William Blake. I would even go so far as to say they were not just acquaintances but friends, although this isn't certain. What is certain, though, is that William Blake illustrated Mary Wollstonecraft's *Original Stories*, a children's book of moral education. And it's generally assumed that Mary Wollstonecraft's writing influenced some of William Blake's work.'

Mr Ashcroft picked up the book and turned the pages until he got to the poetical lines inscribed at the front of it.

'Blake agreed with Mary Wollstonecraft's views. Personally, I think William Blake was a very modern man for his time, advocating for the rights of married women and believing in sexual equivalence in marriage. But that's beside the point. The important thing is he had a relationship of sorts with the author's mother and that's what's important regarding this specific book.'

At this point in Mr Ashcroft's monologue, the ginger cat in the bowl behind him lifted up its head and stared across at them with unblinking piercing green eyes, as though weighing up if the strangers in his master's room were trustworthy or not. Elinor tried not to get distracted from Mr Ashcroft's discourse, which was hard when she was yearning to get up and stroke the furry bundle watching her so avidly.

'Have either of you heard of fore-edged painting?'

'Sorry, what was that again?' asked Leo, puzzled by the sudden change of subject.

'Fore-edged painting. Spelt F-O-R-E.'

Again Leo and Elinor silently shook their heads.

'A fore-edged painting is a painting that is found hidden

inside the gilt edges of rare books. You can only see a fore-edged painting when you fan the book, otherwise it isn't visible. I think I can tell you why the spine of your book was so damaged, Elinor.'

Mr Ashcroft bent the book rigorously so the pages fanned out at the opposite end to the spine. He then gripped the book tightly and turned it round to show Elinor and Leo.

Elinor and Leo bent forward to look at it and to their mutual surprise saw a picture painted on the edges of the book.

The painting was of a large monster with yellow skin and white eyes, with his arms raised as he confronts four other figures, all of whom look absolutely terrified. The two women in the picture are twisted round and reaching for the door, the old man is staring blindly with his mouth open and the young man is holding a stone in his hand, looking as though he's about to hurl it towards the monster.

The colours of the painted figures were bright and vivid and the background behind the figures consisted of swirling lines of dark blue, white and green, adding to the drama of the scene. The figures' emotions were sharply portrayed with caricature-like definition.

'Wow, that's truly amazing!' exclaimed Elinor, enchanted by the book's hidden secret. She looked up at Mr Ashcroft who was watching her reaction with a pleased smile.

'There's still more, if you can just bear with me,' said Mr Ashcroft. 'I think this fore-edged painting bears a marked resemblance to William Blake's artwork. He wasn't just a poet, he was also an artist. The style of this is very similar to his paintings. I think it would be worth getting it verified.'

Mr Ashcroft let the book settle back into its original shape and turned the pages until he came to the front of the book.

'This is a second edition of *Frankenstein*, printed in 1823. William Blake died in 1827. It's quite reasonable to assume that he would've had a copy of Mary Shelley's book, given his ties to her mother. I also think it wouldn't be surprising if he'd inscribed the front of the book with lines from his poem and painted that picture on the edges of it. You'll have to get it all checked out but I think you'll agree it's very exciting to imagine there's a possibility that William Blake might have painted this picture.'

Silence descended as Elinor and Leo took in this information. Mr Ashcroft beamed at the two of them happily with the real enthusiasm of a dedicated bibliophile, delighted to have made the discovery.

He picked up the book again and indicated the spine to them.

'You can see now why the spine would've been so damaged. To fan out the book and see the picture you have to put a substantial amount of pressure on the binding. I've managed to fix the spine using the leather that was there originally, which is fortunate. It keeps the book as authentic as possible,' he said proudly.

'Do you know who would be able to verify the picture?' asked Leo, his mind turning as ever to practicalities.

'Personally I would take it to British Library or the British Museum for authentication. I can write a letter for you to take with you, explaining the premise for this book.'

Leo nodded his thanks as Elinor, completely stunned, continued to gaze at the potentially valuable book in front of her. It was amazing to think how this book, seemingly so unique now, had been carelessly tossed into what was essentially a junkyard sale.

34

'Weather tom good. V light offshore wind. Fancy a dawn patrol? T.'

Elinor read the text with mixed feelings. She liked her lie-ins. Sacrificing a lie-in would have to be worth it.

Then that deep yearning to be free and reckless touched her heart. If she could learn to ride the big waves she'd be able to conquer her anxieties. She was sure of it.

She texted: 'Sure. What time?'

Within seconds the answer pinged back.

'7. See u there.'

Elinor groaned at the thought of getting up for seven o'clock but if the sea happened to be empty of cocky surfers it would be well worth it.

She'd have to get her surfboard fixed to the car as there was no way she'd make it on time to Constantine Bay tomorrow morning otherwise. Her surfboard was currently standing upright in the garage next to the old antique surfboards used by Leo's family in days gone by.

Leo, noting her dedication to her surfing lessons on Saturday mornings, had taken her by surprise one day by driving up to Trenouth with a surfboard attached to the roof rack. He'd gone to Newquay and bought her an expensive all-round one, the R2 by Chemistry.

It was, he'd insisted, a belated Christmas present. Elinor had been overwhelmed by his generosity and felt very tearful at the time of receiving it but Leo, uncomfortable with displays of emotion, had brushed off her thanks brusquely. It did him good, he'd said, to see her find a hobby that was making her happy again.

Now it was the middle of January and she was looking forward to trying out the surfboard on some serious waves.

When she woke up the next morning and peered out of her bedroom window she could glimpse in the breaking daylight a few restless seagulls balancing on the air currents, but the long clumps of grass were only lightly caressed by the wind, suggesting that the day was going to be a relatively mild one as far as the wind factor was concerned.

She raced to get her swimsuit and wetsuit on, dashing into the kitchen to grab the thermos of coffee Leo had already prepared for her and throwing a banana into her bag before heading out of the house.

Once she'd dumped her things in the car she returned to the hallway where her surfboard was reposing in preparation for a sharp exit. Within a couple minutes she had it strapped on to the roof of Leo's car and was trundling down the road, heading towards to Constantine Bay.

This early in the morning rabbits were out in force, eating their grassy breakfast, birds were flurrying with fixed intent from the safety of the Cornish hedges on the search for insects, and a hedgehog had started an epically brave voyage across the road in front of her.

Cursing impatiently, Elinor slammed the handbrake on and got out of the car with a towel. As she approached the prickly adventurer it suddenly curled itself up into a protective ball. Elinor picked it up carefully and, reaching over a stile a little further up the road, deposited the rogue on safer pasture. Running back to the car she continued her journey, anxiously looking at the clock and hoping Tony wouldn't give up waiting for her. Such light winds as there were today weren't going to produce the kind of waves he liked...

Elinor parked in the vacant field next to Constantine Bay. The parking hut was closed this early in the morning so she might well be getting away with free parking today. Leaving her bags in the boot of the car and wearing her surfing boots, she scoffed big mouthfuls of banana as she unstrapped her surfboard. Within five minutes she was making her way to the water, scrunching up her eyes in an attempt to see if she could spot Tony anywhere. His car had been parked up at the field so she knew he was out there somewhere.

From a distance, she could see a couple of dark heads bobbing in the water. The waves weren't as big as she'd expected, they were only three feet high at most. One of the figures, catching sight of her, waved vigorously. She spotted Tony's bright head of fair hair as she came closer, and waved back at him.

She was walking unhurriedly now to the water's edge, slowing markedly as she neared the restless waves. It was quite a thought to immerse oneself this early in the cool temperatures of the unpredictable sea. And for some absurd reason she felt more vulnerable without the lifeguards on duty. She knew most of the surfers were just as able and willing as lifeguards to help someone in trouble but she still preferred the reliability of professional lifesavers.

Quelling her own unprofessional qualms, she took a deep

breath and strode confidently into the water, trying to portray that she had the balls Tony had spoken about in the pub.

She felt the icy fingers of water seeping into the wetsuit to form a thin insulating layer. Soon the water was deep enough for her to be able to hoist herself up onto the surfboard so she was lying flat and paddling through the swaying water.

'You're late,' rebuked Tony a short while later, with a crooked grin on his face as he paddled across to her, adroitly avoiding a wave about to break.

Bobbing up and down, Elinor shrugged as though she couldn't care less.

'It's not that late.'

Tony looked down at his watch pointedly.

'We were supposed to meet at seven!'

'I'm not going to waste time discussing my lateness,' she said mock sternly, starting to paddle out again towards the incoming waves and moving past him. As she repeatedly dipped down in a duck dive to avoid the breaking waves racing to smother her, she sensed Tony's determined paddling close behind her.

She felt the flow of blood building in her veins with the exercise. As her arms worked hard to paddle against the waves the warmth rapidly spread to her extremities. Unprompted, an odd image popped into her mind of her veins spreading out like an oak tree, the warm blood pumping upwards from the ground and moving up through the thick branches and the narrow twigs.

She was already sensing the rhythm and frequency of these waves, which she knew could change at any moment with the whim of the wind. She was starting to feel exhilarated, any doubts or fears getting relegated to the back of her mind as her excitement built.

'Whoa! I would stop around here, Elinor, or you'll be paddling forever to keep up with the waves,' said Tony's voice behind her.

Elinor obediently paused for a moment and sat herself up on her board, a leg dangling down on each side. She quickly scanned the lie of the ocean around her.

Tony was right. She was beyond the waves that were breaking inland and if she went much further out she wouldn't have the stamina to chase the waves until she was ready to mount them. She allowed herself to rock with the movement of the restless sea, rising and falling over the unformed waves, and turned to face the shoreline.

It seemed a long distance away.

She sighed.

'I'm going to go forward a bit.'

'Good idea,' agreed Tony.

They both turned and paddled a short distance towards the shoreline. Elinor gauged she'd be able to catch a potential wave at this range.

She twisted round to watch the waves as they came at her from behind.

'Try this one coming in,' advised Tony. 'It looks to be a right.'

Elinor knew he meant that the wave was going to break from right to left, as viewed from the beach, so she would have to surf to the left of the wave to surf it. She started to paddle furiously as she felt the wave approaching behind her and as she felt the top of the wave nudge her upwards she quickly popped up onto her board. She was so intent on getting the direction of the surfboard correct that she unconsciously dug the nose of her surfboard into the water.

She knew straightaway she'd made a mistake.

Within seconds, the back of her board went up and she was launched off into the air. She smacked into the ocean beneath with the wave crashing on top of her.

Time seemed to slow down suddenly as she felt herself held down under the remorseless water. She'd disappeared into a mute world, her body spinning around so much she had no idea which way she was facing. She'd vanished into a vortex. Her arms and legs hung loose as she felt powerful forces grab hold of her and shake her unmercifully. She waited, saving her strength for the moment when she felt the watery monster weaken and loosen its grip on her.

On her ankle she felt the tugs of her faithful surfboard, bucking and riding the chaos its owner had mistakenly unleashed on it.

As soon as she felt the wave move on and the pull of the next wave dragging her back, she started to fight against her underwater jailer and pushed upwards quickly to get a breath before the next wave collapsed on top of her.

Her chest was starting to burn with the need to get some oxygen.

She reached the surface and took some deep breaths of sweet air before hearing the approach of the next wave rumbling above her. She sank down under the water to let the wave pass over and started to swim vigorously away from the shoreline, out of the reach of the powerful rollers.

After a couple of minutes she kicked upwards again and popped up behind the breaking waves.

'My God, Elinor, are you alright?' asked an anxious voice

next to her.

Tony, lying flat on his board, reached down a hand and put it under her arm to support her as she trod water.

Elinor felt embarrassed but grateful at his concern.

'Yeah, it was a rookie mistake. I feel mortified.'

'Don't be. We've all been there. Still, that was a pretty dramatic wipeout.'

Elinor nodded, still panting after her exertions. Her heart was racing in her chest. She wasn't sure that was helping her catch her breath.

After a moment she reached up and grabbed a hold of her surfboard, pulling herself up onto it and sitting astride it.

She looked towards the shoreline and then behind her.

'Seriously? You're thinking of going again? So soon?' asked a bewildered Tony, reading her thoughts.

Elinor turned to look at him.

'Of course,' said Elinor, genuinely puzzled by his caution. 'I had to summon all my courage to try out these waves and if I don't get to ride even one, I'm not sure I'll ever come back. I need to surf today and I'm not leaving until I do.'

She turned back to watching the waves and after a minute she started paddling forward to the zone she judged best to catch a roller.

35

She was gliding through the wave, cutting through the wall of water as if it was made of soft butter. She was sliding downwards on her flight, the wind brushing gently against her face and running the tips of its fingers along her scalp.

Elinor felt like an Amazon riding her horse into battle, at one with the surfboard that was obeying every tilt and turn she placed on it. The elements were all on her side now and for once she was mistress of the ocean, not a helpless victim.

After three wipeouts, she'd finally managed it.

She was riding the wave, speeding ahead of the giant white snake of breaking surf chasing her from behind. In the distance she heard Tony's cheers egging her on as she raced towards the shoreline.

Within seconds she felt the wave lose power, and as she came closer to the shore her surfboard sank lower and lower towards the surface of the beach. Eventually the wave moved forward to kiss the shoreline before vanishing into oblivion. Elinor jumped off her surfboard, landing softly on the water. She stood upright watching her wave until the dregs finally disintegrated into the other waves chasing it from behind.

'Elinor, that was amazing!' shouted Tony after a moment, putting his arms around her and holding her in a tight embrace. 'You did it!'

Elinor grinned foolishly as she turned towards him. He must have followed her in on another wave.

'I know. I managed a three-foot roller for the first time! It was awesome! Bitchin', as you would say.'

Tony grinned back at her.

'Feeling like a proper surfer now, are we?'

'Yes! YES!' Elinor yelled happily, putting her arms up in the air in a victory salute and dancing on the spot.

Tony laughed and before Elinor realised what he was up to he'd bent his head and kissed her on the lips. Recklessly, she leaned back her head and wantonly tasted the saltiness of the sea on his lips before her mind fully comprehended what was happening.

Unfortunately for Tony, within a minute she suddenly stiffened in dismay and instinctively pulled away. She felt utterly taken aback at what had just happened, reeling with shock.

Feeling her sudden rigidity, Tony quickly let her go and looked at her in consternation.

'Sorry, Elinor. I didn't mean to offend you.'

Elinor realised she was standing stock still with a look of utter horror on her face. She suddenly felt overwhelmed with shame and also a measure of compassion for Tony, who had no idea of how messed up she really was inside.

She shook her head vigorously, trying to clear her blocked ears and her confused mind at the same time. Her wet hair swung backwards and forwards, half hiding her embarrassed face.

'Don't worry about it, Tony. Let's just forget about it, shall we?'

Tony nodded but Elinor didn't miss the puzzled expression

on his face. Her heart sank. He hadn't missed her initial eager response and was no doubt wondering what was going on. She wasn't sure she had the answer to that one herself.

She turned towards the waves and, without a backward glance, started to pull her surfboard out towards the surf zone again. For her, this was the best way to move on, focusing on the immediate danger of the powerful rollers and forgetting the past and future.

Living inside of those exciting split seconds when she was riding the waves made her feel she could conquer the world. And escape from all her complicated problems too, of course...

For the rest of their stay in the water Tony gave her a wide berth, although Elinor had no doubt he was still keeping a protective eye on her from a distance.

An hour later, when the ocean was filling up with the black bodies of other surfers, he swam across to her as she sat astride her surfboard taking a break from the relentless sea. She'd managed two more wipeouts and three more rides on the rollers. She was starting to feel exhausted. A banana wasn't enough fuel to keep her going in this unpredictable sport.

'Elinor, the waves are stacking. I think it would be wise for you to quit now. You don't want to have to handle five- or six-foot waves today.'

'You're right. It's time to quit. I'm absolutely starving anyway. My stomach hasn't stopped rumbling for the last half hour.'

'The Hut does good fry-ups if you fancy some high-energy fuel. That café basically makes its living off us surfers in the winter.'

Elinor wrinkled up her nose with mock scorn.

'I thought doctors weren't supposed to be encouraging high-fat food these days.'

Tony looked mortally offended. Elinor began to realise he had a substantial amount of professional pride and wasn't going to find any derogatory reference to his profession amusing.

'It's all right to treat yourself now and again. I don't recommend it routinely,' he said finally, manfully keeping his ire in check.

'I was only winding you up, Tony. I really don't think you get my sense of humour. I'm happy to go to The Hut if you'll join me,' Elinor said lightly, trying to placate him.

'I'm up for a laugh but not when it involves my job or things I care about,' said Tony seriously, looking at her intently and not budging from the sensitive subject matter.

There was an awkward pause where neither of them knew what to say.

Avoiding the accusatory look in his eyes, Elinor punched him in the arm.

'OK, OK! Sorry for casting doubt on your professionalism. Come on, Tony. Let's go get some food before I pass out with hunger,' she pleaded.

All of a sudden Tony smiled at her with genuine amusement and Elinor felt the relief wash over her. She'd never have put Tony down as insecure or sensitive but she was seeing a new side to him today. However, his smile contained a wealth of warm emotion. Elinor thought it was like the sun breaking out from the cover of a grey cloud. His smile literally lit up his face. Tony, she decided, was an interesting paradox.

They both started to paddle towards the shoreline, lazily letting the push of the waves give them impetus. Before long they'd started the walk back to their cars to get their wetsuits off and throw on some warm clothing, before rewarding themselves with a feast fit for a king as Elinor perceived it, her mouth salivating in anticipation.

36

The Hut turned out to be more of a metal and concrete shack than a hut. It was hidden out of sight down a path that ran from the car park and alongside the golf course. It was buried behind large overgrown gorse bushes in what was an obvious attempt by the golf club to hide an eyesore.

Even with the numerous caravans that arrived here in the summer, The Hut had to win the most ugly habitation prize. It looked like a three-sided spaceship had landed in North Cornwall.

The monstrosity was triangular in shape with thick, ugly concrete walls that stretched up to a flat, corrugated iron roof. The dull grey walls were pockmarked with holes and covered in graffiti. A black painted metal door was the entrance to this unprepossessing café. A plywood board with 'The Hut' painted on it in red letters was crudely attached above the black door with wire.

Elinor was intrigued to think of its premise. Who had given this unsightly building planning permission and why? Had this ugly edifice been some kind of shelter or storage facility in World War Two? It certainly had the look of it.

Elinor had already heard the tales of unexpected airborne enemy troop landings in Cornwall and of bombs raining down on areas like Bodmin during World War Two. Back then, beaches around the Cornish coastline were lined with mines, barbed wire, anti-tank obstacles and road blocks to prevent any enemy machinery gaining access further inland. Leo had told her how during the war his father had once seen a stray cow (which had accidently wandered onto Treyarnon beach) blow up before his very eyes. It had unfortunately trodden on a landmine.

Ugly concrete observation posts had littered the Cornish coastline, but most had now been taken down, and although this hideous metal building might have had something to do with those dire days when function took priority over beauty, it was hard to understand why it was still standing today, an eyesore to anyone within its circumference.

Tony was clearly not into the aesthetical side of things. He'd already disappeared into the interior of The Hut without a backward glance, the door swinging shut behind him with an ominous clunk.

The smell of cooked bacon had briefly assailed Elinor's nostrils when the door had opened, distracting her from her contemplation of the exterior. She'd been staring dazedly at the strange building, unable to make sense of its architecture, but the enticing allure of bacon finally won her over. She decided it was time to eat and pulled open the heavy door.

She blinked under the harsh glare of a myriad of ceiling lights. The owner was clearly making up for the lack of daylight with excessive interior lighting. As her eyes grew accustomed to the brightness she saw that she was in a large room that was decorated with spartan taste. There were only three tables with an odd assortment of wooden chairs attached to them. The walls were painted white and at the back of the room there was what looked to be a hand-painted crude fresco of the ocean, with a couple of surfers riding the waves.

Tony was already sprawled on one chair, flicking through a newspaper that he'd purloined from somewhere.

'Tony, have you ordered breakfast?'

Tony glanced up from the sports section of the newspaper.

'No. It sometimes takes a while for them to make an appearance, I'm afraid. José and Elena, who run this place, have a temperamental relationship with the café. They're from Andalucia in Spain and they work to their own timetable. They're very laid-back as far as time and clients go. But they do make the best English breakfast in Cornwall.'

Elinor groaned. Her stomach was starting to growl angrily with hunger.

'Why on earth would you cook English breakfast when you're Spanish?' she wondered aloud.

Tony shrugged.

'It sells. That's probably why. This place is never going to attract the Rick Stein clientele of Padstow.'

Elinor waited impatiently for five minutes, and when nobody appeared she got up and walked through the beaded doorway at the end of the room, to see if she would be able to attract someone's attention. If she waited much longer she felt she'd start to eat Tony's newspaper or even Tony himself.

She walked down the corridor and poked her head through the door at the end. A large, very clean and professional kitchen greeted her eyes. It had gleaming metallic surfaces, white tiles and not a crumb in sight.

Hissing and bubbling on the top of the glistening oven was a large frying pan with several bits of bacon in it.

Elinor quickly did a double take. She was struggling to believe what she was seeing.

The bacon was burning.

It was turning black at the edges and puffs of grey smoke were winding upwards as the oil spluttered and splattered out of the pan.

Elinor gasped, sudden fear overwhelming her. Her first instinct was to call for Tony but the words wouldn't come out of her mouth. She stood frozen in horror and in a blind panic for what seemed to her to be an age, watching helplessly as the plume of smoke thickened and the bacon slowly charred, turning into a black crisp.

She heard a snore behind her. Turning around quickly, she saw a young man fast asleep on a chair. His head, with its white chef's hat on, was leaning back against the wall and his mouth was wide open in an unattractive pose, making him look not unlike a dead fish.

A second snore brought Elinor to her senses.

Without a moment's hesitation she ran across to the saucepan and switched off the gas. Lifting the pan away from the source of heat, she put it down on the metal surface, leaving the bacon to hiss loudly to itself as it congealed into a sticky burnt mass. She turned to face the man against the wall. Oblivious to any danger, he looked perfectly at peace with himself and the world.

Angry, Elinor went over to him and shook his shoulder roughly.

'Ay! Qué pasa? Qué pasa?'

The man sat up, his eyes blurred and confused.

'Your bacon was burning! You could've started a fire and

180

burnt the place down!' cried out Elinor irately, for once in her life willing herself to be a virago. This man deserved everything he had coming to him.

'The bacon! *Madre mia!* The bacon!' he yelled, jumping up and running to the stove.

He stared at the black mass in dismay, putting both hands up to his cheeks.

'*Ay, Dios!*'

'What on earth did you think you were doing falling asleep with the bacon frying?'

The man looked at her in despair.

'It has been a bad night for me. Me and my wife, we argue all night. She threatens to leave me and go back to Spain.' He spread out his hands. 'I've put all I have into this place and I can't leave now.'

Elinor watched him in bemusement.

'So you're José?'

'Yes, I'm José Mendive. The best chef in Cornwall.'

Elinor suddenly felt an irrational but overwhelming desire to laugh. A reaction to the fright she'd just had, no doubt.

'Look, José. You have to pull yourself together. Drink a shit-load of coffee or something. This can't happen again or you really will lose everything you have. If things had got out of hand just now, how would you have explained it to an insurance company? I don't think falling asleep after a row with your wife would pass muster with them somehow.'

Crestfallen, José nodded miserably.

'I know. It's terrible. I am so sorry, *Señora*. Let me make it up to you. What is it you're wanting today?'

Again resisting the urge to laugh, Elinor looked sternly at him.

181

'I've been surfing for a good hour and a half this morning and I'm famished. My friend Tony and I wanted a cooked English breakfast, which apparently you're meant to do to perfection. So please, I beg of you, before any other surfers turn up, could you please cook us some breakfast without falling asleep again?'

'*Sí, sí*. Of course. No problem. Go back through, *Señora*. I'll have your breakfast done in twenty minutes, at most.'

Elinor turned to leave but then a thought occurred to her. She looked up at the ceiling.

'Hang on a minute! Don't you even have a fire alarm in here?' asked Elinor in consternation, her voice rising with disbelief as she examined the bare ceiling stretching to the other side of the room.

José said nothing, watching her with an expression of ludicrous dismay on his face.

'José, I don't think it's legal for you to be running a café without a fire alarm. For Pete's sake, man, call the local fire station and ask them to install a fire alarm for you. Seriously. If you don't do it, I'll have to report you. This place is a potential death trap.'

'What's going on?' asked Tony, sticking his head in the doorway and sniffing suspiciously at the smell of burnt bacon.

José looked pleadingly at Elinor, begging her silently with his eyes not to tell Tony what had just happened.

She hesitated before she spoke, choosing her words carefully. She had no desire to destroy José's livelihood and she wasn't sure Tony would be tolerant or accepting of what had just happened. He was far too puritanical.

'Everything's fine, Tony,' she said a little bit too quickly, going over to the doorway and trying to push him gently back out into the corridor. 'I distracted José with my chat and he managed to burn the bacon. He's going to start again and says it won't take long.'

'He burnt the bacon? It looked to me like he'd thrown the whole lot into the fire. What on earth did you say to him?'

A devilish imp of mischief danced at the corner of Elinor's mind.

'Well, you know, I was just trying to use my feminine charms to get him to hurry up and concentrate on our breakfasts. I think he was so overwhelmed, he lost track of what he was doing.'

Tony wasn't buying it. His eyes narrowed as he stared at her suspiciously, trying to fathom what had been going on and wondering why she was lying to him about it.

'*Sí, sí*. Tony, it's true. I promise. She's a very beautiful woman. Just look at her. She took my breath away. I'm so ashamed. Me, a married man, should not be *destraido* like that. I am appalled. So ashamed,' said José, entering into the discussion with all the exuberance of a true Spaniard. He hung his head down in shame, not meeting their eyes.

José should go into amateur dramatics, thought Elinor, her lips twitching again as she watched him. He obviously had a hidden talent for this kind of thing.

Tony looked thoroughly taken aback. After looking at the pair of them for a disbelieving minute he shrugged, giving up on trying to understand what was going on.

'Right. I guess we'd better go back to our table, Elinor.'

Elinor nodded, heaving a silent sigh of relief as they retreated back to their seats.

Twenty minutes later they began to tuck into their English

breakfast, presented free of charge by José who was now beaming from ear to ear, as though nothing untoward had happened that morning.

As she ate, Elinor stared pensively at the mural at the other end of the room. It was very crude. She'd be able to do a much better job on it, she mused.

The food was delicious and beautifully cooked, as Tony had said. Given the quality of the cooked breakfast it was a shame everything else fell below par. She thought José and Elena could do with some help to jazz the place up. The Hut might then attract some serious clientele, like the golfers from Trevose Golf Course.

As she munched her way through her plate she started to visualise what she would do to the interior and exterior to make the place more appealing.

She was still thinking about it when she walked to her car after breakfast.

If Tony had noticed she was distracted he didn't comment on it, which she appreciated. She felt very comfortable around him when he made so few demands on her but she sensed this was only a temporary arrangement. A partial truce...

She wasn't sure how long that would last. There was still a lot of unfinished business between them and she was sure Tony was just biding his time before he tried to change the boundaries in their relationship again.

37

'José, I could paint you a better mural for your restaurant,' said Elinor, diplomatically avoiding calling The Hut a café, given that José had declared himself 'the best chef in Cornwall' at their last meeting.

José looked dubious.

'You're an artist?'

'Yes, I'm a good artist actually, José. Look at these photos of my work,' said Elinor calmly, lifting up her mobile phone and passing it over. José studied the photos carefully and then passed the phone to his wife who was sitting next to him.

It was a quiet morning at the café and they were all seated at one of the tables in the dining area of The Hut. Earlier that week, Elinor had arranged the meeting with José and Elena. She'd mentioned it cautiously, hoping desperately that they wouldn't mind, as she had some creative ideas that she thought might be helpful to them regarding their business.

Elena had been very open to having a chat with Elinor and full of enthusiasm to hear her ideas. After the embarrassment of being caught asleep in the kitchen, it was obvious José didn't have the stomach to object.

Elinor had developed an immediate liking for José's wife when she met her.

She discovered Elena was a vivacious character, open with

her feelings and thoughts, so you always knew exactly where you stood with her. She looked very young. Elinor didn't dare ask her age but Elena could've passed for a girl in her late teens.

She was an elegant, pretty girl with a mass of thick, curly brown hair and enormous, warm brown eyes. 'Bambi eyes', as Elinor's mother would have described them. Elena had a natural grace about her, so even dressed in jeans and a shirt she looked impeccably smart. Completely oblivious to her own attractiveness, she had no affected mannerisms.

José, who was sitting next to her, appeared distinctly dishevelled by contrast. His hair was a mess, there were dark shadows under his eyes and he had a five o'clock shadow on his face. He looked like a man who was under a lot of pressure. He was older and more careworn than Elena but it was soon obvious who had the stronger personality in the relationship.

After studying the photos on Elinor's phone, Elena and José turned simultaneously and looked at the mural on the back wall of the café.

'How much would you charge us for painting a new mural?' José asked Elinor suspiciously, apparently thinking Elinor had her own selfish agenda with this meeting.

'I wouldn't charge you. If you'd like me to paint the wall I'd do it for free.'

The two of them stared at Elinor with puzzled frowns on their faces. Almost as if she'd suddenly sprouted horns on her head, Elinor thought ruefully.

'Why would you paint a mural for us for free?' asked Elena bluntly.

Elinor squirmed uncomfortably on her seat.

'I'm not working properly at the moment and I've loads of

spare time. Besides I love hanging around these beaches and I'd enjoy helping you guys out. But I warn you, I'll be asking for free food and paint during the time I work here,' she added, grinning cheekily at them.

Elena looked at her pensively for a moment and then turned to speak to her husband.

'I think it's a good idea, José. If Elinor wants to help us out *eso sería estupendo*. It would be nice to have a better fresco on that wall,' said Elena softly, stroking her husband's arm persuasively.

José shrugged fatalistically, as though there was nothing more to be said if that's what his wife wanted.

'What picture would you put on the wall instead? Would you still paint surfers?' Elena asked Elinor, as though Elinor's co-operation in the project was already a fait accompli.

'That's up to you guys. Personally, I'd do something with a more universal appeal. I know most of your clientele surfs but you might be able to broaden your customer base. I would paint a view of Constantine Bay with Trevose Head in the distance, or else a view of the golf course with St Constantine's holy well and ruined church. Both of these might have a broader appeal.'

José and Elena mulled this over. It was clear to Elinor that José wasn't keen on any changes but that Elena, having reached the end of her tether with their business enterprise, was willing to consider more lateral solutions to their slow trade.

'I agree with you, Elinor. I think it's a good idea. I'd be very grateful if you would do this for us. For me, personally, I'd prefer a painting of the golf course. It's so pretty.'

Elinor cleared her throat.

'Wonderful! I can work on it even with the restaurant open. It won't be a problem. The other thing I wanted to mention is that this lighting will be great for when I'm painting but it's not so good for the kind of intimacy and comfort people expect when they have a meal. Speaking as a client, I would consider maybe putting in lighting that's a little more discreet and subtle.'

José was looking decidedly unhappy at this suggestion.

'See, *idiota*, I told you! Now do you believe me? She's saying the same as me!' said Elena angrily to her husband. 'We have to make this room better or we'll lose our business!'

José turned to face Elinor with a rebellious look on his face.

'We just don't have the budget for big changes like that. That's the main problem here.'

But Elinor had thought about this at length and was one step ahead of him.

'My uncle Leo has a lot of retired friends who used to be in the trade. I'm sure they'd be happy to do some work at a very reasonable cost. I could sound them out if you're up for it.'

'"Sound them out"?' asked Elena, confused by the phrase.

'I could ask them to look at it, once you've decided what you'd like done, and then you could see how much they would charge to do the work,' explained Elinor. 'I'm certain they wouldn't charge much for it.'

Elena started to look more cheerful, in direct contrast to her husband who sat dolefully next to her without saying a word.

'Thank you, Elinor,' said Elena politely, pointedly ignoring her husband. 'I think it's a great idea. I want also to buy some more tables and chairs for this room. Nicer ones.'

Elinor nodded in wholehearted agreement.

Elena and Elinor eyes met for a moment as José sat with his arms crossed and a frown on his face. They smiled at each other like fellow conspirators. They were both reading from the same page. Elinor could see Elena had the upper hand in her marriage, so no doubt José's objections would be swept away by Elena's determination to transform the café.

'I believe there's an Ikea in Exeter, which would be an economical place to go shopping for new tables and chairs,' proposed Elinor, helpfully.

'Would you come with me to choose them?' asked Elena, tentatively.

Elinor smiled.

'Yes, I'd love to. I was also going to mention that you could see if Leo's friends could do something to fix the outside of the restaurant for you. I get you can't change the building but that black door could be replaced or painted over and you could use a better sign. You could also try growing a creeper to disguise some of the wall's graffiti and holes. One of Leo's friends is still working in his retirement as a gardener. I'm sure he'd have some helpful suggestions.'

Elena clapped her hands together in delight.

'Yes, that is a fantastic idea. I like that very much. Let's do it!' she said, lifting up her hand to smack it against Elinor's.

José said nothing. It really was quite funny to see how depressed he looked next to his enthusiastic, vivacious wife.

Once more, Elinor studied the notepad where she'd penned all her ideas. She wasn't sure why José and Elena's business had grabbed her interest so much but she reckoned José's superbly cooked English breakfast had something to do with it.

As a true foodie, she couldn't ignore the injustice of such skilful cooking going to waste in what was little more than a derelict shack. Although if this whole ridiculous crusade of hers was for the sake of honouring José's cooking, she must surely be losing what little sanity she had left.

'By the way, another thing that you might want to consider is to rethink the name for the business. The Hut is not a good name for an up-and-coming restaurant.'

José put his hands up in protest.

'Oh, no. That cannot change. No way.'

Elena rounded on him, descending into Spanish in her agitation.

'And why not, *tonto*? The Hut is a stupid *nombre*. You show off so much but this place is called The Hut. *Una cabaña*. Bah! It is not a good name for a restaurant. It is nothing.'

'It is what the surfers have always called it,' insisted José.

'But we don't just want surfers eating here, José. It's not enough business. We want the golfers and the people who go to the caravans in the summer. You don't have a proper restaurant if you only get hungry surfers coming here.'

José stiffened, his pride offended by his outspoken wife.

'Well, you could discuss that another time maybe,' suggested Elinor hastily, not keen to get in the middle of a marital bust-up. 'My next idea, and the last, you'll be glad to hear, is that once you're fixed up you might want to advertise your business at the clubhouse at Trevose Golf Club. You're right next to the ninth hole. This would be an ideal pit stop for golfers for a bite to eat as they make their way around the golf course.'

At this José brightened perceptively. It was clear he was finally beginning to see how this would heighten his prestige in the area.

38

Elinor had started painting a new mural at The Hut almost immediately, and two weeks into the project she could see she would only need another couple of days before it was fully completed.

She'd enjoyed immersing herself in the project. Working in the dining area she inevitably attracted the interest of the diners, and she felt she'd become better acquainted with the surfing community as they dropped in to get a drink or some food. Even Richard Glynn, that notorious surfer-farmer, had exchanged polite pleasantries with her one morning, leading her to think that he'd been painted blacker than he really was. Not that she'd dare to suggest such a thing to Leo.

Another side benefit to painting The Hut's mural, Elinor thought, was that she was also creating future publicity for her artwork and that was no bad thing. Not that she'd really managed to get entrenched into her art again but she was sure the day would come.

So far she only had two finished oil paintings, which were hanging at the art gallery in Truro where Barbara predominantly exhibited her work.

Barbara, who always sold her pictures for an astronomical amount of money, had insisted that Elinor put a high price tag on her two paintings too. Elinor didn't think she had a hope in hell of selling either for an astounding ten thousand pounds, but as the exhibition was Barbara's show to run she'd accepted her commands meekly.

Tonight was the opening night at the Kestrel Gallery for Barbara's exhibition, and both Barbara and Elinor had been handing out invitations like sweeties in the hope that a few of their friends and acquaintances would make the effort to turn up.

Elinor suddenly heard a loud bang as the door to The Hut opened and shut again. Someone with a decisive, confident step walked up to her ladder but Elinor didn't turn, in the futile hope they'd let her continue painting in peace.

'Hello, Elinor.'

Lost in her thoughts, she still would have recognised that deep voice anywhere. It was Tony.

Elinor smiled to herself and glanced down at Tony from the top of the ladder where she was occupied in putting the finishing touches to a cloud. She was getting used to the constant interruptions that occurred when she was absorbed in her painting work but still resented them at times. However, she was always happy to have a chat with Tony.

'Hi.'

Tony was standing with his feet apart and his hands on his waist as he surveyed the mural.

'You've done a good job on that wall.'

'Thanks.'

'Although I'm not sure I'm a big fan of you poshifying the place,' complained Tony. 'You're either going to scare off the surfers or else price them out.'

Elinor glared indignantly at him.

'For heaven's sake, Tony, it's not me doing up this place. José and Elena want this done for the sake of their business.'

She turned back to her painting in a huff.

'And probably for the sake of their marriage too,' added Elinor as an afterthought, as she carried on dabbing delicately at her cloud.

'That doesn't explain why a gang of retired men, looking suspiciously like Leo's friends from the pub, have been buzzing about the place like wasps the last few days, fixing things up. I take it you had nothing to do with that either?'

'I don't owe you an explanation, Tony.'

There was an ominous pause.

'Really?' said Tony with an edge to his voice.

Elinor quickly peered downwards again and saw Tony looking up at her with a great deal of anger in his eyes. Her heart started to thump uncomfortably in her chest. Feeling her hands start to shake with nervousness she decided to stop painting. She wasn't going to ruin her hard work because of Tony's difficult mood.

Damn Tony, she thought to herself, as she carefully put down her easel and paintbrush on the top step and walked slowly down the rickety steps of the ladder.

Tony, who was standing right next to the ladder, didn't move as she reached the bottom rung. She looked up at him sharply as she stepped on to the floor but her irritation was suddenly arrested by the intense expression in his dark brown eyes.

She peeked around his broad shoulders and saw the café was empty.

'Tony, what's going on?' she asked, trying to sound casually interested even though her heart was now pounding and threatening to burst out of her ribcage.

Tony moved a step closer, pinning her against the wall behind her, and before she knew what was happening he had both hands on her waist and was bending down to kiss her lips. Just at the point that his lips brushed hers she put her hands up and pushed him gently back.

'No.'

'No?' murmured Tony, looking into her eyes.

Elinor looked away.

'No, Tony. I'm sorry but I can't.'

'Because of Mark, I take it?'

Elinor stared at him in surprise, completely speechless for a moment.

'Who told you about Mark? Barbara?' she whispered eventually.

Tony nodded.

'Elinor, you can't change the past but you can change the future. I'm sure Mark would've wanted you to do that too. To move on and be happy...'

Elinor looked miserably at him, stubbornly shaking her head.

'You don't understand. In the days after Mark died I remembered everything about him. Every facial expression, every mannerism and every precious moment we had together. But what no one ever tells you is that the only reason "time is a great healer" is because you slowly, bit by bit, start to forget all those things about the person you loved. If I get involved with you Mark's going to fade even more than he already has. I can't let that happen.'

'So you're just going to deny your feelings and bury your natural instincts? How's that going to help you?' demanded

Tony, frustrated. 'I'm not completely stupid, Elinor. Working as General Practitioner you get to read people pretty well. I know what's going on in there right now.'

He pointed straight to her heart.

'I'm sorry, Tony. Please just let it all go,' pleaded Elinor pathetically, inwardly despising herself for her stubborn self-denial.

'Honestly, Elinor, you drive me absolutely mental. I've no idea what weird shit is going on between us but I do know it's driving me crazy. At least you know what I think now. You should relax and see where this takes us. It's like surfing, you don't know where you're going to end up when you start the ride but you take the risk anyway. That's not dishonouring Mark, it's living life to the full while you have it.'

Elinor lifted up her hands in a gesture of defeat.

'OK. I understand what you're saying. I'll think about it but you shouldn't rush me into something I'm not ready for.'

'Fair enough. Let's leave it for now,' said Tony, not looking particularly happy about it. 'Shall I see you tonight?'

Elinor smiled, pleased to be distracted from other more sensitive topics.

'Yes, of course you will, you idiot. I've two paintings up for sale. For a colossal price too.'

'I know. I've already had a look online at the gallery's website. Crazy amount of money artists sell their work for nowadays.'

'Not if you've made a name for yourself like Barbara has. I think she wanted to make sure my work didn't look like cheap tat next to hers,' laughed Elinor disparagingly.

Tony nodded absent-mindedly, his thoughts clearly

elsewhere, and then smiled sadly at her before he walked back to his table, picked up his rucksack and headed out of the café.

Oddly, Elinor felt the sudden urge to cry as he left.

39

Elinor stood next to Barbara, her champagne glass held awkwardly in her hand and her smart high heels starting to make her calf muscles ache. Barbara was dressed in a smart black trouser suit whereas Elinor, by contrast, was wearing a tight-fitting sequin dress she'd borrowed from Elena for the occasion. The silver dress was loose, of course, on Elena but stretched comfortably to fit Elinor's ample curves. Elena had insisted she looked great in it so, against her better judgement, Elinor had taken her at her word.

She was listening politely to the conversation of five guests who'd surrounded Barbara shortly after making an appearance at the Kestrel Gallery's opening night. As the five had made their way determinedly towards Barbara, Barbara had bent her head and quickly whispered in Elinor's ear:

'These are a group of pretentious interior designers but they quite often buy my work for their clients...'

She'd then straightened up and smiled gaily as she greeted them with a double kiss, introducing Elinor to them as her 'fellow artist'.

Out of the corner of her eye Elinor could see Leo, looking proud as punch, strutting about the gallery talking to people he recognised. He was dressed in a smart grey suit and tie. Elinor had wondered where he'd fished it out from, but Leo had explained how Barbara had hauled him over to Plymouth to buy a smart suit years ago. She hadn't wanted him to bring down the tone of her exhibitions with his everyday casual clothing.

This had surprised Elinor, as snobbery wasn't something she would normally have associated with Barbara, but she could see now that underneath her eccentric ways Barbara had a hard-nosed business acumen that evidently contributed to her commercial success.

She zoned back into the conversation just as Barbara said, 'Do have a look around and let me know what you think. I do value your feedback very much and it makes a real difference to any future work I do.'

The others all nodded as if they all knew their opinion was going to be very important to Barbara and turned as one to stroll about the gallery.

'Phew! That wasn't too difficult. I was worried I wouldn't be able to shake them off. To be honest with you, Elinor, the biggest danger in these events is that you can get completely monopolised by one set of people and never get a chance to speak to anyone else.'

Elinor nodded, reeling at the hidden complexities of the art world. She'd made a decent living back in the days when she'd been a full-time artist, as she'd worked on commissions for people and sold her work online. But this prestigious exhibition was on a whole other level of promotion and publicity.

The gallery owner came up to Barbara with a middle-aged couple in tow, beaming from ear to ear.

'Barbara, let me introduce you to Mr and Mrs Coults. They've just bought two of your paintings and were very keen to meet with you.'

Since this introduction didn't include her in it, Elinor moved back politely and left Barbara to carry on the cordial conversation while she wandered anonymously amongst the shoals of people drifting in and out of the gallery rooms.

She walked to a large room at the back of the gallery and glanced briefly over to where her two paintings were hanging optimistically on the dark green wall. Her eyes narrowed as she saw what seemed to be a red dot attached to the plastic sign next to one of them. Thoroughly surprised, she moved to have a closer look.

There was no denying it.

There was a circular red sticker placed on the sign next to her painting. It had sold!

Elinor felt the elation fizz inside her. Ten thousand pounds! Even with the thirty per cent fee due to the gallery that would still leave her with seven thousand pounds in its entirety. For someone like her, who'd been out of work for a year, this was an absolute fortune.

Her mind was buzzing but in the midst of her excitement she also started to wonder who'd conceivably buy the work of an unknown artist at such an extortionate price.

She immediately thought of Leo and her heart sank. She really hoped he hadn't been deceived into paying such a ridiculous price for her painting. Surely he'd know that she would have painted anything for him, for free, after his kindness to her? Feeling troubled, she started to look around to see if she could find him.

She tracked him down in one of the rooms, chatting to Frederick, another of his innumerable friends. She hurried up to them.

'Leo, please tell me you didn't buy my painting?'

Leo turned to her eagerly.

'Have you sold a painting?'

'Yes, it appears so. So it wasn't you after all? Really?'

Leo shook his head.

'No, it wasn't, I'm afraid, Elinor. Although, as you know, I do think they're fantastic paintings.'

'Oh, thank God!' exclaimed Elinor, bending down, a hand above her knee and another clutching at her heart in relief. 'I was so worried you'd gone and squandered a fortune on it!'

Leo patted her reassuringly on the shoulder as Frederick started to laugh.

'Elinor, don't worry. I know I could commission you to paint me a picture any time and you know what that would be of.'

Elinor nodded breathlessly in agreement, suddenly feeling very foolish. The only painting Leo would ever ask her for would be one of Warren Cove, which was where the ashes of his wife, Elinor's Auntie Lowena, had been laid to rest.

'Which just goes to show you, Elinor, that you don't value yourself enough,' scolded Leo as she straightened up again. Elinor groaned inwardly as Leo became fired up. 'Somebody here clearly liked your painting so much they paid ten grand for it! Ten grand! It's bloody fantastic. And there I was thinking we'd have to take your book to the British Museum soon to earn you some kind of a living!'

'What are you talking about, Leo?' interposed Frederick, totally confused by this conversation. 'What book?'

As Leo started to explain to Frederick how Elinor had discovered a potentially valuable book, Elinor caught sight of Barbara waving vigorously at her from the entrance to the gallery. Obediently, she walked over to her, grabbing another glass of champagne on the way.

'Elinor, where did you go? I've had a lot of people asking me who you are,' complained Barbara, instantly making Elinor feel bad for escaping temporarily from the polite chit-chat. 'They've been so intrigued with your work. And I hear one of your paintings has sold too! That's wonderful, darling!'

'I know! I still can't quite believe it. I'm struggling to imagine a painting of a surfer would be of interest to anyone.'

'It's certainly an unusual subject but you've done it beautifully. You deserve to sell both those paintings. They're absolute masterpieces.'

Elinor blushed, not used to getting such lavish praise from someone as acclaimed as Barbara.

'Barbara doesn't hand out such fulsome compliments very often. You've clearly impressed her,' said a quiet voice in Elinor's ear.

Elinor looked up and smiled at Tony who was standing next to her, looking smart in a navy suit and a pale blue tie. Elinor was finding it increasingly funny to see everyone so dressed up. It seemed to add to the superficiality of the evening. All of them were acting a part that bore no relation to their everyday reality.

'Have you just arrived, Tony?' asked Barbara.

'We have,' affirmed Tony, cordially.

Hearing Tony say 'we', Elinor peered behind him and saw Jennifer standing there, looking absolutely stunning as usual in a full-length, light blue dress. The soft chiffon material floated downwards in loose, swirling layers. It was the kind of dress that would have made Elinor look like a frumpy matron but on Jennifer, who was tall and slim, the garment looked regal and imposing. Jennifer and Elinor smiled politely at each other, Elinor assimilating Jennifer's presence with mixed feelings. She was pretty sure that Tony and Jennifer were only mates, but there'd always be a niggling doubt in the back of Elinor's mind telling her that they could conceivably be something more. It didn't seem possible to Elinor that any red-blooded male wouldn't be physically attracted to a natural beauty like Jennifer.

'You need to go and look at the exhibition and see if you can reach into those deep pockets of yours, Tony,' teased Barbara.

Tony grinned at her affectionately, his eyes creasing at the corners in friendly amusement. As more guests came up to talk to Barbara and Elinor, Jennifer and Tony moved off in tandem to saunter around the gallery.

By the time the crowd had died down slightly, Elinor had managed to work her way through five glasses of champagne, three of orange juice, and numerous canapés. That's it, she thought, as she gazed down at her bloated stomach, I have to get back into my running tomorrow. Since she'd started working on the mural at The Hut she hadn't done any exercise and she was worried she was going to lose all the fitness she'd built up so persistently over the preceding months.

Weariness was overwhelming her. She'd spent the better part of six hours standing on a ladder in The Hut earlier that day, and now spending the entire evening standing in her high heels was killing her legs. After a quick survey of the room, she decided to give herself some much-needed respite and disappeared into the storage room at the back of the gallery. She'd been in there earlier in the evening and had spotted a comfortable chair to sit down on.

She sank gratefully into the cushioned chair as soon as she

walked into the cluttered room and quickly removed her high-heeled shoes, ruefully observing the red lines imprinted on the skin of her feet. She leant her head backwards, closing her eyes with a relieved sigh. Before long, she found herself drifting off into blessed slumber so she didn't hear the door to the room open forty minutes later.

She was woken up by the sound of giggles resonating close to her. She opened her eyes and stared in shock at the little crowd in front of her. Frederick, Leo, Barbara, Tony and Jennifer were watching her with a great deal of hilarity.

Elinor sat up hurriedly, feeling a deep blush creeping up her cheeks as she strived to pull herself together. She quickly flattened her hair and reached for her shoes before remembering she'd tossed them to the other side of the room in disgust.

'Are you looking for these?' asked Tony humorously, dangling the pair of silver stilettos in front of her.

Elinor grabbed them ungraciously, quickly putting them on to cover up her ungainly feet, by now red and swollen. To cap it all off, the toes of her tights had ripped open and she had a huge ladder working its way up her leg.

'Has everyone gone?' she asked eventually, looking up at the small crowd of spectators.

'Yes, dear. Everyone's gone. It's been a wonderful evening. I'm just sorry you missed the end of it. We didn't know where you'd got to but thankfully someone said they thought they'd seen you come in here. Otherwise you could've been locked up for the night!' exclaimed Barbara, looking distressed at the thought.

The others clearly didn't feel a similar concern. It didn't escape Elinor's notice that they were all looking like they were gallantly trying not to laugh at her. She was going to have to tell José about this tomorrow. It was almost as though she was following in his footsteps by falling asleep on the job, although with considerably less danger to the public in her case.

She stood up and stretched into a big yawn.

'I'm sorry to have missed the end of the show but I think the six hours of painting at The Hut finished me off today. I'm definitely ready to go home now.'

'Good. That means poor Godfrey can lock up his art gallery and we can all go home for some well-deserved rest,' said Barbara firmly.

Godfrey, who was the gallery owner, poked his head in the door.

'OK, everyone? Ready to go home now?'

Everyone murmured their assent and as one they all walked back out into the main gallery.

After effusive thanks and goodbyes to Godfrey they all split up, Elinor and Leo getting into Leo's old Volvo to drive home to Trenouth. Before they drove off, Barbara bent down quickly to speak to Elinor through the car window.

'Elinor, I want you back in the studio soon. You need to immerse yourself into making paintings again. You're much too talented to be wasting your time on a café mural.'

Flattered, Elinor nodded her agreement.

'Sure, I'll be back at the studio soon. I promise. Thanks for everything, Barbara. You just earned me seven thousand pounds tonight.'

'No, Elinor,' corrected Barbara adamantly. '*You* just earned yourself seven thousand pounds.'

Barbara then stood back and waved as Leo and Elinor drove off.

Watching Barbara in her side mirror, Elinor saw her tall, solitary figure standing for a long moment under the street light, diminishing slowly as the car sped away until she was just a tiny dot on the horizon.

40

Elinor was sound asleep when she was awoken by the tendrils of light sneaking into her bedroom and tracing a pattern on the curtains on the other side of the room. She sat up in her bed, thoroughly confused. She knew it wasn't morning. Why was the hallway light on?

She felt hideously tired. They'd arrived home from the art exhibition at half past eleven, she'd fallen asleep at twelve o' clock and yet it felt like she hadn't slept at all.

She heard a noise in the hallway that sounded ominously like Leo was putting his heavy boots on. Elinor jumped out of bed and raced to open the bedroom door.

She walked rapidly to the front door of the house and, sure enough, found Leo sitting on the hallway bench and working his tight-fitting boots onto his feet.

Leo looked up at her apologetically.

'Sorry. I didn't mean to wake you up.'

'What on earth are you doing?' asked Elinor impatiently.

'I had a call from Sheila Burns.'

'Sheila Burns?' repeated Elinor stupidly, wearily rubbing her eyes and trying to remember who she was.

'Yes. Sheila Burns. Don't you remember the old lady who lives next to the wheat field?'

'Oh! Yes. *Her*. So what's she doing calling you at...' Elinor looked quickly at her watch. 'Two in the morning... Two in the morning! Has she totally lost her marbles?'

'We told her to call if she saw something suspicious, remember?' explained Leo patiently.

'Ah, yes! What has she seen then? Some badgers conga dancing along the road? A fox playing tig with a colony of rabbits?' asked Elinor sarcastically.

'No, although I have to say that would be worth seeing,' said Leo calmly. 'She says the white van's back again.'

With this, Leo bent down and shifted his second boot onto his foot.

Elinor looked at him in exasperation.

'Leo, you can't go searching out there on your own. It's the middle of the night. You've no idea what's really going on or what you could be getting involved in.'

Leo glanced at her amusedly as if to say, 'Do you want to try and stop me?'

Elinor sighed. She knew that look.

'Listen. Give me five and I'll join you. At least two of us will be safer than just one.'

'Elinor, I'm not going to boss you around,' said Leo, pointedly referencing her earlier attitude. 'But are you sure you want to do this? I'm just thinking of your anxiety.'

Unoffended, Elinor smiled back at him.

'Yes, I know. My anxiety with a capital "A". It's always the elephant in the room, isn't it? Well, screw my anxiety. Since I've come down to Cornwall my anxiety hasn't stopped me doing anything I've wanted to do. So it's not going to now.'

And with that, Elinor turned around and went back to her room to get changed.

Ten minutes later they were walking quietly down the road bordering the field of cows, only using the light of the moon to guide their steps even though Leo had his torch with him. They could see the white van glimmering at the far corner of the wheat field with its headlights on and the engine running.

Whatever was going on, it certainly wasn't the most secretive of operations. The rumbling noise of the van's engine echoed intrusively in the silence of the night. No wonder Sheila Burns had been woken up by it.

Leo and Elinor walked into the wheat field by opening the stiff wooden gate and soon found themselves hidden by the high Cornish hedge, which was an effective barrier between them and the van on the other side.

Leo switched on his torch when they stumbled over the tilled earth at the entrance of the field and he began to slowly sweep its light from side to side.

As they started to walk in a single file down the middle of the field, slowly heading diagonally towards the van in the corner, they tried as much as they could to follow the furrows in the ground so as not to damage the wheat too much.

Her senses sharpened by her apprehension, Elinor could feel the spiky burrs of the wheat heads rasping and catching on her trousers and she could vividly hear the quiet swish of the wheat stalks brushing against their legs as they walked through the field. But it was the steady pulsing of the van's engine that dominated the quietness of the night and relegated all the other collective noises to the background.

Elinor felt the tension hit her in the solar plexus. Her legs felt strangely unstable and weak, her neck wobbling like that of a puppet on a string. She felt propelled forward by an irrational impulse while a sensible voice in her head screamed at her to go home and rest in the relative safety of Trenouth.

She started to chew her lip in an effort to calm her nerves, tasting the metallic flavour of blood on her tongue as her dry lips split under the relentless pressure of her teeth.

In her tired and confused state she nearly bumped into Leo as he came to a halt halfway down the field.

She stopped walking and looked cautiously around the enormous field but she still couldn't see what had stopped him in his tracks.

'Elinor, look over there,' whispered Leo, pulling her to him and pointing his torch towards a hawthorn bush at the very end of the field in front of them.

Elinor strained her eyes, trying to figure out what her eagle-eyed uncle had spotted.

She suddenly saw the hawthorn bush move to one side and a figure of a man literally pop out of the ground like a Jack in the Box.

The man scrambled up, letting the bush fall back into place again. Once he was standing, he suddenly caught sight of their torchlight and stood rigidly still as he stared across at Leo and Elinor in stunned surprise. He was young, possibly in his early twenties, and dressed conventionally in jeans, trainers, a thick black jacket and a woollen red hat.

After a nerve-racking minute in which they all remained curiously static, the man lifted up the torch he was carrying loosely in his hand and pointed it directly at them, blinding Leo and Elinor with its powerful light in the process. As they blinked in the torch's fierce glare, they could see the man studying them and then they saw him turn to look anxiously back at the hawthorn bush.

Within moments the bush moved again and a second man came up the same way as the man before him. The second man exclaimed loudly when he caught sight of them but the other man shushed him angrily, still keeping a watchful eye on Leo and Elinor as they stood immobile in the middle of the wheat field.

Elinor looked at Leo apprehensively, wondering how this face-off was going to end. She had no idea what these men were doing coming out of the ground at this hour but whatever it was it couldn't be an innocent occupation, given they were doing it under the dark cover of night.

Elinor pulled on Leo's sleeve.

'I think we should go, Leo,' she whispered urgently, even as a third figure pulled himself up from behind the roughly used hawthorn.

Leo nodded his agreement silently. Taking hold of Elinor's elbow he quickly led her back the way they'd come.

She tripped continually on the uneven mounds of earth and wheat as she tried to keep up with Leo's breakneck speed. She also kept twisting around frantically, trying desperately to keep a cautious eye on the men behind them.

She really didn't like feeling vulnerable and completely exposed to danger. And the truth was that she and Leo were walking away now with their backs towards a strange group of men who'd suspiciously gathered together in the dead of night.

Even though the men were congregated at the other side of the wheat field, she figured it wouldn't be too hard for them to catch her and Leo up if they decided they wanted to. Elinor's ears strained as she listened out for any sudden indication that any of the men might be running after them.

By the time she'd turned around for a third time she could see there were now six dimly discernible figures standing bunched together at the other end of the field, flashing their torches towards her and Leo, watching them carefully as they made a quick exit out of the field.

Once out of the wheat field, Leo and Elinor walked up the road circling the cow field at a tremendously fast pace. The thick, shrouding darkness of the dense night made it difficult for them to see the black tarmac of the road clearly, but it didn't slow them down one iota.

Elinor felt her apprehension and fear begin to subside once they were safely through Trenouth's entrance and back in their front garden once more. Only then did she have the courage to turn around one last time to look at the white van purring away on the other side of the cow field, still with its front lights blazing a yellow path in front of it.

'Elinor, you go in. I'm going to stay up and see what happens with that white van. It can't be staying there all night.'

'Leo, what the hell's going on with those strange men appearing in the field like that?'

'I've no idea. But I do know I'll be speaking to Richard Glynn as soon as I get a chance, and I'll be asking him a few pointed questions.'

'You think he knows what all this is about?'

'To be blunt, Elinor, yes I do. It's his wheat field. If there's a secret entrance into it he'd be the most likely candidate to know about it.'

Elinor worriedly eyed her uncle's worn and wrinkled face,

with his thick grey hair standing up in tufts; he obviously hadn't had time to brush it down after getting up from his bed. He was getting too old for this kind of caper.

'Would you like a hot drink?'

Leo nodded as he sat down heavily on the slate steps leading to their front door.

'Yes, I'd love a black coffee with a dollop of whisky in it, please.'

Elinor glanced down at him anxiously as she put her key in the front door. Leo must be unaccustomedly concerned about what he'd just witnessed to be asking for whisky at this time of the night.

Leo sank his head briefly into his large, gnarled hands, combing his fingers through his shaggy grey hair. When he raised it again his expression was troubled, digging a groove between his thick grey eyebrows.

Elinor opened the front door and trod thankfully into the familiar comfort of the entrance, switching on the lights as she did so.

'Hold on a minute! Here they come,' said Leo excitedly from the doorstep.

Elinor poked her head out of the door and followed his pointed finger.

Sure enough all six men, with their torches waving about madly, were climbing over the Cornish hedge just like Leo himself had done not so long ago, after his initial exploration of the wheat field.

The men jumped agilely down onto the road and quickly let themselves into the back of the van.

Two minutes later the van drove up the road and turned the

corner, disappearing into the darkness with its red taillights fading away gradually like the dying embers of a fire, and leaving Leo and Elinor to the stillness of the night again.

41

Two days later, Elinor had reason to forget all about the mysterious white van and the men in the wheat field as her stay in Cornwall came under imminent threat.

It all came from what seemed to be an innocuous comment from Leo but Elinor knew her strong-willed mother only too well. As soon as Elinor heard his words, she knew that her kind but overbearing mother was already in the process of moving heaven and earth to bring her back to Scotland again.

'Elinor, your mother's been asking me when you're going to go back home to Glasgow.'

Elinor quickly put her knife and fork down. At those words a sinking sensation started to pool at the base of her stomach.

She and Leo had been enjoying a rare breakfast together. Usually Leo was up a good few hours before Elinor so their paths didn't cross at the breakfast table, but on Sundays, by mutual agreement, the two of them decided to sit down to a cooked breakfast.

For Leo this meant kippers and for Elinor a more refined combination of scrambled eggs and smoked salmon. But this morning, after hearing Leo's words, Elinor felt her appetite vanish into thin air.

Her mind started to race into overdrive.

Was Leo getting tired of having her to stay? Was this his

polite way of telling her to move on? Or was her mother about to ruin the happiest period of her life since Mark had died?

Leo continued to munch his breakfast slowly and steadily, his movements calm and unhurried.

'Leo, have I overstayed my welcome?' asked Elinor eventually, in a small voice.

Leo smiled humorously as he chewed his kippers.

'Whatever gave you that crazy notion? It's been an absolute pleasure having you to stay here. But you're only twenty-eight, Elinor. A young lady. You've your whole life before you. I'm not sure being cooped up here in the Cornish countryside, with your seventy-year-old uncle, is a healthy thing for a young lady like you.'

Elinor felt a knot form in the middle of her throat. Tears began to slide down her cheeks unheeded. How could she explain to Leo that Trenouth felt like home to her now?

'Why didn't Mum mention this to me? Why is she trying to get you to pressure me to leave?'

Leo looked a little uncomfortable.

'She knows you've made huge strides in dealing with your anxiety since you've been here. I think she feels you now need to pick up the threads of your life once more and return to the old life you had before everything fell apart. And I suspect she was also worried you might react badly to that suggestion.'

'Too right! Of course I would react against it. I'm happy for the first time in ages and she has to try and wreck it all for me?'

'That's enough of the over-dramatic talk, Elinor. You need to learn to speak of your mother with some respect. You know she only has your best interests at heart,' growled Leo, with a note of warning in his voice.

'If she had my best interests at heart she wouldn't be forcing me to leave.'

'You're a grown adult. No one has the power to force you to do anything you don't want to do. As long as it's legal, of course,' countered Leo placidly.

Elinor wiped her eyes with a napkin and drank some tea, her mutinous emotions swirling around inside of her. She felt like breaking something to release some of the anger boiling within.

'All I'm going to say is that you should think about the life you left behind. And start thinking about what you want to do with yourself in the future,' said Leo convincingly. 'You shouldn't just let things drift and life pass you by.'

'Leo, you want to know what I think? I think Trenouth feels like home to me now, not Glasgow. Surfing's given me a sense of purpose and a release from my anxiety. How am I possibly going to be able to carry on surfing if I go back to living in the West End of Glasgow?'

Elinor let out an angry sob.

'And Barbara's helping me return to my painting again. How can any of this be a bad thing? Everything that makes my life worth living is here now. And you can tell my mother I'm still healing and recovering. I don't understand how Mum thinks a few months is enough time for me to suddenly go back to where I was before my anxiety kicked in.'

Leo nodded in agreement.

'And on top of everything else,' added Elinor aggrievedly, 'Mum's been supporting me financially up until now. So she can pull the strings at any point in time and so yes, she can force me to come home if that's what she really wants me to do.'

'Hold on just a minute there, young lady. You should be

grateful to your mother for supporting you. Not everyone's lucky enough to have such a supportive family. And as far as being beholden to her goes, you're going down that road far too fast if you ask me. You sold a bloody expensive painting at that exhibition the other night. That should keep you going for a while...'

Leo pondered the problem for a moment.

'And there's no reason why you can't restart your art career,' he added confidently. 'Plus, don't forget your *Frankenstein* book. That alone could potentially earn you quite a bit.'

Elinor smiled tremulously for the first time since the conversation had been broached. Her uncle was one of the most independent people she'd ever met and he was always going to be able to find a way to avoid Elinor being beholden to anyone, even if it was her own mother.

'It still wouldn't earn me enough to be able to find a place to live here on a clifftop near you, Leo. And that's all I want to do at the moment, if you can put up with me. I'm not ready to move back to Scotland now, if ever.'

'That's fine by me. As long as you've thought things through properly, I'm happy with your decision. Your mother will no doubt have a few choice words to give me on that subject but she'll come round in the end.'

They both returned to eating their breakfast with renewed vigour, relieved to have things finally settled between them. Silence reigned peaceably for the next five minutes.

Once Leo had finished his kippers, he pushed his plate away and poured himself a cup of black coffee.

'On quite another topic, I've been thinking of visiting an old school friend who lives in London. He has a smart flat in

Baker Street.' Leo lifted his blue mug and took a swig of coffee. 'The visit's been long overdue and I also considered that while I was staying there I could arrange to take your book to the British Museum. If that's OK with you.'

'Yes, absolutely. It'll probably take a good few months to get to auction so the sooner the better, I guess.'

Leo looked across at his precious bookcase. He'd placed Elinor's book in amongst his prized collection of seafaring books.

'I don't even know if the book will end up at auction,' he remarked. 'I've no idea how these things work. There's a chance, I guess, that the British Museum or the British Library might want to purchase it for their collection. I have to say, I'm not entirely comfortable with keeping a rare and valuable book sitting inside my bookcase. Although in all the years I've lived here I've never had anyone try to break into the house.'

He swallowed some more coffee.

'I take it you're OK with me selling the book for you?'

'Yes, of course. I only bought it on a stupid whim in the first place because I liked the poetical lines written at the front of the book. Now I know those lines were by William Blake I can just buy a book of Blake's poetry.'

Elinor drank a sip of tea and made a face. Her tea was now tepid. She hastily put her mug down again.

'When were you thinking of going up to London?' asked Elinor apprehensively, not enamoured by the thought of living in Trenouth without Leo around. He was as much a part of the house as the foundation was.

She wasn't sure she'd be comfortable staying in Trenouth on her own. It was, after all, a very isolated and exposed spot during the winter and early spring.

'I was thinking of going this Wednesday and coming back on Sunday. Are you going to be all right on your own? Because I'm sure Barbara would be delighted to have you stay with her.'

'I know. She would happily have me stay,' agreed Elinor. 'It'll be fine, Leo. I'll work it out. As you said, I'm old enough now to deal with myself.'

Leo looked doubtful, as though he wasn't sure Elinor was in a good enough shape as yet to be able to make any sensible decisions.

Elinor patted his arm reassuringly.

'Honestly, Leo, I'll be fine. The days will fly by and before I realise the time's gone, you'll be back here again.'

42

'There you go, José and Elena. It's all finished now,' said Elinor, having dragged the couple away from the kitchen to look at the finished mural.

Elena clapped her hands together gleefully. José studied the mural cautiously but finally smiled in what Elinor could only take as approval for her work.

'I love it, Elinor. Really. It's *muy bello*. We must have a celebration night for this, do you not think?' asked Elena.

Elinor nodded her agreement.

A lot of work had been done over the course of the last two and a half weeks. Leo's friends had thrown themselves into the renovation project with wholehearted zeal and the finished result was impressive.

Four large hanging lights in stylish wickerwork lampshades had replaced the ceiling lights. A new cherry wood floor had been put in overnight so as not to disturb any daytime trade. Comfortable fabric chairs in various shades from cream to mocha to chocolate brown were grouped around circular tables and in the far corner, right next to the mural, there were three groupings of coffee tables with two-seater sofas for those who wanted to sit for an informal drink or snack.

The exterior had been covered with trellises and the fast-growing New Zealand broadleaf planted at regular intervals around the building. The door had been painted a pale shade of green and above the flat roof a large triangular sign, fully visible from the golf course, had been placed, with the restaurant's new name, 'The Ninth Hole', painted on it in a tasteful script.

Elinor was sure some golfers were bound to complain about the now overtly visible sign but as far as she could make out José and Elinor, as owners of the commercial building, were perfectly entitled to put up a sign on its flat roof.

It was still early days and there had been no clear change to the amount of custom José and Elena received so maybe an opening night wasn't such a bad idea, thought Elinor. A little publicity never did any business harm.

Elena and Elinor by mutual consent sat down together to weave some kind of a plan for the party night, looking at dates while José made a sharp exit back to the kitchen. At the start of the morning they'd pencilled in 23rd February as the big date, with Elinor agreeing to design the invitation cards. Elena assured Elinor that she and José would take care of the food and drink supplies.

Elinor decided she would ask Leo if he had any golfing pals who were members of Trevose Golf Club. It would be great if they could entice a few golfers along to try out the newly decorated venue. If she knew anything about the golfing community, it was that word of a new watering hole with tasty food would spread like wildfire. Golfing wasn't a team sport but it certainly was a sociable one.

Elinor made her way home, strolling along the edge of Constantine Bay to have a look at the surfers who were out in force by now. It was mid-morning and the offshore wind was strong, which in turn had encouraged a large number of surfers to turn out. She wondered if Tony would be out there but she doubted it. He seemed to prefer to turn up early when the water was quieter.

For the last two weeks Elinor hadn't received an invitation from Tony to join him surfing or, in actual fact, any text at all. She'd texted him once or twice but there had been absolutely zero response. Complete silence reigned in their communication with each other. A stand-off of sorts...

She looked out to sea, watching the waves as the wind tugged brusquely at her ponytail and gently prodded her back. She felt like the wind itself was trying to encourage her to move into the sea, buffeting her forward as though to say, 'You should be out there.'

Elinor was in no hurry to return home to an empty house. Leo had been gone for two nights already and the house felt lonesome without him. She couldn't have felt more alone if she'd been stranded in the middle of the Sahara Desert, as ludicrous as that sounded.

She didn't know why she hadn't approached Barbara, and decided it was probably her pride that was at fault. She felt that she would be behaving like a small child who was scared of the dark if she called Barbara begging for companionship. After all, Barbara was used to living on her own so how could she empathise with Elinor's riotous fears?

But she also knew she was sometimes too hard on herself and that her ever-present anxiety made things trebly difficult.

She was currently exhausted from lack of sleep. In her solitary state, she'd woken up several times during the night with her heart beating madly in panic, imagining the worst with every single creak and crack, as the old house stretched and shrank its limbs with the changing weather and its erratic heating system.

It felt like the next two and a half days until Leo arrived back were going to drag.

She looked at the surfers enviously. It felt like such a long time since she'd been out there, gliding manically on the waves like they were doing now. Glancing at her watch she saw it was nearly eleven o'clock. Perfect for a pre-lunch venture out into the waves...

She started to walk purposefully back to Trenouth.

43

'Elinor, don't you think the weather's too wild for you to go surfing today?' asked Jennifer bluntly, as she stood in the shallows with her wet blonde hair streaming down her back and her surfboard tucked under one arm.

'No. I'll be fine,' said Elinor firmly, holding her surfboard defensively in front of her as she prepared to enter the ocean.

Elinor stared aggressively into Jennifer's clear blue eyes but Jennifer was a tough cookie and wasn't afraid of a challenge. She reached out a hand and held on to Elinor's surfboard, much to Elinor's annoyance.

'I really don't advise you to go out to the surf zone. I'm telling you the waves are too strong for you.'

'Look, Jennifer, I appreciate the friendly advice but I'll be fine.'

'Elinor! I'm telling you as an experienced surfer that you won't manage the waves today. The others would agree with me on this one. Tony would've warned you too if he'd seen you.'

This was the final straw for Elinor.

'He would, would he? Well, Tony's not here now and nobody else is paying the slightest bit of attention, so why don't you just let me get on with it? With due respect, you're not my mother, you know.'

To Elinor's satisfaction Jennifer flinched at this.

Elinor had no idea what had come over her but she felt the pent-up emotion of the last few weeks bursting out of her. Her two sleepless nights were playing havoc with her reason. What on earth was she doing picking a fight with Jennifer, of all people?

Jennifer reluctantly removed her hand from Elinor's surfboard.

'Fine. Just don't say I didn't warn you,' she said quietly, making Elinor feel incredibly guilty and foolish in the process.

Jennifer then walked majestically out of the water and onto the sandy beach, heading towards the car park. Elinor watched her leave, feeling wretched. She'd have to apologise profusely to her later.

She turned back to the ocean, putting her regrets to the back of her mind. She felt the adrenaline and excitement build up in her as she felt the fresh sea spray hit her face. The roar of the waves seemed to her to be beating on a war drum inside her head, challenging her to get back out into the ocean and fight.

The red lifeguard flags were positioned to the left hand side of the beach so Elinor moved towards the right. She stood for a while, watching the sea, trying to gauge the waves and the wind.

She immediately spotted the rip current, which today was a wide channel of dark, choppy water beating a path straight out to the surf zone. Mick had taught them well.

The waves were the largest she'd seen yet and they were thundering at an incredibly fast pace towards the sandy beach. How on earth was she going to be able to paddle fast enough to keep up with them?

Jennifer had a point warning her, but then again the life-guards were on duty today so how bad could it really be?

Elinor started to wade into the water and then carefully, so she didn't get in the way of any of the surfers twisting and turning ably on the incoming waves, she began to duck dive under the waves as she made her way out to the surf zone.

Conditions that day were very different to what she was used to. For a start, her arms had to work a lot harder to pull her through the tormented sea and when she duck dived she struggled to make any leeway against the surprisingly strong pull of the waves drawing her backwards, each one of them striving viciously to carry her shoreward.

By the time she made it to the surf zone her muscles were screaming silently with the pain of pitting their strength against the forces of nature. She felt she'd reached the end of her endurance and had no idea how she was now going to find the strength to surf back to shore again.

She rocked backwards and forwards violently as she sat on her surfboard. Keeping an eye on the fast-moving waves, she wondered for the first time if she should have heeded Jennifer's warning.

All she could hear in her brain at that moment was her mother's voice, chanting like a mantra, that pride comes before a fall. She knew a well-grounded or mature person would have at this point conceded defeat and made their way by the safest means possible back to the beach, saving their strength for another more lenient day. But she'd never been one to give in to the promptings of her better self.

Her obstinacy came to the forefront. If she gave up now, her argument with Jennifer would have all been for nothing. And she was yearning to surf again. Never mind that the craving had hit her today, on a hideously windy day with the waves crashing in from what Elinor estimated was often a six-foot height and moving at a good twenty miles an hour.

She knew she wouldn't have the strength to continuously attempt to ride the rollers streaming in towards land, so she would have to give it her best effort and then leave the rest for another day.

She caught sight of two wave peaks moving rapidly towards her and angled herself so she was in the right position to paddle furiously to try and catch them. She lay down and dipped her hands down into the water, starting to paddle aggressively as fast as she could.

Within a couple of minutes she felt herself sliding down into a trough before rising upwards again as the wave behind her pulled her upwards. As soon as she felt herself rise on the wave she continued to paddle furiously a few more times and then quickly pushed her body upwards, sliding her back foot first and then her front foot forward in between her hands, before standing up with her knees bent.

As soon as she stood up she knew she'd been too late.

She started to tilt back into the trough between the waves and lost her balance. She was hit with the full force of the second wave that was stretching up ominously behind her. As she slipped from her surfboard she felt her left hand ram itself at an awkward angle against the hard surface of the board, pain instantly firing up the length of her arm as she was tossed unceremoniously into the water.

What felt like the weight of an elephant or a mid-sized truck slammed on top of her, pushing her deeper than she'd ever been previously. Her ears began to hurt excruciatingly as the water pressure weighed in on her discomfort. Her left arm felt like it was on fire and the leash was tugging hard on her ankle as though someone had grabbed it and was pulling fiercely and repeatedly on it. She was shaken like a rag doll, a headache starting to spread across her forehead as the cold started to bite.

Forty seconds later, she felt the crushing roller that was holding her down lighten somewhat, and she knew she had to get to the surface for another breath before the next wave smothered her again. She kicked wildly with her legs, fighting against the turbulence in the water and trying to slice through the currents swirling around her. She managed with a great deal of effort to move slowly upwards, feeling more and more desperate as her lungs started to burn with the need for more oxygen.

When she managed to break through the surface of the water she gulped madly at the air, not caring if another wave was about to slam down on her head. And she did manage to take a few breaths before another wave rained down. Unfortunately for her the wave had broken. She felt herself shoved under the water again, shaking like a feeble piece of flotsam as she was spun around and around.

She no longer felt she had the muscle strength to fight her way through this second ducking. Inside her head, as she hung limply under the water, she felt strangely calm and philosophical. She knew she was fully at the mercy of the ocean and there was nothing she could do about it. Maybe this was now the end of the road for her...

All of a sudden she sensed a hand tucking itself under her arm, pulling and jerking her upwards to the surface, the iron grip squeezing painfully on her flesh. As she burst through the surface of the water again, she felt herself being dragged roughly onto a floating board and pulled shoreward.

Her chest was heaving with the deep breaths she was greedily gulping down. She opened her eyes after a moment and looked at the yellow board she was clinging onto tightly with her right hand.

The lifeguard.

He was now competently cutting across the choppy water, pulling her along with him. She felt her leash dragging on her foot. Hopefully her surfboard would be trailing along behind them.

The lower part of her left arm was still in excruciating pain and she knew that she'd done some serious damage to it. Miserably, she waited until they reached shallower waters and then slid off the board, her feet finding the soft sand. The lifeguard put his hand under her arm and walked with her out of the water.

As soon as she reached the edge of the dry sand she fell onto her knees. Her head was spinning wildly and she started to retch. Thankfully, she had next to nothing in her stomach.

After a while, once the nausea had passed, she sat down on her calf muscles and looked up. The lifeguard was crouched down next to her, watching her with concern.

Elinor smiled at him weakly and then looked around the beach self-consciously, wondering who else had witnessed her getting rescued by a lifeguard.

She could only imagine the scorn of the other more competent surfers as they watched her get tossed by the ocean that was too strong for her and then, in the ultimate indignity, saw her rescued by a lifeguard. And all because she was cocky enough to think she could manage these conditions.

In the distance, a man in a black wetsuit with an unruly

mop of short blonde hair was making his way quickly across to them. As he came into closer focus, she groaned.

It was Tony.

She really didn't feel up to getting a scolding today. She put her head down again, pretending not to have seen him.

'What's going on?' Tony asked anxiously as he came up to them.

'Hi Tony, you're just the man we need,' declared the lifeguard thankfully. 'This lady was wiped out by a wave and then she seemed to be struggling to keep her head above the water, so I went out to help her. But as soon as we reached the beach she seemed to get dizzy and she's been retching for a while. I don't know if it's concussion or not.'

'OK. Thanks, Dave. Leave her to me, I'll take care of it.'

Relieved, the lifeguard got up and went back to his post.

Tony proceeded to ask Elinor a number of questions that she recognised straight away as being related to concussion. He asked her if she could follow his finger as he moved it from left to right. As he started to test her eyes with various exercises she started to feel increasingly upset.

'Look, Tony,' said Elinor impatiently, grabbing hold of his hand to stop it moving. 'It's not my head I'm worried about. It's my left arm! It's killing me just now with the pain of it.'

Tony looked down at her left arm and saw that it was hanging limply by her lap. He tried to pick it up but as soon as he touched it she yelled out.

'Ow! Bloody hell! No, don't touch it. It's sore!'

There was a long pause as they stared at each other.

'Elinor, I think the best thing for you to do right now is to go to Newquay Hospital and get your injuries looked at.

You might need an X-ray done. Do you want me to call Leo for you?'

Hearing Leo's name, Elinor felt the tears start to her eyes. Irrational thoughts started circling in her head. What on earth was she going to do with Leo's car, which was sitting in the car park?

'Leo's not here,' she said in a small voice. 'He's in London and he's not coming back until Sunday.'

'No problem. I'll take you up there myself, then. Can you stand up?'

Elinor nodded brusquely and stood up quickly, carefully putting all her weight on her right arm, before Tony even had the chance to bend down and help her up.

Tony then crouched down to undo the leash on her ankle and picked up her surfboard.

'Where's your surfboard?' asked Elinor in surprise.

'I didn't bring it. I wasn't planning on going surfing,' answered Tony shortly. 'I only came out here today because I received a call from Jennifer. She told me you'd insisted on going out in very rough surfing conditions and she was worried about you.'

Elinor didn't have anything to say to this. She walked slowly across the beach towards the car park, wallowing in self-pity and self-recriminations. That day, the whole length of Constantine Beach felt like the walk of shame to her.

44

'She was right, you know.'

'Who?'

'Jennifer. Who else?'

Tony didn't bother replying to this.

They were both sitting on bright blue plastic chairs in the waiting area of Newquay Hospital's Minor Injuries Unit, waiting to be seen.

Thankfully, it was a Friday and still within GP surgeries' opening hours, so the place wasn't too busy.

Elinor was dressed in a loose jumper and a pair of baggy trousers. She'd given up on trying to get her long sleeved T-shirt on.

Because of the pain in her arm, Tony had insisted on cutting off her wetsuit with a pair of scissors. Normally this would have utterly distressed Elinor, as good winter wetsuits weren't cheap, but she was too worn down to care any more. She'd sat quietly on the car seat as Tony fetched the scissors from his first aid kit and started to slice through the tight-fitting, rubbery material.

Elinor was feeling completely exhausted. Tony had given her some ibuprofen for the pain in her left arm but it was barely taking the edge off it.

Without consciously being aware of what she was doing, she leant against Tony and dropped her head against his arm in weariness. Tony didn't move or object, so they stayed like that until the nurse called them through.

An hour and a half later, the pair of them walked tiredly out into the hospital car park.

It was now three o'clock in the afternoon and Elinor had a cast on her left hand and lower arm. The X-ray had shown that she'd cracked her wrist and the nurse had informed her it would probably take up to eight weeks to heal. No more riding the waves for the time being.

There might be no more surfing for the short term but Elinor could only be thankful it was her left wrist that had cracked, as she'd still be able to paint with her right hand. Without both surfing and painting, she knew she would have soon sunk into morbid depression.

'Where now?' asked Tony, as they sat in his car.

'Trenouth, please,' said Elinor, puzzled by his question.

'They've said you have mild concussion so you shouldn't really be alone for forty-eight hours, Elinor,' said Tony wearily, as if talking to a troublesome child. 'Is there anyone you'd like to call to stay with you?'

Elinor shook her head silently, cringing slightly at the rush of pain in her head as she did so.

'What about Barbara?'

'No. Please don't call her. She's got a lot on at the moment. Thursdays she's at the day care centre all day and I know that tomorrow morning she was going to visit her sister in Penzance.'

Tony looked across at her with a frown on his face.

'OK, then,' he said reluctantly. 'Look, I've got to be at Porthcothan tomorrow morning to help out at the surf school, but I can pack a bag and stay with you at Trenouth tonight. Tomorrow morning you can come and watch us at

Porthcothan, or I can drop you off at The Ninth Hole with José and Elena for a few hours.'

Elinor nodded mutely.

Her head was aching badly, whether from the hammering she'd taken in the water that morning or from her two nights' insomnia she wasn't sure. All she wanted to do right now was curl up on a bed or a sofa and sleep...

Tony looked anxiously at her, started up the car and drove off. Elinor stared out of the front window of the car in a daze.

They arrived at Tony's flat in West Hill, Wadebridge, half an hour later. Elinor wearily followed him into the modern, cube-like building and then up some stairs to the top-floor flat.

She could tell she wasn't looking too good because of the concerned glances Tony kept firing across to her, as though he was expecting her to keel over at any moment.

'Right,' he said as he opened the front door. 'Why don't you make yourself comfortable in the sitting room?'

He pointed down the corridor to a door at the far end.

'In the meantime, I'll rustle us up some food. You look like you could do with some nourishment.'

'Thanks Tony, for everything. And I'm sorry for screwing up your day.'

'Now I really know you're not well! I don't think I've ever seen you so docile.'

Elinor smiled back at him weakly and made her way to the sitting room.

Apart from a unit filled with books across one wall, the decor in the flat was very minimalist. It really looked as though Tony spent hardly any time at home, which was probably the case given his wholehearted involvement in surfing.

After briefly studying the numerous photos on the bookcase, Elinor surmised he probably had a very active social life too.

She sat down on a comfortable leather recliner seat, tilting it so she was lying back and looking out at a view of Wadebridge from the large window. Then she swivelled around slowly on the chair, wanting to inspect the room out of curiosity once more, and suddenly noticed with amazement that her painting from the gallery was hanging up, in pride of place, above the fireplace.

It stood out magnificently against the brilliant white wall of the room and it suited the minimalist decor. The colours in the painting gleamed like jewels against the background light provided by the large windows of the sitting room and the looseness of the brushstrokes on the canvas were nicely juxtaposed with the angular, geometrical lines in the room.

Despite how beautiful the painting looked in its new location, she felt shocked and mortified that Tony had spent ten thousand pounds on one of her paintings. She wondered why he hadn't told her.

She got up and walked back to the kitchen.

'Tony, why didn't you tell me you'd bought my painting?'

Tony looked up from the saucepan where he was stirring some soup. Two plates with buttered bread were on the kitchen table.

'I didn't realise I was obliged to let you know,' he commented, smiling to himself.

'No, but... You know, if you'd let me know you wanted it, I could have sold it to you for so much less.'

'And rob you of your publicity at the gallery? That wouldn't have done your artistic career any good. You need to take a leaf out of Barbara's self-promotion book.'

'Well, anyway, I'm very honoured you thought my work was worth ten grand, Tony.'

'You should be. It's not every day I splash out that kind of money. Still, it's a lovely painting and I'm very happy with it.'

Elinor giggled.

'I'm open for commissions if you want any other pictures painted.'

'Don't push your luck, young lady. One's enough for me. The soup's ready now. Come on, let's get some food down us.'

Tony looked at his watch.

'Lunch at half three. We're going for continental times today.'

Eating the lentil and bacon soup delicately, savouring every mouthful, Elinor felt the strength returning to her body. It really was extraordinary the impact wholesome food could have on you when you hadn't eaten for near enough eight hours. And yet, as her stomach worked to digest her lunch, overwhelming tiredness hit her.

Elinor reached for a piece of bread and noticed Tony watching her worriedly, having wolfed down his soup and bread earlier on.

Looking at Tony's empty bowl and plate Elinor felt a pang of guilt. She wasn't the only one who'd been hungry.

'Elinor, you look completely and utterly drained. Why don't you have a nap in the spare bedroom and we can head over to Trenouth later? I've plenty of work I can catch up on here.'

'That would be wonderful if you don't mind too much. I'm so overtired I'm not even sure I'll be able to nap, but a rest would be appreciated. I haven't slept well since Leo left for London and it's beginning to catch up with me.'

'Why's he in London?' asked Tony, frowning as though this was a thoroughly inconsiderate thing for Leo to do.

'He's visiting a friend of his and he's also trying to get a book I found at a book sale valued and sold.'

Elinor reached out for her plate and grabbed a piece of buttered bread with her right hand.

'I bought the old book because I liked the few lines written in the front of it,' she recounted, before taking a big bite of bread. She chewed and swallowed it quickly, eager to finish her tale. 'And now it turns out that the book expert, here in Wadebridge, thinks the written lines and the painting on the edges of the book are by William Blake. And so it turns out the book might actually be worth something.'

'I'm sure you weren't expecting when you came to Cornwall to be painting with a well-known local artist. Or to be learning to surf, for that matter, or to be finding a valuable book completely by accident...'

Tony paused for a moment, lost in thought.

'And also taking part in a prestigious art exhibition in Truro,' he added.

Elinor laughed with a mouth full of buttered bread, wincing slightly at the ache in her cranium.

'No, I hadn't expected any of that. Cornwall's such an amazing place. The strangest things have happened to me since I've moved here. And I haven't even told you about the tunnel Leo's found in Wine Cove or the helicopter we found outside our house one morning.'

'Well, you can save that for later,' said Tony firmly, standing up as Elinor finished her last morsel of bread and taking the dirty dishes to the sink.

Elinor drank the remnants of her glass of water and then stood up as well. Tony walked her to the kitchen door.

'Right, let's get you some rest. See the door that's open at the end of the corridor? That's the spare bedroom. Make yourself at home.'

Elinor nodded her thanks but before she walked out of the kitchen she couldn't help turning back and wrapping her arms around Tony's back in a quick, appreciative hug as he stood washing the dishes at the sink.

She walked gratefully down the corridor and into the spare bedroom. Within five minutes of folding the duvet around herself and lying back on the soft pillows, she felt herself drifting off.

For the first time since Leo had left for London she was feeling safe and secure.

45

Elinor felt a pat on her back and ignored it, snuggling down deeper into the warm nest of her duvet. The patting gradually increased in vigorousness until at last she opened her eyes and turned to stare up at Tony fiercely.

'What?' she demanded angrily. She could still feel the mists of sleep clouding up her brain and stubbornly refusing to dissipate.

Tony put his hands up in mock surrender.

'God, Elinor, don't ever let me catch you when you've just woken up. You're an absolute tiger! It's six o'clock in the evening now and I was just wondering if you wanted some dinner? And what's the plan for tonight? Are you wanting to head over to Trenouth?'

Elinor sat up and rubbed her eyes.

'I don't know... I'm so, so tired,' she added unnecessarily, yawning loudly.

'I gathered that,' said Tony, looking like he was trying not to laugh. He sat down on the bed and waited patiently for Elinor to elaborate.

She looked at him disconsolately.

'Right now, all I want to do is sleep.'

'OK, fine,' said Tony, giving up. 'Look, come and have some of the pasta I've cooked up and then you can head straight back to bed if that's what you want.'

'But I don't have a toothbrush or any of the stuff I use at bedtime. Or my pyjamas for that matter.'

'I've got spare toothbrushes in the bathroom cabinet and you can borrow my pyjamas tonight.'

Elinor made a face. Tony was so much taller and broader than her. Any pyjamas he gave her would be falling off her, surely?

After trying unsuccessfully to come up with a better suggestion, she eventually shrugged and reluctantly got herself out of bed.

She docilely followed Tony to the kitchen, ate a bowl of pasta and then disappeared again shortly afterwards to get her face washed with soap, her teeth brushed and to change at breakneck speed into a pair of Tony's pyjamas. She always carried her medication in her handbag so she swallowed her two Sertraline tablets. Thankfully her handbag had been retrieved from the boot of Leo's old Volvo before they left Constantine Bay, because a few hours' delay in taking her medication could make her feel very sick indeed. In a record thirty minutes she was tucked back up in bed again.

Some houseguest I am, she thought to herself ruefully. But within a few minutes the warmth of the bed dragged her down to the land of nod again...

When Elinor woke up again her room was in complete darkness except for a narrow sliver of light coming from the corridor. For a brief moment she wondered where she was until she suddenly remembered the events of the last twelve hours.

She turned her head to look at the window. She reckoned it must be late at night, given how dark it was outside the window, and she was grateful that Tony had helpfully left the hall light on.

Her wrist was starting to ache painfully again; the ibuprofen she'd taken earlier in the evening had worn off, leaving an uncomfortable throb.

Elinor reached across and switched on the bedside table light, blinking in the sudden glare of it and feeling the brightness momentarily hurt her head. Her watch told her it was one in the morning.

She picked up the packet of paracetamol that Tony had left with her and popped another tablet in her mouth, swallowing it down with some water. Then she leant back on her pillows and for want of anything better to do stared at the wall opposite her bed, waiting patiently for the painkiller to kick in.

She found the quiet stillness of the night slightly unnerving, accustomed as she was now to Leo's old bungalow. There was rarely a time during the wintertime when you didn't hear the wind gusting or howling against the solid walls of his house. And rarely was there a time during the night when you didn't hear the house expanding and shifting on its ancient timbers.

Forty minutes later Elinor was still lying in bed, wide awake and thoroughly fed up. Because of her anxiety, there'd been many nights over the last year when she'd been left unable to sleep, lying awake until the early hours of the morning. As she was already on strong medication for her anxiety, she'd been averse to crawling back to the doctor and begging for some sleeping tablets. So for a long time she'd managed her erratic sleep with over-the-counter sleeping tablets, both herbal and artificial.

Elinor hated the night. For some reason its emptiness made everything worse for her.

She couldn't understand why, but in the dead of the night negative emotions and thoughts became magnified and distorted. The smallest of her fears and worries grew to an unsustainable size during those sombre hours. Like the genie in Aladdin's lamp or the evils of Pandora's box, it often felt at night as though supernatural powers beyond her control had been unleashed and were taking hold of her emotions and mental health.

Tonight, as she lay there in her bed, Elinor relived the mortification of her behaviour towards Jennifer the day before, as well as all the inconvenience she had thrust upon Tony since her accident. She tortured herself with recriminations and self-loathing.

It was Friday night, and she was sure if it hadn't been for her Tony would've been at the pub with his friends. And what was Jennifer going to think when she found out about this?

She felt a complete and utter fool.

She started to cry forlornly, letting the tears slide down her face as she reached out for a tissue to wipe her nose.

In the end, she decided she couldn't stand the emotional pain any more. Physical pain she could deal with but the emotional pain was far, far worse. She could only describe it as a knife twisting in her chest.

She got up and went out into the corridor, looking for Tony's room. She saw his bedroom door was slightly ajar and she quietly pushed it open, tiptoeing into the room. When she peered at the bed she could see Tony was sleeping on his side, with his back to the door.

Without even considering the fright she could be giving him, she lifted one side of the duvet and slid herself into the bed, huddling up to his back and reaching up to rest her left hand carefully over his waist.

'Elinor, what the hell are you doing?' mumbled Tony irritably, not moving an inch but his muscles tensing under her arm.

Elinor buried her face into his back and didn't reply.

Tony turned around slowly until he was staring into Elinor's face, his brown eyes glinting in the light from the hallway.

'What's wrong?' he asked in a gentler tone of voice.

Elinor just looked at him pathetically, tears running down her face. He lifted his hand and gently wiped the tears away with his fingers.

'Don't cry. Tell me, what's wrong?'

'I think I'm just feeling overwhelmed with guilt at how I behaved towards Jennifer and I'm feeling awful at putting you to all this inconvenience too. All because of my stupid pride and arrogance. I should've never gone out into the ocean with the conditions as bad as that. I don't know what in the world I was thinking.'

She sobbed.

'And I'm really wishing Leo was here. He calms me down so much.'

Tony reached an arm around her and pulled her close, so her head was now resting on his chest. He stroked her back softly and she felt the warmth of his body slowly loosen the tension in hers. She buried her nose in him, breathing in his musky scent.

It wasn't long before she started to giggle.

'Tony, honestly, it doesn't take much to get you excited,' she said, feeling a hard bulge against her hip.

Tony looked down at her and grinned widely.

'What do you expect, Elinor? You know perfectly well what you do to me.'

Elinor squirmed a little further up the bed and then reached across to kiss Tony tenderly on the lips. He responded eagerly, kissing and tasting her lips as though starting a long and slow voyage of discovery.

He took his time, as though testing her resolve and commitment, but in the end it was she that moved them on, by pulling off her clothes and impatiently reaching out to take his off too. Almost as soon as Tony reached for her naked breast, she was moaning impatiently for him to fill her.

After that, time sped quickly by and before long the pair of them were coiled up around each other and drifting off to sleep once more.

46

'For goodness' sake, Elinor! I'm away for four days and look what happens to you.'

'I know, Leo, but at least you're back now. I've missed you. Cornwall's not the same without you.'

Leo leaned back contentedly on the dining chair and took a bite out of one of Elinor's freshly made scones.

'I missed you *and* your cooking,' said Leo humorously, through a mouthful of scone crumbs. 'I missed my home very much too. And of course, the coast hereabouts. The great thing about going up to London is that it reminds me of how special it is here.'

Elinor nodded and took a swig of coffee.

She couldn't regret anything that had happened while Leo had been away because it had brought her and Tony together. But it had taken fairly extreme measures for that to happen and she wasn't eager for any more drama in her life. She'd learnt her lesson in caution.

Leo's reassuring bulk emerging from Barbara's car had been a truly welcome sight. Leo's solid and familiar presence always emitted an aura that suggested everything was going to be OK and that things were going to return to normality once more.

With Leo back it looked like life at Trenouth was going to resume its steady rhythm again, only now Elinor had the added bonus of a relationship with Tony to brighten up her days with...

'Well, any exciting news while I've been away?' asked Leo, swirling the dregs of his coffee around at the bottom of his mug.

Elinor glanced suspiciously at him but he was busy concentrating on his coffee.

'Did Barbara tell you about Tony and me, Leo?'

Leo burst out laughing.

'Yeah, she did! Of course she did. You didn't think you two could keep something like that from her, did you? In another life she would've worked as an undercover spy.' Leo smiled across the table at her. 'Couldn't be more delighted for the pair of you. Your mother's certainly not going to get you returning back to Scotland in a hurry, is she?'

'No, she certainly won't but that's already been decided. Speaking of my mother, how did you get on with valuing the book?'

Leo patted his jacket as if trying to remind himself where he'd put something. Then he reached into his inside pocket and pulled out a folded envelope, tossing it on to the table in front of Elinor.

'There you go. That's the receipt for the book and a cheque for fifteen thousand pounds.'

'Wow,' said Elinor, greedily opening the envelope and pulling out the cheque. 'That's amazing! So they established the book belonged to William Blake, did they?'

'It took them a couple of days to get back to me but yes, in the end they had the experts look at the handwriting and the fore-edged painting. I think it was fairly conclusive. William Blake has apparently quite a distinctive way of painting and drawing. "Unique" is what they said. Which made the whole process simpler, thankfully.'

'I really feel we should be giving some of this to Stephen Ashcroft, who discovered the fore-edged painting in the first place.'

Leo scratched his five o'clock shadow meditatively.

'You know, Elinor, you could have a point there. I've given Stephen a lot of good custom over the years but it's also true that if it hadn't been for him we wouldn't have discovered how special that book really was. The only thing is I doubt he'll accept anything for it.'

'What should we offer him?'

'Leave it with me. I'll have a chat with him when I'm next in Wadebridge.'

Elinor restrained herself from telling him that she herself would realistically be spending some time at Tony's flat in Wadebridge too. The relationship was so deliciously new and she had no idea as yet how things would change on a daily basis for them both.

She now had the added problem that she couldn't drive anywhere either.

She'd sent Tony a couple of soppy text messages that morning but he was at work and she had no idea when he'd have time to reply to them.

In the meantime she planned to request a lift from Leo to Barbara's studio or else make her own way there. She was desperately pining for some studio time. Barbara had kindly given her a spare key so she could let herself in whenever she wanted.

'Leo, I wanted to ask you if you were planning on going to

St Merryn sometime?'

'Yes, I'm heading there this morning. I need some lubricating oil for the garage door. Are you wanting to go to Barbara's studio?'

'Yep.'

'No problem. Eleven o'clock OK for you?'

'Perfect. And by the way, Leo, don't forget José and Elena have their opening night this Friday.'

'Ah, yes, that's right. Will Richard Glynn be there?'

Elinor regarded Leo worriedly. One of these days he was going to end up in trouble. Curiosity killed the cat and all that. But it was pointless trying to tell Leo this because, quite simply, the man had no fear.

'I guess he might be. He's a regular customer of theirs,' she answered reluctantly.

'Good. It's about time I spoke to him about that tunnel. Before I report it to the authorities, that is.'

'I'd be careful, Leo. He might not like you prying into his business.'

Leo shrugged nonchalantly.

'If what we saw that night is part of his business, then he's definitely up to something dodgy,' he said serenely, wiping the scone crumbs from his jumper.

'But what exactly was going on that night? That's what I can't compute. We don't even know if it *was* dodgy or illegal.'

'I think those men came out of a tunnel leading from the cave in Wine Cove to the wheat field. And there's a cleat in that cave for a boat to be tied to. Personally, I think somebody's bringing in men clandestinely into the country. And, yes, I told Barbara that was far-fetched so I'm not sure anyone will believe me either.'

'You have absolutely no proof,' said Elinor.

'No. I don't. But to be honest with you, if with a friendly warning Richard Glynn stops whatever he's involved in, that's good enough for me. And that tunnel needs to be closed up. It's only asking for trouble keeping it open. I'm sure the local council will agree with me on that at least.'

Elinor didn't want to be cynical but she couldn't help thinking that if Richard Glynn was making money out of these men, why would he stop with a word of warning from Leo?

47

Elinor pushed the hair out of her face wearily. She'd been working in the studio for the last seven hours with barely a break. Adele was blasting out of the radio in the corner but other than that the studio was empty. The only background noise was the wind puffing gently against the windows and the trees outside.

She was lost in her painting, unable to let it go. Every time she looked at it, there was something else she wanted to add to it or amend. This was the negative side of her work. It absorbed her totally, sucking every last ounce of mental energy from her.

She'd had to learn, to her cost, when to stop. If she carried on painting after her brain was burnt out with too much effort, she ended up making bad mistakes as a result of poor judgement. The trick was to stop before she ruined a perfectly good painting with over-thinking.

She reckoned that she was just about at the point when she should stop. She was painting the clifftop at Warren Cove for Leo. Trenouth was in the painting, too, perched at the top of the steep cliff. The only thing that was annoying her at that precise moment was the positioning of the spring flowers. She'd scattered the bright flowers amongst the grass but it didn't look quite right. However, she was so tired she knew if she carried on she risked making things worse. The flowers could be amended in the morning...

She reached across to smudge the slate roof tiles on Trenouth a little more.

As she did so she heard the click of the door opening behind her and automatically assumed it was Barbara. Until, that is, two muscular arms wrapped themselves around her and Tony rested his head on her shoulder. She leant back contentedly, enjoying the embrace. If she'd been a cat she would have purred.

'What are you working on now?' asked Tony interestedly.

'I'm painting this for Leo. He's always said he'd like a picture of Warren Cove. It's where his wife's ashes have been laid to rest. But I'm stopping now. I've been working at it for the last seven hours and I'm shattered.'

'Not too shattered I hope,' said Tony mischievously, kissing her on the side of her neck.

Elinor smiled and put her brush down.

'I'd be careful if I were you. I'm known for getting oil paint in the strangest of places.'

Tony looked down hastily at his shirt and tie. Elinor smiled to herself. She'd noticed he was fastidious with his clothing. One of the idiosyncrasies she was learning about him.

'You're OK I think,' she said, reassuring him.

She stood up and pulled off her overalls, arching back to stretch her spine and neck in the process. Tony impatiently pulled her close and started to kiss her mouth with avid attention. Elinor's overalls dropped unheeded onto the floor with a quiet swish as she reached up a hand to touch his cheek.

As she started to explore Tony's mouth with her tongue she heard the door click again.

'Really, you two! Get a room, will you?' said an amused voice from the doorway.

Elinor and Tony pulled apart guiltily and turned around.

Barbara, dressed in a bright red coat that clashed with her pink-striped hair and wearing knee-high purple boots, was smiling at them both from the doorway. Elinor humorously noted the difference in the raiment Barbara wore when she was not trying to impress well-connected clients. There were two sides to this woman and she knew the one she preferred.

'Hello, Barbara. How was your day? I hope you don't mind but Tony dropped in on me.'

'Of course not. It's lovely to see you both. How's your painting going?'

'Good. I should have it finished in a day or two,' said Elinor, standing back to let Barbara see.

'Beautiful. Sublimely gorgeous, Elinor! Leo's going to love it.'

'I hope so! I've certainly worked hard enough on it.'

'Yes. Although when you've finished it you'll need to get back into making paintings to sell, Elinor. You must try and get into your vocation again. Did I hear correctly that you received a couple of commissions recently as a result of the art exhibition? Godfrey, the owner of the Kestrel Gallery, informed me yesterday.'

Tony looked surprised and delighted for her in equal measure. Elinor felt a warm feeling envelop her as she observed how pleased both Tony and Barbara were for her.

'Yes, that's right. I've been asked to do a picture of Tintagel Castle and one of Bodmin Moor. I've yet to speak to them so I don't know if they want a specific angle or view. Or if they'll give me the artistic licence to do what I want, which would be nice.'

'Good excuse for a trip to Bodmin Moor for the pair of you,' observed Barbara, patting Elinor's arm briefly before going over to her easel and depositing a bag next to it.

'I've been to Tintagel Castle with Leo but I've not been to Bodmin Moor. I don't really know much about it,' said Elinor.

'Me neither,' remarked Tony unabashedly.

'You're just like Leo,' accused Elinor. 'If it doesn't have seawater you simply have no interest in it. For goodness' sake, you live here! You should know a little of the culture.'

'I'm not sure Bodmin Moor has much culture,' replied Tony, sitting down on a stool.

'Tony, that's shocking! Of course Bodmin has culture. Loads of it, in actual fact. Prehistoric, medieval...' said Barbara, genuinely horrified at his ignorance. 'Jamaica Inn ring any bells for you? There are ancient villages and farms. There's also Dozmary Pool there, which has myths about it related to King Arthur's sword, Excalibur. Apparently it's where King Arthur picked up Excalibur from the Lady of the Lake. And there are the rumours about the Beast of Bodmin too, of course.'

'There are stories about King Arthur everywhere,' said Tony dismissively. 'I wonder if the people who commissioned the painting are King Arthur fans? Maybe they're modern-day witches or wizards. Loads of those hanging around.'

'That's true,' agreed Barbara.

Barbara started emptying oil paints out of her plastic bag and on to her worktop.

'I often think people must think I'm a New Age witch of some sort,' Barbara remarked amusedly, sorting out the different coloured oil paints.

'Nonsense!' scoffed Elinor.

'I'm deadly serious,' insisted Barbara. 'I'm an eccentric. An eccentric, elderly woman who lives on her own with a cat. In the olden days I definitely would've qualified for the stocks or being burnt at the stake.'

Tony and Elinor looked at each other, trying not to laugh.

Barbara was indomitable. It was hard to imagine anyone getting the better of her. If she'd lived in another age, no doubt she would have figured out a way to escape punishment of any sort, especially if it was unjustly due to her unconventionality.

'Oh, go away, you two lovebirds! *Stop* making fun of me!' cried Barbara, trying not to laugh, as she watched the pair of them exchanging glances. She leant back on her workstation, smiling broadly but with her arms crossed protectively in front of her.

Tony stood up and stretched, giving Elinor the sudden and irrational desire to pull his shirt off and explore his torso. A year of abstinence after Mark had died had not gone unnoticed by her libido.

'Barbara's right, Elinor. It's getting late and I'm getting hungry. Shall we head to Trenouth?' asked Tony wearily.

Elinor nodded, not missing the quick look of forlornness passing over Barbara's face.

'Barbara, why don't you come back to Trenouth and join us for some dinner?' asked Elinor kindly.

'I can drop you back off on my way home,' added Tony encouragingly.

'But aren't you staying over at Trenouth?' Barbara asked him, very surprised.

Tony grinned as Elinor's face turned crimson. No matter how much she tried, Elinor still couldn't get used to Barbara's outspokenness.

'I would normally, but I'm working at the out-of-hours unit from ten o'clock tonight, so I've to get back,' he explained, as Elinor looked at the floor in acute embarrassment.

Barbara looked at the two of them fondly and smiled.

'All right, then. If you don't mind me joining you, that would be lovely. I never could resist a chance to tease Leo about his cooking. I take it he is cooking?'

Elinor chuckled.

'He is, Barbara. But I'm afraid you'll not get much of a chance to make fun of his cooking tonight. It's mussels with garlic and white wine sauce on the menu. In honour of Tony, I can only assume...'

48

Elinor was regretting signing up for the opening night at The Ninth Hole. That was the problem with anxiety. It sometimes slumbered and gave one a false sense of security, only to rear its ugly head at the most inconvenient moments. José and Elena, of course, knew nothing about Elinor's battles with anxiety and her mental health. And now Elinor was standing in the middle of The Ninth Hole's kitchen and feeling the panic in her seeping slowly into her frazzled mind.

She was covered from top to bottom in self-raising flour, having split the bag when she was in a fluster earlier. José and Elena had asked Elinor to cook some miniature sticky toffee puddings for the night, a dish she could do with her eyes shut back home in Trenouth but ever since she'd stepped into the kitchen at The Ninth Hole everything had gone strangely wrong.

She'd barely two hours to go before the guests started to arrive and her latest batch of puddings looked like a burnt offering fit for the bin. She rubbed her tired eyes. She didn't know where she'd gone wrong but before she'd arrived the kitchen had looked like a thing of beauty, with neat canapés laid out on the work surfaces ready for the night ahead.

Now it looked like an excitable team of three year olds had been let loose in the kitchen after stuffing themselves full of Haribos.

And her stress was making it worse. She knew she was going to have to give up on the miniature puddings that Elena and José had requested of her and she hated herself for letting them down, but as she became evermore overwrought she knew she could easily end up doing something stupid. Not as stupid as falling asleep with the bacon frying, but near enough...

She sighed.

She reached across to pick up her three baking trays and carried them off towards the sink to scrape the burnt sponge out into the bin.

Elena and José were due to arrive at any moment with the drinks and glasses for the night's celebration.

The kitchen door swung open and Jennifer walked in, carrying a tray piled high with plastic containers filled with what looked to be various homemade salads.

Elinor put her baking tray down abruptly and looked guiltily at her.

She and Jennifer had made up after Elinor had called her from Tony's mobile and apologised profusely for ignoring her well-meaning advice. Elinor had been surprised at the calmness with which Jennifer had accepted her apology. Most women she knew would have harboured a long-standing grudge as a result of what had happened. But then again, Jennifer wasn't 'most women'.

'Elinor, are you OK? My God, what's happened?' asked Jennifer, glancing around her with a look of wonder on her face.

'I've screwed up again. I've made a total mess. José and Elena are going to kill me. I've burnt all the sticky toffee puddings. I don't know what happened...'

Jennifer surveyed Elinor inscrutably for a moment, making

Elinor want to squirm under her gaze.

'OK. I think the best thing is for us to clear up the mess,' Jennifer said slowly. 'Then I suggest we do what my mother always told me to do in a situation like this. I suggest we head out to Marks & Spencer and buy the puddings. We can pass them off as homemade. It's what she always used to pull out of the hat when she couldn't be bothered to cook for a dinner party.'

'Yes, but what do we say to Elena and José?'

'I think they'll be too busy to notice, to be honest with you. As long as we clear up this bomb site, it'll be fine. Trust me.'

Elinor smiled ruefully, remembering the momentous events that had occurred not so long ago when she hadn't trusted her.

'OK, Jennifer. Let's do it.'

The pair of them raced into the utility cupboard and started to clean up the mess, pouring buckets of filthy water down the utility sink, wiping grease off the normally shining work surfaces and throwing away all the unwanted ingredients.

Half an hour later Jennifer and Elinor were driving to Marks & Spencer on their last-minute rescue mission.

They came back with the boot filled with mini eclairs and profiteroles from an Iceland store and a number of full-sized cakes from M&S. By the time they arrived at The Ninth Hole Elena and José were in the dining room arranging the drinks and glasses, fussing over the decorations and laying out the tables at one side of the room with the canapés. They barely glanced up when Elinor and Jennifer walked in the door.

'We've had to buy some of the puddings, I'm afraid,' said Jennifer brazenly, confronting Elena and José with the truth in her forthright way.

'No, why?' protested José, looking understandably distressed at the thought of shop-bought food getting served up on their opening night.

'I'm sorry, José. I totally messed up with the mini desserts,' said Elinor contritely.

'Elinor, it's fine. It'll all be fine,' intervened Elena hurriedly before José could protest any more. 'Everyone will be so drunk by then that nobody will notice what the puddings are like.'

'I don't think you need to worry, José. My mother regularly serves up these cakes at her dinner parties and everyone thinks she's cooked them,' persisted Jennifer.

José waved his hands in the air agitatedly.

'Enough, enough. Don't tell me any more or I'll have *un ataque cardíaco*. Take it away to the kitchen.'

Jennifer and Elinor hurried off like two guilty bandits making off with The Ninth Hole's takings.

Once they were in the kitchen, they quickly plonked the bags on the work surface.

'You OK?' Jennifer asked Elinor.

Elinor nodded solemnly and then peeked up at Jennifer. For a moment both of them said nothing and then they burst out laughing. They were shaking with huge gusts of laughter and clinging desperately on to the workstation in the middle of the room when Elena came back into the kitchen.

'Well, this is a good start to the evening,' she said complacently, without batting an eyelid at their mirth.

Elinor could only feel admiration for Elena's intensely laid-back attitude. The roof could've fallen in tonight and Elena would still be putting a positive slant on it. When Elena was on good form there was clearly no getting her down.

Elena started taking the cakes out of the bags and went to fetch some platters to display them. Elinor and Jennifer helped her lay everything out and then Elinor helped Jennifer set out the different kinds of salad into serving bowls, carrying them through to the dining area where the other savoury food was neatly laid out.

By the time they'd finished there wasn't much left to be done. Elena and José were paying three local teenagers to work as waiters for the night, so all Jennifer and Elinor had to do was to go home and get ready for the party.

Elena good-humouredly shooed them out of the door with strict instructions to get dressed up and not to turn up late.

49

It didn't take long for Elinor to get ready.

She had splashed out some of her new-found cash on a tight-fitting black dress with a large split up one leg. She felt Tony would probably approve of her using the money from her painting in this way.

She smiled to herself as she put her make-up on. So many times she'd shrivelled up with shyness when she'd gone to social events but for once she was looking forward to tonight. Tony was coming to pick them up and would no doubt be by her side for the evening. It was amazing what a difference having a partner made to one's life.

We weren't made to be solitary creatures, she mused to herself. Apart from Leo, of course. That man had to be an exception. She'd never met anyone who was more comfortable in his own skin or in his own company.

She heard the doorbell ring and went to answer the door.

'Hello, gorgeous,' said Tony, reaching in to kiss her on the lips.

He stood back and she saw the light of his desire in his eyes as he surveyed her.

'You look beautiful, my love. That's a very sexy dress.'

'I thought you'd like it,' said Elinor, with self-satisfaction.

She moved aside and let Tony in to the house. She shut the

door behind him, keeping the cold wind outside.

'Hello, Tony, how are you?' asked Leo affably, turning up in his only grey suit (the same one he'd worn for the exhibition) and shaking Tony's hand amicably.

'I'm very well, thank you. Doesn't Elinor look amazing?'

Leo turned to observe her and nodded.

'Yes, that she does. Of course, an expensive dress bought with your money always helps,' said Leo cheekily.

'Leo! I hope you're going to behave yourself tonight,' said Elinor, whacking him on the shoulder.

'That'll depend on who's there,' said Leo cryptically. 'Right, we'd better get going.'

They left Trenouth and by the time they reached The Ninth Hole they found the car park was already a third full. Elinor was certain most of the cars belonged to Leo's more punctual friends. The surfing crowd tended to be more lackadaisical and unreliable with their timekeeping.

Tony parked his car on the grass and then went across to help Elinor out of the car, with an old-fashioned courtesy that she knew was sure to win Leo's approval. The three of them walked up to the doorway but as soon as Tony opened the door they were almost blasted off their feet by the volume of the music.

'What the?' asked Tony, stunned momentarily by the sheer magnitude of the noise.

A minute later the music was turned off.

José appeared in the doorway looking flustered.

'Come in! Come in! Good to see you! Sorry we are having a few problems with the music system but it will soon be fixed. I paid for a local DJ but he's *mierda*. Sorry, I mean crap... Elena is fixing him.'

Elinor peered into the dining area and saw Elena, dressed up in a dashing red and black Spanish flamenco dress, arguing vociferously with the DJ. She went across straight away to see if she could help her, feeling immediate sympathy for her plight. Elinor was used to things backfiring on her...

'Elena, are you OK?'

Elena turned fiery eyes her way.

'No, this man is an imbecile. How's anyone going to be able to talk when he plays music this loudly? Leo's friends are in the kitchen while we try and change this. I do not want them going home because it's too loud.'

Elinor looked at the DJ, who was looking mutinously at Elena.

'Can't you play the music quietly?' Elinor asked the DJ.

Elinor could see the effect her voice had. The DJ's face visibly cleared at hearing Elinor wasn't a 'foreigner'. Elinor felt her temper rising. Where did José and Elena find this dimwit?

'My loudspeakers aren't made for this size of room. I can't play music any quieter. They just don't get it.'

Elinor looked around at the two enormous speakers that were positioned on each side of the room. Elinor gazed at them for a long moment, her mind trying desperately to find a resolution.

'Elena, you can't have music blasting out at top volume during the party. You have a music system here, don't you? Can't you use that?'

'Yes, but what about him?' asked Elena, gesturing to the DJ dismissively. 'We paid him to play the music.'

'I know, Elena, but it's really not going to work with this guy. The volume that hit us when we came in is going to cause some serious hearing damage. I mean, you want the party to be a success, don't you?'

Elena nodded disconsolately.

'Don't you have any music ready prepared that you could run through their music system?' Elinor asked the DJ as a last resort.

The DJ's face lit up as he thought this proposition over.

'Yeah. That might work. But I need to see their system first.'

Elena clapped her hands.

'Oh, that is good. Come and see.'

Elena dragged the DJ off to see their music system, which was installed in the hallway between the dining area and the kitchen.

'What's wrong?' asked Tony, puzzled, as he came up to Elinor with a glass of champagne for her.

'Teething problems with a prat of a DJ,' answered Elinor, gratefully accepting the glass.

'Oh! And where are all the others?'

'In the kitchen until the music's fixed, apparently. I think we should fetch them through or this evening's going to end in disaster.'

'I'll go fetch them. Elena looks like she could do with some TLC,' said Tony as he watched Elena bustling back into the dining area. He disappeared off into the hallway.

'He says he can play the tunes through his phone on our system,' said Elena, shrugging. 'It's better than nothing.'

Two minutes later the muted sound of The Script's 'Hall of Fame' rang around the dining area. It was definitely an improvement.

Elena grabbed a glass of champagne from a tray the waiter

was carrying.

'That stupid man! Does he think we all want to listen to only his music and not be able to talk at all? I told him it was an opening night at a restaurant! Not a disco!'

She swallowed her champagne glass in two big gulps and then took another glass.

'Bah! I am not going to let that idiot spoil the night! We're going to have fun, aren't we?' she asked Elinor conspiratorially, smiling determinedly at her.

'Yes, Elena, we'll have a great night. You wait and see.'

Sure enough, an hour later the place was heaving with people and the noise of the chatter was soon overriding the background music. The Greek goddess Nemesis herself, thought Elinor amusedly, couldn't have planned Elena's retribution on the hapless DJ better than that.

50

It was close to eight o'clock when Elinor saw Richard Glynn walk in through the door. Her heart sank. Knowing how determined Leo was to confront Richard about his suspicions, she had a horrible feeling the two might cause a scene and ruin the party for everyone else. She resolved to keep an eye on the two men so she could try and intervene if things got out of hand. Not that Leo was ever going to listen to her, but she might be able to rope in Tony.

She'd told Tony all about Leo's discoveries and his suspicions about Richard Glynn. Tony was inclined to dismiss the whole thing as pure fantasy, refusing to believe Richard would ever try anything illegal, but she knew Tony would get involved if an argument broke out between Leo and Richard.

Elinor went and stood with Leo as he chatted with his friends at one corner of the room. It didn't take him long to notice Richard helping himself to a drink from the table at the entrance. Elinor saw him stiffen like a terrier in pursuit of its quarry. Leo waited until an opportune moment arose in the conversation and then excused himself, turning to head across the room.

Elinor reached out quickly and pulled on his arm.

'Leo, are you going to speak to Richard?'

'Yes, why?'

'Can you let me come with you, please?'

Leo looked cross.

'Oh, come on, Elinor. I'm a grown man, you know,' he said exasperatedly.

'I know. But I was there too, remember? I want to know what's going on just as much as you do.'

'OK,' said Leo, accepting her explanation. 'But I don't want you interfering, right? And you don't need to fret about me, I'm well capable of looking after myself.'

'Fine,' said Elinor, relieved he was allowing her to tag along with him.

They went up to Richard, who looked puzzled to see them approaching him.

He was a tall man but not as big as Leo. He had Celtic black hair and his eyes were clear blue. His features were harsh, his skin weathered to a tan and he carried himself with awkwardness in his suit. It was clear he was more at home out in the fields than at a social gathering. Similar to Leo, except Leo preferred the water to the soil.

'Hello, Richard.'

'Hello, Leo,' said Richard cautiously. He was clearly wondering what it was Leo wanted to speak to him about.

'This is my niece, Elinor,' Leo said awkwardly, feeling introductions were needed.

'Hello, Elinor,' said Richard politely, nodding his head towards her.

'We were wondering if we could have a word with you about something. It's a little awkward, I'm afraid. We were just wondering if you could try and explain to us what's going on.'

'Sure,' said Richard, pulling out his bottom lip. Looking

briefly at the group next to him, he gestured towards the door.

'Would you rather we talked in private?'

'Yes, that would be a good idea,' agreed Leo.

Without saying anything more they all walked outside. Elinor shivered. Even with all the alcohol she'd drunk, she felt the chill in the wind.

'So, what is it you wanted to ask me?' asked Richard impatiently, as he watched Leo struggle with himself to begin the conversation.

'It's a little convoluted so bear with me,' said Leo eventually. 'You might've heard we had six men, who didn't speak a word of English, arrive on our doorstep in the middle of the night. That was in November. Then I heard from a friend that someone down the road from us had been noticing a white van turning up in the middle of the night, and this lady said she heard men talking a "foreign language". All of this, right next to the wheat field.'

Elinor had read about people going pale under their tan, but until that moment she'd never seen it. Richard Glynn had gone a shade paler as he stood watching them fixedly, a ghastly expression of horror on his face. Both Leo and Elinor knew straight away that Richard was aware of or complicit in what was going on.

'Anyway, I discovered a tunnel in Wine Cove,' said Leo, continuing implacably. 'But what worried me were the signs I saw of it being in active use. Torches in a waterproof bag, a cleat in the wall to moor a small boat. It looked very suspicious to me. So we went to speak to the lady and gave her our phone number to call if she saw anything of a clandestine nature taking place.'

Elinor and Leo looked expectantly at Richard but he said nothing. He was staring at Leo as mesmerised as a snake confronted with a wily mongoose.

'So she called me one night, saying the white van was back again,' continued Leo. 'Elinor and I went into the wheat field to see if we could figure out what was going on. And sure enough, we saw men coming out of a hole behind the hawthorn bush. Would you mind telling us what's going on? Because I do feel I have to report this to the authorities but it would be good to have a proper explanation.'

Richard licked his dry lips and again said nothing. Elinor could see his mind was whirring in many different directions as he thought about plausible reasons he could give them for what had happened.

Clearly none came to mind, because his shoulders suddenly dropped as if in defeat. They clearly weren't confronting a hardened criminal.

'What do you want to know?' asked Richard, stalling for time.

'Are you running a small smuggling operation into this country? With illegal immigrants?' asked Leo, going straight for the jugular.

Richard licked his lips nervously again. He then shrugged.

'I needed the cash at first,' he confessed, finally.

Elinor and Leo waited for him to elaborate.

'It's been a dire year for crops because of the weather. The politicians all bang on their drums about climate change but it's us farmers that are on the front line of it. And then again all of us farmers are struggling with the price of milk. The supermarkets are crushing us. I mean, four pints for little over a pound. It's insane...'

Richard's voice tailed off as though he'd realised his attempts to justify his actions weren't really going to cut it with Leo.

'How much money were you getting for doing this?' asked Leo, a frown between his eyebrows.

'About three grand a time.'

Elinor nodded, impressed at the amount of money people seemed willing to hand over to complete strangers for the chance to get into a country illegally.

'They just want to work. They're not a burden on the state. Half this country wouldn't function without cheap labour.'

'Yes, but it's illegal, Richard. A crime, in other words. As I'm sure you're well aware,' remarked Leo, angrily.

Leo rubbed his face wearily.

'Christ, Richard. What on earth? I mean how could you think you'd get away with this?'

'I did get away with it until you two came along,' said Richard aggressively, standing with his legs apart and his arms crossed defensively in front of him.

'How long's it been going on for?' asked Elinor.

Richard looked at her as though he'd forgotten she was there.

'I was approached by a fisherman at Padstow about four months ago.'

'And where are these men coming from?' asked Leo curiously.

'Where do you think?' answered Richard sulkily. 'France, of course. Where else?'

The door to The Ninth Hole opened behind them and Tony poked his head out.

'What's going on, guys? Everything OK, Elinor?'

Elinor looked quickly at Richard and straight away saw that

he didn't want anyone else involved in their conversation.

'We're fine, Tony. We'll be finished in a minute.'

'OK. Don't take too long, it's cold out there.'

The door clicked shut again, leaving the three of them standing outside with the wind gently ruffling up their hair and gusting against their chilly bodies.

'Richard, I am going to report that tunnel to the authorities and get them to close it up,' said Leo firmly. 'I'll say that I've seen teenagers using it and it's not safe. But what you're doing has to stop. If I hear or see anything suspicious going on, anywhere, I'll be going straight to the police next time. Understood?'

Richard nodded, looking relieved.

'Next time you're in financial trouble try legal ways of resolving it, OK?' insisted Leo. 'You're an intrinsic part of the countryside around here and a good farmer. Don't throw it all away. Try talking to us next time. We might be able to help you out.'

Richard released a long sigh of relief, reaching up a hand to his forehead and tilting his head backwards as if unable to believe his good fortune.

'Leo, thanks for this. I really appreciate it. I'm done with the whole thing anyway. It's cost me several nights' sleep and a lot of stress. It's not worth spending my life looking over my shoulder, waiting for someone to catch me out. I'm just glad it was you. And yes, next time I'm in dire straits I'll come to you for some advice.'

'Good lad,' said Leo, patting Richard on the back as though he was a young boy.

Leo turned and looked at Elinor.

'Right. I need to get home soon. I'm not as young as I used to be. Elinor, are you staying on?'

Elinor was finding it hard to keep up with Leo's sudden change of conversation.

'Umm. What? Yes, I was going to stay longer but I'm sure Tony's happy to take us back now. It doesn't bother me.'

'No, no,' insisted Leo. 'I'll head back on my own. I could do with the fresh air. I'll just go in and get my torch.'

Before Elinor or Richard could say anything, he walked off back into The Ninth Hole.

'Elinor, I'm sorry you got caught up in this,' said Richard, tentatively.

Elinor understood what reassurances Richard was looking for from her.

'It's OK. I won't say anything. I'm hardly blemish-free anyway. I've done plenty to be ashamed about in my life and made many mistakes, although thankfully nothing illegal.'

Richard flinched at the word 'illegal'. It certainly didn't sit comfortably with him. Elinor wondered what twists and turns life had given Richard to encourage him go down the road of illegal smuggling. Just like it was in Cornwall two hundred years ago, Richard's smuggling seemed to be an act of survival or desperation.

51

'Tony, where exactly are you taking me?' asked Elinor curiously as Tony took a left hand turn, instead of a right towards Trenouth. It was nearly midnight. Having helped José and Elena tidy up after the party at The Ninth Hole, they'd left later than they'd intended.

Elinor was beginning to feel drowsy too.

'I've a surprise for you.'

Elinor turned on her seat to observe him.

'Didn't anyone tell you I don't like surprises?'

'No, they didn't,' said Tony. 'And no, I'm not going to tell you what it is. You're just going to have to lump it until we get there. Which won't be long.'

Elinor gazed out of the front window in a huff, wondering what he was up to. They drove past Booby's Bay and then they were driving down a single-track road towards Trevose Head, the headlights of the car lighting the way directly in front of them. But although they couldn't see much in the darkness, Elinor could sense the wash of the waves and the wildness of the sea all around them.

A hundred questions were rotating madly in her head but she kept her mouth tightly shut. If Tony gave her any more of his wise guy backchat she'd be strongly tempted to slap him.

Tony drove right up to the lighthouse, turned in at the

entrance gates and parked next to a small cottage.

'Here we are,' he said, switching off the motor.

Elinor looked out at the bleach-white lighthouse and the neat cottage next to it. She'd walked on Trevose Head before, keeping to the footpath as requested by the National Trust so as not to disturb the birds' nests, but she'd never actually walked up to the lighthouse that was owned and managed by Trinity House.

'Tony, why are we here?'

'I've booked us Verity Cottage for a couple of nights. I thought we could do with a short break and I'm a little tired of working out the logistics to and from Wadebridge and even staying over at Trenouth.' He shrugged. 'I thought you might appreciate something a little different.'

Elinor placed her hand over Tony's and reached over to kiss him on the lips. Maybe surprises weren't so bad, she thought, when someone as thoughtful and considerate as Tony plans them.

They got out of the car, Elinor clasping her coat tightly to her, as the wind was stronger here on the headland and it was cutting straight through the flimsy material.

'What about Leo, Tony?'

'He knows all about this. And I've a bag packed by him for you here, but you'll have to excuse him if he's picked the wrong clothing out for you or put lots of extraneous stuff in it. He did his best.'

Elinor chuckled. Goodness knows what she'd find in the bag, but who cared?

Tony opened the door and they made their way inside. The cottage was beautifully neat and tidy. Elinor felt herself relax as soon as she saw how comfortable it was.

Tony had a quick look around the rooms and then selected the bedroom which had a view straight out to the sea. They could hear the water slopping, gurgling and hissing close by the walls of the house. Elinor wasn't used to hearing the ocean as close as this. Trenouth was hundreds of metres above sea level, situated near what used to be the remains of a clifftop fort. But here at Trevose lighthouse the sheer power of the ocean could be heard close by, like a living, breathing monster. Leo would have loved it.

They were so tired they collapsed into the bed, only to be woken in the early hours by the cheerful song of the skylark, ringing happily through the bright morning. Before Tony could reach out to her and pinion her in his arms, Elinor rushed to the window and pulled the curtains open. She looked down at the swirling, foaming water licking the rocks below them and at the sun reflecting shining points of light across the ocean that stretched away to infinity.

She turned to Tony.

'It's utterly beautiful. I could spend all my days looking at this and never grow weary of it.'

'I could say the same,' said Tony, watching her naked body with a deep lust in his eyes.

Elinor giggled and seductively walked back to bed to celebrate the beauty of the natural surroundings with a carnal act that now felt as natural to her as the coast...

'Imagine living here as a lighthouse keeper,' murmured Elinor later, as she lazed in bed, comfortably held in the close embrace of Tony's arms and looking out at the blue sky outside the bedroom window.

'The lighthouse didn't become unmanned and automated until 1995, so it wasn't so long ago that someone lived here as the lighthouse keeper.'

'No,' said Elinor wistfully.

'Are you thinking you wish you could be a lighthouse keeper? You're turning into another version of Leo,' observed Tony, thoroughly amused. 'You're falling under the spell of the ocean. Once you're under its enchantment it's very hard to escape its clutches.'

Elinor turned around to look pointedly at him, her head resting comfortably on the pillow.

'So says the man who's obsessed with surfing.'

'True. But I do spend more than half my life away from the seawater, surrounded by people. Life as isolated as the one Leo leads, or that of a lighthouse keeper, wouldn't be for me. I need to be with people.'

Elinor shrugged, still staring intensely into Tony's deep brown eyes.

'People, they're everywhere. There are fewer and fewer places in the world where you can be truly alone. I love the feeling when it's just nature and me. When there's nothing else out there. That's when I can breathe.'

Tony grinned at her passion.

'It still wouldn't suit me. We're different in that respect. It's just as well I like being with people as my job means I've to work with patients all the time.'

Elinor bent down and kissed him on the nose.

'Come on; let's not waste the morning. Let's get out there and enjoy the day.'

Tony reached out and caressed her breast softly, feeling its contours tenderly and rubbing her nipple with his thumb until it hardened.

'I don't see this as wasting the morning, Elinor,' he said, determinedly reaching over to kiss her on the lips.

Elinor gave up. She let the softness of his lips melt into the deepest part of her mind as she gave way to the urgings Tony was deliberately stirring up in her. She might be lost under the enchantment of the ocean but this man, who'd broken through all her barriers and stolen her heart, also bewitched her...

52

Elinor soon learnt that Tony liked springing surprises on her. Her habitual anxiety meant she liked to control every aspect of her life so living with Tony's unexpected outings took some adjusting to. But in the end she decided it was good for her to adopt some flexibility and to have a more chilled-out attitude towards the unpredictable events in her life.

Tony always tried to bear in mind her particular wishes and desires. If it hadn't been for that she would have given him a much harder time. How could she ever be annoyed with him when he'd gone to huge efforts to organise something he thought she'd enjoy? And for the most part he succeeded.

Their relationship had a strange elasticity to it. Elinor could only picture shoelaces to properly describe it. At times she and Tony were tied up tightly together, synchronising their time together with fierce intensity, and at other times the laces of their relationship were hanging loose, each of them doing their own separate thing and getting involved in their own interests and work.

She wondered if one day, once her wrist was fully healed, whether they'd be able to co-ordinate their passion for surfing. But that was an intriguing question for the future. Despite not being able to surf she often did go and sit on the beach, watching the surfers cruising on the waves with a hidden longing.

On the days Tony went out surfing, she would arrange to meet him afterwards to go to The Ninth Hole for a bite to eat. Often they found they needed to book a table because, as Elinor had envisaged, the golfers had discovered the comfortable eatery on their way around the golf course. So now the golfers were in direct competition with the surfers for a seat at The Ninth Hole, much to Tony's disgruntlement.

But Elena and José, of course, were delighted with this state of affairs and Elinor loved to see their cheerful demeanour as they served their clients.

Emotionally, Tony touched sensitive and vulnerable chords in Elinor that hadn't been played for a long time. Sometimes in his unconscious way he pushed things too far, his expectations of her were at times too high, and Elinor felt the shadow of failure and self-recrimination hover over her mind. But Tony, like Leo, never over-thought or over-analysed things, and so her mind was never encouraged to spiral out of control. Like the Biblical parable of the house built on the rock, Elinor felt she was on solid ground with the stability Leo and Tony brought into her life.

One Saturday Tony surprised her with a trip to the Minack Theatre in Porthcurno. It was an open-air theatre built into the rock which was in the most romantic location imaginable, perched high up on the cliffs with a stunning backdrop of the Atlantic Ocean.

The atmosphere was strangely informal, with people bringing picnic baskets and bottles of wine to the performances.

Tony and Elinor sat in the theatre at the end of March, in eager anticipation, to watch a production of *The Glass Menagerie* by Tennessee Williams.

Concentrating on the performance, Elinor found herself identifying strongly with the role of Laura, the mentally fragile sister in the play. In the production, Laura played with her glass menagerie, which was in itself a metaphor for her extreme vulnerability. Elinor found she was relating completely to Laura's desire to isolate herself from the outside world and to shield herself from its unkindness.

As the light darkened, the backdrop of the sea started fading and the lights focused everyone's attention on the actors, so Elinor felt herself increasingly sucked into the play in a most unhealthy way.

Later on, she didn't feel able to explain to Tony how she'd found the performance deeply moving but also extremely painful, tearing away at parts of her that she'd tried so hard to keep strong and complete.

She sat silently in the car on the way home, feeling raw and exposed but Tony, as was the norm with his forthright character, bludgeoned his way through her defences.

They'd been driving home for twenty minutes when he suddenly stopped the car on a side road and switched off the engine.

'What's wrong, Elinor?'

'I'm a little tired, that's all.'

Tony reached across and turned her chin towards him, searching her face with his anxious gaze.

'Not true. What's happened?'

Elinor lifted up her hand and pulled his hand away.

'Nothing, Tony. Nothing's wrong,' she said adamantly. 'We should get going.'

After an awkward moment, during which they sat in total

silence, Tony started up the car and drove off. He drove them back to his flat in Wadebridge as had been arranged between them before the theatre showing.

He quietly lifted Elinor's rucksack out of the car boot and they walked soberly up the stairs to his flat.

He opened the door and let Elinor in first. Elinor didn't miss his surreptitious glances at her as she walked wearily into the hallway.

As Tony disappeared into the bedroom to dump Elinor's bag, she wandered slowly down the corridor like a dazed sleepwalker. As soon as she reached the lounge she sank down into her favourite chair, the leather recliner. She gazed despairingly out of the window, trying to distract herself by watching the lights of the town below her. The tiny square lights outside the sitting room window were sharp little points of humanity, bravely fighting against the insidious darkness, reminding Elinor there was still life out there and a life worth living.

Insensibly, Elinor began to feel slightly better.

'Elinor, what are you doing sitting in the dark? You're starting to really worry me,' said Tony, perturbed, as he entered noisily into the lounge, disturbing the stillness of the night with his vibrant presence.

He walked up to Elinor's chair and leant over the top of it. Elinor reached up and grasped hold of his hand, pulling it to her cheek, taking comfort from its warmth.

'I'm sorry, Tony. But that play was a little too close to the bone. It gets me every time I read that play, but seeing a live performance like that, it shattered me with its pathos. *The Glass Menagerie* is a stroke of genius. Those glass figurines... It's exactly what you feel when you come out of a nervous breakdown. Broken, shattered, splintered. And even when they patch you up with medication, psychologists and psychiatrists, you're still damaged, fragile goods and always will be.'

'I'm sorry, Elinor. I should've researched the play a little more, but I'm no student of English Literature, as you can see from my bookcase.'

Elinor smiled wryly. Tony's bookcase consisted solely of sports biographies, mixed in with a few specialised books and files on medicine.

She stroked his hand, loving the feel of his solid fingers and the veins that stood out firmly from his skin.

'It'll be fine, Tony. Anxiety's totally unpredictable and irrational. How's it possible I can go surfing and nearly drown in a crazy, wild sea without having a single panic attack and yet suffer and struggle through a theatre performance? It makes no sense.'

'I understand what you mean. I see a lot of patients that find the unpredictability of their mental health the hardest thing to deal with. They don't know from one week to the next what is going to trigger the next episode, if they'll manage a week of work or not. Anything associated with anxiety is a horrible mental illness to have.'

'In one way having a relationship with you is hard because although I know you deal with patients with mental health issues, it's never the same as living it. And yet I am so thankful you're so grounded and rooted in yourself. It's a trial, I am sure, for you to have me by your side.' At this point Tony made a grunt of denial. 'But you're so substantial it helps me to break through the lies my mind feeds to me. Your presence pulls me out of the alternate reality I live in during my worst moments...'

They both stared out of the window silently for a few minutes.

'Are you going to make some space for me, greedy guts?' asked Tony eventually, getting down to what mattered to him the most and dealing with things, as always, in a more practical frame of mind.

Elinor smiled delightedly and stood up so Tony could take a seat on the recliner. She then dumped herself on his lap, letting him wrap his arms around her in a cocoon, sheltering her from the adverse winds roaring inside her mind.

By the time they went to bed her mind was shrouded in tranquillity once more, which promised to lead to a good night's sleep. Consigning what had been an unsatisfactory evening to oblivion, she willed herself to look ahead to the future. Tomorrow was another day...

53

The following day Tony and Elinor let themselves into Trenouth and made their way to the kitchen for a cup of tea. Tony would be heading back to Wadebridge later to prepare for the start of his working week but he liked to linger as long as possible once he'd dropped Elinor off at Trenouth.

They both enjoyed jumping down from the Cornish hedge and making their way along to Fox Cove for a breathtaking view of the surrounding countryside. Fox Cove was a beautiful cove with a sparkling white sandy beach at low tide and a long oblong rock in the middle of it that to Elinor's mind looked like an exact copy of a granite submarine. It was their favourite spot and Tony liked soaking up the beauty of it before beginning a hectic day in the enclosed environment of the surgery.

Today, as Tony and Elinor walked along the corridor to the kitchen, Elinor suddenly heard a familiar and feminine voice shout out:

'Is that you, Elinor?'

Elinor's heart dropped to her feet and she quickly clasped Tony's hand, looking up at him with horrified eyes. Before Elinor could say anything to him, a rotund woman with strawberry blonde hair appeared in the doorway to the dining room and grinned at the pair of them. She was dressed in a miniskirt and a revealing top, her face liberally plastered with make-up.

Her bold appearance was similar to what you'd expect of a madam from an upper-class sauna.

She came forward quickly with her arms open and gave Elinor a hearty embrace, squeezing her inanimate body with a great deal of vigour, before turning to Tony and subjecting him to the same treatment without the least hint of bashfulness.

'Hello, my darlings! I'm so, so happy to see you both.'

'Mum,' said Elinor, shell-shocked and struggling to get her words out. 'I wasn't expecting you. I mean, Leo said nothing.'

'I know,' said Elinor's mum, smirking with self-satisfaction. 'He had no idea! I took a flight to Newquay this morning and gave him a call from there.'

'Morwenna, stop frightening your child,' scolded Leo, making an appearance at the doorway. Elinor turned and fixed Leo with a meaningful look, which Leo returned complacently with a twinkle in his eye.

Elinor let her shoulders drop as her mind assimilated her mother's unexpected arrival.

'Tony, this is my mother, if you hadn't already guessed.'

'Pleased to meet you, Mrs Campbell,' said Tony courteously.

'Oh, gosh! Isn't he lovely, Elinor?' gushed Morwenna, batting her eyelids coyly at Tony in the most provocative way.

Tony looked completely taken aback and for once was speechless.

Mortified, Elinor gave her mum a determined push towards the dining room.

'Hands off, Mum! Honestly, you're an absolute embarrassment.'

They walked through to the sitting room, with Morwenna turning around briefly and giving Tony a lurid wink as he brought up the rear.

Once the others had sat down, Tony took a hot drinks order and escaped to the kitchen to get the kettle boiling.

Elinor turned to her mother and shook her head disapprovingly.

'You're going to frighten him off, Mum. You're overdoing it.'

'No, really, Elinor. I'm sure he's taking it in the spirit it's meant. It's not every day I get to meet such a handsome young man.'

'I can hear you!' shouted Tony through the kitchen hatch, before any more embarrassing confidences were shared.

Morwenna chuckled loudly.

'That's OK, Tony,' she yelled back. 'I've nothing to hide. And I've always been very attracted to modest young men.'

Elinor groaned.

'Mum, what are you doing here? And how long are you staying for?'

For the first time, Morwenna seemed to be a little disconcerted.

'I'm here to see you, of course! A week at Christmas wasn't enough for me. I never dreamt that you'd make Cornwall your home or that you'd stick to the place like a limpet. That wasn't my intention when I asked Leo to take you in.'

She turned heavily on the sofa to look at Leo.

'I blame you, Leo. You've taken my daughter from me.'

'I've restored your daughter to you, you mean,' growled Leo, unimpressed by his sister's accusation.

'Mum, are you sure there's nothing else going on?'

'All I wanted to do was to visit my only daughter,' protested Morwenna indignantly, not quite meeting Elinor's eyes.

'I presume you've taken time off work?' asked Elinor, puzzled

286

and wondering why her mother would turn up in the middle of the semester.

Morwenna worked as a hugely popular and successful lecturer in moral philosophy at Glasgow University. University rumours had it that Morwenna once managed to convert two-thirds of a first year class to vegetarianism during one of her lectures.

Subsequently, there'd been several complaints made to the department from the students' disgruntled parents, but these were brushed off by Morwenna as the result of society's latest creation: 'helicopter parenting'.

Morwenna bent her head to one side and looked at her daughter pensively.

'My students are on study leave this week, my love, and my PhD students can be managed remotely in any case... Thanks for the concern, though,' she added sardonically.

Tony brought through the drinks and handed them out. There was an uneasy silence as they all drank from their mugs.

Elinor pondered what kind of things would occupy her restless and dynamic mother during her stay. She didn't think walks along the coast would have much appeal. Anything could happen when her volatile mother was at a loose end, so it was important to find something to distract her.

'Elinor tells me you're interested in palm reading,' said Tony, curiously, after a few minutes.

Morwenna leaned over to him enthusiastically.

'Yes. Would you like me to read yours?'

Tony quickly tucked his hands into his pockets.

'No, I'm fine, thank you. But a lot of the surfing community are very into that kind of thing. That New Age stuff's big business here in Cornwall.'

'There's nothing "new" about palmistry,' rebuked Morwenna. 'It's been around for thousands of years. From before Christ was born, in actual fact. But, yes, I've heard that mystical things are immensely popular here in Cornwall.'

Silence fell once more until Tony eventually stood up and gathered up the mugs.

'Right, I'd best get going, Elinor. Nice to meet you, Morwenna.'

'Likewise,' said Morwenna, nodding at him with a small smile on her face.

Elinor was disappointed. She knew Tony had been expecting to stay longer at Trenouth. He was beating a hasty exit and she had no idea what his reasons were for doing so, but she sincerely hoped her mother wasn't scaring him away. Her mother's bark was always worse than her bite. Although on this visit she seemed to be even more full-on and over the top than usual. Strange. What was she up to? Elinor didn't know why but she could already foretell that her mother's visit was only going to bring trouble and misery.

54

Watching Barbara and her mother greet each other was like watching two stags circling each other, eyeing up each other's weaknesses, and ready to lock horns on the slightest pretext. Barbara, normally so friendly and effusive, was bristling with hostility. It didn't help that that Morwenna, almost as soon as she'd walked in the door of Barbara's studio, had chosen to aim the most insulting and barbed criticisms at Barbara's half-finished painting.

'Oh, Elinor. Please don't tell me this horrific, psychedelic painting is yours? My darling, what's happened to your art? I mean, look at it! It looks like a two year old has been having fun with a box of crayons. And what's it of, anyway? It looks to me a bit like a dustbin with its lid on the ground...'

'It's actually my painting and it's of Bedruthan Steps,' said Barbara, between tightly compressed teeth.

'Oh! Oh dear! I'm so sorry. I'm really mortified,' said Morwenna, holding her hand to her mouth in dismay. 'It was such a shock to see that painting, you see. Elinor's work has always been so refined and detailed...'

Elinor was starting to wish the floor would swallow her up.

'My name's Barbara Bligh,' said Barbara, holding out her hand but at the same time glaring at Morwenna aggressively.

They shook hands fleetingly, as if each found the other

contaminated by a hideous virus.

'I'm Morwenna, Elinor's mother. I'm sure she's told you all about me. We're so close,' effused Morwenna, grabbing hold of Elinor's arm and clinging to her determinedly.

'Mum! Get off! What's got into you?'

'What do you mean, my darling?' asked Morwenna, wounded. 'I was just giving you a motherly cuddle.'

She spotted Elinor's painting and sidled up to it.

'Ah, yes, this one I can see is by you, Elinor. There's no comparison. The talent in this one is so evident. It's of such superior quality...'

Elinor gasped at the malice in her mother's voice. Her mother was never malicious or mean. She always stood up to bullies of any kind. What on earth had come over her?

'Elinor, would you and your mother like a cup of tea or coffee?' asked Barbara in a resigned voice.

'Ehh. Yes, that would be nice,' said Elinor, flummoxed by her mother and struggling to think straight any more.

There was suddenly a loud crash as something big collided with the tiled floor.

Barbara was staring in disbelief over Elinor's shoulder. Elinor whirled around and saw her painting lying face down on the tiles.

'Mum, what have you done?' yelled Elinor in distress.

She raced across the floor to pick up her painting and as soon as she lifted it up she saw it was ruined. Oil paint always took a long time to dry and the picture had been freshly painted a couple of days earlier. It was now smeared from top to bottom and had left half its paint on the red floor tiles. The painting was unrecognisable and completely ruined. Elinor felt like sobbing. Her clumsy mother, in a matter of seconds, had destroyed hours of work.

Barbara still looked utterly appalled but Morwenna seemed to recover from the shock of the ruined painting pretty quickly. She walked rapidly across to Elinor and gave her a big hug.

'Don't you worry, darling. I'm sure it's fixable. You'll get it back to what it was. I'm so sorry. I hadn't realised how unstable the easel was,' she said, glancing across at the fallen object, which had toppled forwards onto the floor.

Elinor shook her mother off angrily and went across the room to place the painting safely against the wall in the corner. She then ripped off a large quantity of paper towel and poured white spirit onto it, falling onto her hands and knees to wipe up the sticky oil paint from the floor. She scrubbed ferociously at the stains. Tears had started to her eyes and she couldn't speak she was so distressed. Each oil painting was a unique work of art and she knew, no matter how hard she tried, it would never be the same as the one she'd lost on the tiled floor.

'My goodness, you've certainly managed to shake things up since you've arrived,' commented Barbara, in an arctic tone of voice.

'I don't need any sarcasm from you,' answered Morwenna crossly. 'You poor excuse for an artist.'

'Barbara! Ignore her, please!' called Elinor from the floor, where she had sat back up in surprise at the words coming out of her mother's mouth. Barbara, who looked like she'd been a hair's breadth from pouncing on Morwenna and beating her to a pulp, took a deep breath and moved to the other side of the studio.

Elinor stood up.

'OK, Mum. We're leaving now. Enough's enough. I don't know what's come over you,' said Elinor, her voice starting to break with emotion. 'Your personality's completely changed and I really don't know who you are any more. If you carry on like this, I'm going to have to take you to the doctor to get tested for Alzheimer's.'

'Good idea,' chipped in Barbara from her corner, unable to resist the temptation to stick her oar in.

Elinor pushed her mother out of the door before she had a chance to say the last word.

As they walked up the side path and towards Leo's Volvo, Elinor felt her anxiety building as she wondered what had happened to her normally kind mother. When Elinor had seen her at Christmas she had been her normal, bouncy self but it seemed that within the space of a few months she'd turned into a complete stranger. One, moreover, who seemed to be completely unaware how antisocial her behaviour was.

She had to talk to Leo about this when she had the chance.

55

'I love palm reading, Mrs Campbell!' enthused Elena, looking at Morwenna with childish eagerness. 'I even went one year to the Mind Body Spirit festival in London. It was amazing. So interesting! There was everything there from graphology to yoga to tarot reading. Mindfulness, of course, and Buddhist teaching. And then of course, the paranormal people... I wasn't so sure about them. They were a little weird.'

'There's plenty of the paranormal enthusiasts in Scotland. Edinburgh especially,' said Morwenna with a modicum of pride. Elinor didn't see how having a city full of ghosts was something to brag about but she kept quiet, happy to see the two enthusiasts gelling over a cup of coffee. Her mother had been very unpredictable recently so it was nice to see traces of her old self finally emerging.

'Nowadays there's even what's called the Extreme Paranormal Underground Ghost tour in Edinburgh,' said Morwenna confidentially. 'They go to Greyfriars Kirkyard as part of the tour. You know, Greyfriars Kirkyard is supposed to be the world's most haunted cemetery after dark. And in the Old Town there are the underground vaults where apparently they sealed in people dying of the plague. Loads of ghosts seen there.'

Elena shivered dramatically, enjoying herself hugely.

'That is too scary for me! I'd die of a heart attack if I went on that. I know I would! Mrs Campbell, I think we should do a palm reading event here! What do you think? We could get some of the surfers along. Many of them like this kind of thing.'

And just like that it was agreed that a palm reading afternoon was to take place on Friday that week, at The Ninth Hole. Elena was going to send out emails to everyone who'd signed up for The Ninth Hole's newsletter, inviting them along for an afternoon's palm reading and tea.

Elinor could only be thankful that her mother had a focus for her stay now.

Things had been fairly uneventful for the last couple of days, much to Elinor's relief, but she had a feeling that, like a volcano, the other side of her mother she'd seen recently was bound to erupt to the surface again.

Pleased that her mother had the palm reading event to occupy her mind with, she felt a little more comfortable leaving her to her own devices for a bit. Her mother never did things by half so there would be things like the palm reading costume to be decided on, products like hand sanitiser to be bought, and Elinor was certain Morwenna would be reading up on palmistry to make sure she was on point during Friday's sessions. Now that her mother seemed to be on good form once more, Elinor started to relax a little for the first time since her arrival.

Leo had burst out laughing when he'd heard about the horrible morning Elinor had endured at Barbara's studio with her mother. He bluntly dismissed Elinor's fears that her mother might be starting to have Alzheimer's, telling her not to be stupid. He tried his best to reassure Elinor, explaining that Morwenna had a very responsible job and there was no way she would've been able to get away with having Alzheimer's when so many people depended on her.

So everything more or less seemed to be on an even keel until the day Tony was due to return to Trenouth.

That day was a Wednesday in the middle of March and the early morning had been full of promise.

Elinor had opened up her curtains and gazed out at the blinding sunshine, feeling her heart open up like the petals of a flower unfurling in the warmth of summer. The seagulls were showing off their best acrobatics in front of her, diving and twisting like miniature aeroplanes, weaving expertly on the different air currents. Thrift was covering their Cornish hedge in a pretty pattern of pink pom-poms, the oversized heads bobbing and wobbling in the wind.

Everything on the coast seemed to be screaming out, 'It's spring at last!'

Elinor took in a long, deep breath and loosened the muscles in her neck. Her wrist cast had been taken off the week before and she was looking forward to chasing the waves in Constantine Bay once more. Her surfboard had been in the garage, unused, for almost seven weeks. Too long... Elinor decided to go and check it over later and make sure it was ready for its next outing.

She threw on her dressing gown and slippers and left the room to have some breakfast.

Elinor realised her mother wasn't at home, which was a little odd. She wandered slowly into the kitchen, noticing the bungalow was strangely silent without her vibrant presence. She quickly made herself a cup of coffee and then went to open the front door so she could sit on the slate steps and bask in the sunlight.

As soon as she opened the front door she saw Leo's Volvo had gone, which presumably explained her mother's absence. Elinor couldn't see her mother going for a morning stroll along the cliffs or down to the beach. She was the most sedentary person she knew.

Elinor swallowed the last dregs of her coffee and then left her mug on the slate steps.

She walked over to the garage and, with a great deal of effort, twisted and lifted the big metal door. Leo never locked the garage because in his view there was never any need. In all the years he'd lived on the clifftop his house and garage hadn't been broken into once.

She walked into the dusty space, brushing past the cobwebs that seemed to be an integral part of the garage and heading towards the back wall where the surfboards were positioned.

She placed her hands on her surfboard, checking expertly to see if it needed a new coat of wax and if any damage had occurred while she'd last been out to sea with it. During her last surf she'd been so consumed with the pain in her wrist, she'd never actually checked her surfboard afterwards.

She ran her hands gently across the surface of the board and when she reached up to its nose she perceived a bumpy ridge stretching across it. She turned the surfboard around and saw that the nose had completely cracked from side to side.

Elinor frowned.

Surely Tony would have warned her there was obvious damage to her surfboard? It wasn't the kind of thing a dedicated surfer would miss or forget because all of them formed close bonds with their surfboards. It was just the way it was. People became attached to their cars in much the same way.

Anyway, she was clearly going to have to take it to Newquay for repairs, at the first available opportunity.

She put the surfboard carefully back against the wall.

It was time for a jog along the coast to shake the fidgets out of her before her mother arrived back at the bungalow. With this in mind she raced to get dressed and within ten minutes she was jumping down from their Cornish hedge onto the narrow path that bypassed the clifftop.

She wandered along to the side of Warren Cove to have a look and see what mood the ocean was in, an unbreakable habit since she'd begun to surf.

As she watched the waves, rocking back and forth, she heard a shrill, faint wailing coming from somewhere close by. It puzzled her. It certainly wasn't a seagull's rasping cry. She was still struggling to place it when suddenly she heard the vigorous flapping of birds' wings.

She was familiar with *that* sound. The flock of doves that normally resided inside the cave roof at Warren Cove had been disturbed and in a blurred flurry of white they circled the cove and flew off at breakneck speed.

Elinor walked further along the cliff for a better view of the cove. She strode past the old grass trenches that were the remains of an ancient clifftop fort and looked down into the cove once more.

The tide was coming in, that much was obvious.

And on the pebbled beach, far below, there was a little boy, who could only be at most eight or nine years old, sobbing his heart out.

She recognised him. He was the next door neighbour's grandchild, who often stayed with his grandmother when the need arose for some childcare. Why he'd be here on a Wednesday when he should've been at school, Elinor had no idea. But there wasn't time to think about that now.

'Hellooo!' she called down into the cove.

The boy stopped crying suddenly and looked up in confusion. He soon managed to spot Elinor's head protruding from the side of the cliff, with the sharp sight small children so often have.

'Are you OK?' yelled Elinor. It was a stupid question to ask but she wasn't sure if anyone else was down there with the boy.

'I'm stuck,' shouted back the boy tearfully. Elinor's heart sank at his words. 'I got down here but I'm too scared to climb up. I'm scared...'

The boy began to break out into gulping sobs again.

God, thought Elinor, I don't know if I can climb down the steep cliff path. Leo would've done it in a flash but then again Leo wasn't at home. She knew Warren Cove had one of the easier cliff paths around this part of the coast but she had no head for heights, as had been proven the last time she tried to descend it.

She looked down again and noticed that already the seawater had inched up the beach. It wouldn't be much longer before the path out of the cove would be cut off completely. When the tide was fully in, the water was deep and dangerous in this cove, with strong currents at the entrance waiting to pull the unprepared out to sea.

Elinor ran up to the start of the path and started to climb down, not allowing herself to think about what she was doing. It was purely an instinctive response and she yielded to it. She knew that even if she'd left the boy to find help, she would never have been able to live with herself if something had happened to him while she was gone.

She had no choice but to climb down into the cove.

56

The start of the descent was easy enough. The top half of the cliff was earthy, with clumps of tough coastal grass to hold onto if she needed to. At the beginning the path was a gently descending zigzag, but before long she reached about a third of the way down and then it became steadily steeper and rockier.

Loose pieces of slate slipped away from the cliff face as she climbed downwards. She could hear the small fragments chinking against the cliff face as they bounced down hundreds of metres to the cove below.

It was at this point that Elinor began to stiffen with fright.

When she felt the hard, uneven granite under her hands and had to stretch with her feet to find a foothold, she began to panic. Stopping for a brief moment, she took deep breaths to try and steady her pulse.

The sobbing at the bottom of the cove had ceased, which gave her the encouragement to keep going. The boy clearly had faith in her accomplishing the descent and helping him out of the situation he found himself in. Somehow this implicit trust in her made her feel braver and encouraged her to believe she could manage what only a day ago would have been unthinkable.

She crawled slowly down the steep cliff face, not daring to look down but focusing solely on securing a safe grip for her hands and her feet. The mass of water at the entrance of the cove was heaving heavy sighs as it lapped and sucked at the rocks around it.

Seagulls were perched on precipitous ledges on the cliff wall, preparing for nesting time. They watched her descent with cold eyes, utterly scornful of her feeble and awkward movements, totally unthreatened by her poor agility.

At last, Elinor felt her hands touching the rough barnacled surface of the cliff rock and knew she was safe once more. She'd reached that lower fringe of rock that was always underwater when the tide was in.

Jelly-like, red-brown beadlet anemones dotted these slippery rocks, shaking like tiny blancmanges and belying their aggressive, hidden strength until the seawater covered them and their tentacles emerged to prey on drifting food.

Coloured periwinkles were scattered across the rock face too; some were large and barnacle-encrusted whereas others were delicate, miniature shells. Their shell colours ranged from deep, chocolate brown to lighter creamy brown, white tinged with green algae to Elinor's favourite bright orange or yellow.

The sturdy, pyramid domes of limpets also decorated these granite rocks, as did the blue-purple mussels. Thin, frail threads attached the mussels to the rock, whereas the limpets' muscular feet were bound to the rock with such strength it was like breaking through adhesive glue to pick one up.

Elinor moved downwards until she felt her feet touch the shifting stones of the beach.

At that point she stood up and looked back up at the sky. The cove seen from this angle, with its steep, dark grey walls encircling and towering above her, made her feel very claustrophobic.

Elinor soon discovered that down here at the bottom of the cove, the noise of the pounding seawater, the seagulls' screams and the shifting loose beach pebbles all echoed and were magnified threefold. It was like standing within an amphitheatre.

'Hello.'

Elinor turned around quickly and looked at the small boy behind her. His freckled face was tear-stained but he was smiling happily at her now. His spiky short brown hair reminded her of a half-fledged bird, as did his thin knobbly knees.

'Hello. What's your name again? Your grandmother's told me but I've forgotten.'

'I'm called Conan.'

Elinor had to restrain a smile. She didn't think anyone could possibly look less like Conan the Barbarian. She shook her head angrily. Her mind was drifting off at random tangents again, as it was prone to do when it was stressed.

'Hello, Conan! I'm Elinor Campbell. Your granny's next door neighbour. She'll be wondering where you are, so I think we should try and get you up to the top again, don't you?'

Conan nodded but tears started shining in his eyes again. Clearly the boy was utterly terrified at the thought.

Elinor bent down and put her arms around him.

'Look, Conan, I'm the most scared woman you'll ever meet. When I tried to come down here four months ago, I had to stop halfway down and my uncle had to help me climb back up. So I'm just as scared as you are. But you know something? You made it all the way down here and actually the climb back up is meant to be easier.' Elinor didn't know if this was true or not, but she was happy to tell a few white lies if it got Conan motivated to climb upwards. 'I'll be right behind you to talk to you and help you all the way, OK?'

Conan nodded silently.

'Right, let's get going. The sooner we start the better,' said Elinor, glancing at the restless seawater.

And with this the two of them started the ascent. Elinor chattered to Conan with an endless stream of inanities as they made their way slowly upward. At the same time as talking to Conan, she was trying to focus on securing her grip on the rock face and was frequently taking deep breaths so her fear didn't paralyse her as it had on so many other occasions.

'So, Conan, why aren't you at school today? By the way, I would try holding on to that rock over there.'

Conan, who'd stopped as his ascent was blocked by a large rock, obediently sidestepped it and reached across to pull himself up onto another rocky outcrop.

'The school called my mum because I had a temperature and wasn't well.'

Elinor, following close behind him, found it hard to pull herself up onto the rocks and could only be thankful for the muscles she'd built up when she was surfing.

'Mum was really mad because she had important stuff to do at work today, so she dropped me off at Granny's house. But Granny's not well either; she's in bed with bad arthritis...'

As Conan's voice faded a little, Elinor looked up sharply and noticed the distance increasing between them. Conan was more sure-footed than Elinor and was racing ahead of her.

'Hold on, Conan. I'm not as fast as you. You're really good at this and you're doing really well. Bear with me and I'll catch you up... That's it. Sorry, what made you escape from your granny's and go down into the cove?'

'My cousin dared me to go down last weekend when we were having lunch with Granny. He's called Edward.'

'So did you go down to the cove last weekend?'

'No, I was too afraid to. And Edward made me feel really bad. So I thought I'd see if I could do it today.'

'I understand.'

By this time they were nearing the zigzag earthy path leading on to the clifftop. The last stage, thought Elinor thankfully.

Now they were near the top, clumps of grass and clifftop flowers were coating the rock face on either side of them. With only a few more steps, they were both able to stand up and walk their way to the surface along the narrow, dusty path.

As soon as she set foot on the clifftop, Elinor flung herself down backwards onto the thick cushioned grass, staring up at the blue sky with intense relief. Such was her euphoria she felt as though the ground was moving and shaking beneath her.

Conan peered across at her anxiously.

'What's wrong? Are you OK?' he asked, standing next to her in confusion.

'I'm brilliant, Conan,' gasped out Elinor as she laughed insanely. 'Do you know, I would've never been able to do that if it hadn't been for you?'

Conan waited politely but it was clear he didn't know what she was talking about.

Which was just as well, thought Elinor. It really wouldn't have taken much for her to have chickened out and left Conan's rescue to someone else.

She stood up.

'Right, Conan. Let's get you back to your granny. Do you think she'll have even noticed you weren't there this morning?'

she asked, looking at him with a twinkle in her eye.

Conan smiled engagingly back.

'I don't know. I hope not.'

Unfortunately, their hopes weren't realised.

As soon as Elinor rang the doorbell Conan's granny yanked open the door and stared at them in disbelief, a hand raised to her chest.

'Oh, thank God! Conan, my love, where did you go? I was beside myself with worry. I was on the verge of calling your mother.'

At this, Conan looked seriously alarmed.

'Granny, you didn't call her, did you?'

'No, no, I didn't. But you can't disappear like that without a word of warning.'

'I know, Granny. I won't do it again.'

His granny reached across and pulled him into a hug. That should be punishment enough, thought Elinor amusedly, watching the expression of distaste on Conan's face.

'Right,' said Elinor. 'I'd best get going. I'm glad everything's sorted now.'

She stepped away to make her way back to Trenouth.

'Wait!' called Conan's granny. 'Where did you find him?'

Elinor paused for a moment. Conan was looking at her apprehensively.

'Oh, he wasn't far. He was only a few metres away. Conan seemed to be doing some nature exploring but you can ask him about it.'

'Oh, right. That's a surprise. I can't say I've ever seen him show much interest in nature before. Thank you for bringing him back. I was so worried.'

'No problem.'

Elinor raised a hand and then climbed back over the Cornish hedge of their garden. She then ambled five metres further down to make her way over the hedge leading to Trenouth's garden.

She was desperately keen to let Leo know about her bravery that morning. She knew he'd appreciate better than anyone else the massive challenge she'd undertaken by climbing down and up that cliff face.

57

'I'm very impressed, young lady. I never thought I'd see the day you'd make it down to Warren Cove. Especially not after your first attempt.'

Elinor drank a few mouthfuls of Yorkshire Tea as she sat on the sofa in Trenouth's living room. She sat back with a contented sigh, letting her head roll comfortably on the sofa's headrest.

'I know. I don't know what came over me. For one long moment I had to choose between my fear and anxiety and a small, vulnerable boy. A boy, moreover, who was in distress and, potentially, in danger too,' recalled Elinor, ashamed that there would even be a choice between the two. However, she now accepted that this was the debilitating nature of poor mental health.

She ran her forefinger over the top of the mug as she thought through the morning's events.

'I'm so glad Conan won over my fear. It goes to show that I'm recovered enough to override my instinctual panic. Which is fantastic. It's given me a real confidence boost.'

Leo ruminated for a moment.

'I had assumed surfing on those waves had given you a confidence boost in that regard,' he commented at last.

'Yes, it has done. Of course it has. Surfing frees me from fear because you have to think in the present and concentrate on outwitting the waves. Maybe that's what happened this morning. I had to act quickly and not over-think things. It's clear proof that the book *Feel the Fear and Do It Anyway* works.'

Leo rolled his eyes up to the ceiling in disdain.

'All that psychobabble. It is no wonder half the world has gone mad these days. When I was younger we were all so busy trying to survive and get by that we never had the leisure to get ourselves into those kinds of problems. Self-harm, suicide attempts, mental health issues... I'm pretty sure if you talk to anyone who comes from a Third World country, they'd be astonished to see how rampant these things are in the West.'

Elinor didn't say anything. Leo had been more than kind and patient with her mental health issues, but even he had limits to his tolerance.

She swigged the remains left in her mug of tea, lost in thought. Her erratic mother had texted her at lunchtime, letting her know she was delayed in Exeter. Where on earth was she?

'Leo, what's my mother up to? She's still not back from her shopping trip.'

Leo looked at his watch.

'You're right. It's nearly five o'clock. Most unusual. But then again, that's your mother for you. What are your plans tonight? Isn't Tony going to drop by?'

'Yes, I think he's planning to take me out for dinner at the Pig's Trough. But I haven't really had a chance to run it by Mum yet.'

'Oh, you don't have to worry about her. We've plenty of food in the house. She'll certainly not starve. Get yourself out there with Tony. Your mother's been monopolising a lot of your time.'

'I still don't think everything's quite right with her, Leo. I'm not sure what's going on. Would you mind trying to pry it out of her? I know something's bothering her.'

'I'll try but Morwenna's never been one to confide in me,' said Leo matter-of-factly, shrugging his shoulders. 'We've always been too different. Chalk and cheese, that's the two of us. You can't determine who you're going to get on with in your family.'

'You can say that again,' agreed Elinor, thinking about her Scottish cousins who seemed to her to regularly detest their siblings. Being an only child had its advantages.

They both heard a car driving up the gravel driveway and come to an abrupt halt. A car door opened. Elinor got up and looked out of the window.

'It's Mum! Good grief, it looks like she's bought up the contents of a costume department. Where the hell did she get all that from?'

Leo joined her at the window and watched bemused as Morwenna started carrying her things to the front door.

He left the room abruptly and walked quickly down the corridor to the front door. Once he'd opened the old door, he stared down at the pile on the doorstep.

'Morwenna!'

Morwenna lifted her head up from inside the car.

'Yes?'

'What's all this for? You're supposed to be leaving on Sunday! Are you planning on taking it with you?'

'No, of course not. Don't be so stupid, Leo. It's only for the palm reading afternoon at The Ninth Hole on Friday.'

Leo's frown cleared.

'Oh. I see. Are you renting all this stuff, then?'

Morwenna stood up with her hands on her hips.

'No, I'm not.'

'But, Mum,' faltered Elinor, thoroughly taken aback. 'This must have cost you a fortune.'

There was a blue velvet cloak that from its label looked to be from a vintage shop, a small, round marquetry table, a large tapestry hanging with magical symbols on it and an expensive-looking purple ball dress on a covered hanger from the John Lewis department store in Exeter.

Leo, who was usually frugal to a fault, sniffed in disgust and stalked back into the bungalow, not wanting to have anything to do with such pointless extravagance. Elinor, by contrast, was again wondering what had come over her mother. She knew her better than Leo and she wasn't normally a spendthrift. Was this a midlife crisis?

She bent down and picked up the ball dress, as well as the velvet cloak, and carried them through to her mother's bedroom. After laying them out carefully on Morwenna's bed, she returned to the front door to find the pile had grown again and showed no signs of slowing down.

By the time Elinor had helped carry it all into the bungalow, Morwenna's bedroom looked like a car boot sale. There were boxes of milk chocolate witches, a trio of fishermen's blue glass floats, silver bracelets with stars and moons hanging from them, a CD of Berlioz's *Symphonie Fantastique*, a box of little purple linen bags (normally used as favours at weddings), lavender air freshener, numerous candles, unusual silver candle lanterns and a rolled-up rug.

Elinor gazed at everything in shock as Morwenna, who was looking very pleased with herself, pottered about the room checking on everything.

The doorbell rang and Elinor raced out of Morwenna's room to answer the door, hoping and praying it would be Tony. When she saw his familiar features, she launched herself into his arms.

'Whoa! Elinor!' expostulated Tony in surprise, as he nearly lost his footing on the doorstep. 'What's going on?'

'My mother,' said Elinor, burying her face briefly in his soft cashmere jumper and clinging on to him as though she were clinging on to the last remaining piece of sanity in the world.

Tony's lips tightened into a thin line. So far he hadn't said a word in disparagement of Morwenna but Elinor could tell he didn't rate her very highly. Her flirtatious mannerisms when she'd first met him hadn't done her any favours.

'Let me dump my bag and you can tell me all about it,' he said shortly, stepping into the bungalow.

Tony walked down the corridor briskly. Once he'd entered into Elinor's room, he dropped his bag onto a chair and impatiently took Elinor into his arms. Before she could open her mouth he started kissing her hungrily, teasing her lips apart with his tongue. Elinor indulged him for a few minutes but then decided she wanted to talk to him about her mother and ask for his advice.

Every time Elinor tried to speak, though, he mischievously covered her mouth with his lips and prevented her from doing so. Soon they were laughing so much they were both forced to stop kissing so they could draw breath.

They sank down together onto the double bed so they were lying side by side, holding hands and staring up at the ceiling as they let their gusts of laughter peter out.

'I needed that,' said Elinor, wiping away her tears of laughter with her free hand.

Tony lifted the hand he was holding and kissed it tenderly.

'I can tell you what else I'm needing.'

Elinor groaned and rolled her eyes comically.

'It's OK, I can guess,' she said cheekily, rolling onto her side so she was facing him. 'Are we going out to dinner?'

'Yes,' said Tony, looking at his watch. 'I've a reservation for eight o'clock. That OK?'

'Yes, of course. Lovely. I haven't told Mum yet but I'm sure it'll be fine.'

Tony frowned.

'I didn't know you had to ask your mother's permission to go out for dinner.'

'No, I don't,' said Elinor hastily. 'It's just that she's been behaving so erratically recently. And I guess she did come to Cornwall to see me, too.'

Elinor found herself running out of excuses.

She wanted to tell him that her mother hadn't been herself recently. And she wanted to explain how, given her mother was being so irrational these days, it would be totally possible for her to object or get offended if Elinor went out to dinner without her...

And that even though Morwenna had taken herself out for most of the day, without any word of warning to Leo or Elinor, it was also entirely plausible that she wouldn't be able to see the hypocrisy in her unreasonable behaviour.

But Tony had had a long day at work and his mind was clearly set on other things. He reached over and pulled Elinor to him, sneaking a hand under her jumper to rub her nipples and stroke her breasts, knowing perfectly well that by his doing so she'd be unable to resist him.

58

'So tell me what's bothering you,' said Tony, taking a meditative sip from his glass of red wine.

They were both seated at a small corner table at the Pig's Trough. It was quiet, which wasn't surprising given it was midweek, but there were enough clients in the restaurant to make conversation comfortably intimate.

In the end, Morwenna hadn't raised any objections to them going out for dinner. She was dressed in her new purple ball gown at the time, so that might have had something to do with it. Either way, Elinor was enjoying the prospect of relaxing over a delicious meal in Tony's company.

'I'm worried Mum's starting to get Alzheimer's.'

'Any reason why?'

'She's changed. Her behaviour is different to normal. I mean, she was always quite full-on, but the rude way she behaved towards Barbara and her flirting with you, it's not like her. It's not the person I knew. And she's been doing some crazy things these past days too.'

A waiter arrived with their starters. He placed the plates neatly in front of them and, picking up their cutlery, they began to eat.

'Such as?'

'Sorry?' asked Elinor, through a mouthful of smoked salmon.

She thought of Leo's eating habits and had to choke back a laugh.

'What exactly has she been doing to make you think she has Alzheimer's?' asked Tony patiently.

'She disappeared off today on a shopping trip to Exeter. Elena has booked her in for a palm reading afternoon, at The Ninth Hole this Friday. So she comes back from Exeter today, having spent literally hundreds of pounds on a bootload of stuff for the palm reading session. A ball dress, a tapestry to hang onto the wall, candles, lanterns, chocolates, a small table, a cloak. I mean, it's utterly crazy for one afternoon event.'

'To you, maybe. But maybe she doesn't see things the same way. Maybe she's just having some fun.'

Elinor shook her head stubbornly as she neatly placed her fork and knife on her plate.

'She's never been one to splurge. She's always been especially careful with her money since she divorced my father.'

'But that was a while ago, wasn't it?'

Elinor took a mouthful of wine as she pondered this.

'Yes, it was a while ago. But call me a cynic, when someone's been a certain way for the better part of their adult life, I think it's unlikely they're suddenly going to change their habits.'

'Rubbish,' derided Tony.

'Rubbish?' repeated Elinor, beginning to feel the heat of her irritation mottle her cheeks. How dare he dismiss her worries about her mother like that?

'Yes, rubbish. We're all changing, all the time. You can't arrest the passage of time and we change with experience. Loads of people end up having a midlife crisis, for example. Maybe that's what this is.'

'Why don't you think it could be a mental condition like Alzheimer's?'

Tony waited until the waiter had cleared away their plates and then he leaned forward, putting his elbows on the table.

'She doesn't suffer from forgetfulness, does she?'

Elinor shook her head.

'She doesn't have any problems communicating? I mean, she doesn't struggle to remember certain words, does she?'

Again Elinor shook her head.

'Does she seem confused or disorientated? I mean, she's not getting lost easily or saying she's waking up in the morning and wondering where she is? That kind of thing.'

Elinor took a moment to think about this and then reluctantly shook her head again.

'Then I'm afraid you can only conclude that she knows exactly what she's doing. To be frank with you, Elinor, I got the impression she was out to rile me from the moment I met her. Don't ask me why but that was my feeling.'

Elinor's forehead creased as he finished talking. Tony reached across and gently rubbed away at the lines.

'Hey, we're out for a nice meal. Put those worries away. I'm sure everything will become clearer with time.'

Elinor reached up and grasped his hand. Holding his hand in hers, she smiled at him tenderly.

'You're right. I'm sorry. This must count as the biggest turn-off ever, talking about your girlfriend's mother over dinner,' she said.

'That would be an impossible feat.'

'What?'

'It's impossible for me to be turned off by you, Elinor. You could talk to me all year about your mother and I'd still fancy you like crazy.'

Elinor blushed under the ardent look in his eyes and picked up her glass of wine to hide her intense pleasure at hearing him voice his passion for her.

The rest of the meal passed by pleasantly and soon they were toying with their desserts. Elinor, who was feeling full to bursting, was enjoying feeding Tony some of her chocolate mousse when he dropped a bombshell.

'Elinor, I'd like you to move in with me. I'm tired of commuting backwards and forwards between West Hill and Trenouth. The flat's empty for me without you.'

Elinor sat back in surprise.

'So soon?'

'What can I say? Life's short. You have to live in the moment. I know you're the one for me. I'm not going to change my mind about that.'

Elinor could well believe that. Tony was like Leo, he had a will as unstoppable as the sea once his mind was made up. She wasn't going to dispute him on that point because she knew she'd end up like King Canute trying futilely to stop the sea's passage. But the very thought of leaving Trenouth was tugging painfully at her heartstrings...

59

The next morning Elinor ambled contentedly along to the kitchen, only to find Tony and her mother were there before her. Tony was holding a mug of coffee in his hands but his stance was rigid and tense. Puzzled, Elinor looked at him and saw his chocolate-brown eyes were blazing with anger. After hesitating for a moment, Tony brushed past her and exited the kitchen.

Elinor turned to her mother and sighed.

'What's going on, Mum? What have you done now?'

'Nothing at all,' protested Morwenna adamantly. 'I've done nothing. And if he says I have, don't believe him.'

'Given your behaviour over the last few days, I think I'd believe him, Mum. What games are you playing?'

Elinor stared sternly at her mother but if she hoped to abash her she singularly failed. Morwenna pouted and shrugged her shoulders.

'If you're going to believe him rather than me, there's nothing else to be said.'

Morwenna put her mug in the dishwasher and stalked out of the kitchen. Elinor walked back to her room, only to find Tony packing his bag. Elinor looked at him in dismay.

'Tony, you're not leaving?' she faltered.

'I'm afraid so. If I stay any longer I might end up belting

your mother. So in the interests of our relationship I think it's best I leave.'

'What did she do?'

'She made a pass at me.'

'Oh, come on, Tony. I can't believe that's true. You must have mistaken her natural tactility for a pass.'

Tony straightened up and glared at Elinor.

'She grabbed my crotch, Elinor. I don't think that was by accident, do you?'

'Oh God, no!'

'Yes, Elinor. I'm sorry but that's the truth. Look, I'll give you a call later on. I'm going to need to cool down first.'

With that Tony picked up his bag and made his way out of the house.

Elinor felt a wave of such red-hot fury overwhelm her that she was sure she'd burst into flames. She stomped down the corridor and angrily opened her mother's bedroom door, without even the courtesy of knocking first.

Morwenna was sitting dejectedly on her bed amongst a complete carnage of miscellaneous items, looking a little like the portrait of General Marius sitting forlornly amongst the ruins of Carthage.

She looked up at Elinor.

'What is it, darling?'

Scowling at her mother, Elinor suddenly felt her rage slowly draining away as she noticed how old and worn she looked in her silk pyjamas and without any make-up. Her mother seemed so vulnerable these days. She seemed to be on a path to self-destruction and at the end of the day she was only making things harder for herself.

'Mum, you can't carry on like this,' Elinor said sadly.

Her sympathetic tone seemed to strike a chord in Morwenna. Morwenna looked out of the window as though trying to restrain her tears. After a minute or two of silence, Morwenna turned to face Elinor again.

'I'm absolutely fine, Elinor. I really don't know what you're talking about,' she said brightly.

At that point Elinor gave it up and returned, defeated, to her room. Three more days to go, she said to herself, just three more days. Then peace will be restored once more.

60

Elinor began to notice her upper shoulders and neck start to ache with the tension. She started to rub the back of her neck, pushing aside her thick brown hair with impatience. Ever since Tony had said he loved her hair loose she'd given up wearing a ponytail, but today she wished she'd tied it up.

She was sitting in the dining room of The Ninth Hole, amongst many of her friends and acquaintances who were waiting to have their palms read.

She'd watched several people walk out of their session with Morwenna in tears and leave in a hurry. Which was a little odd.

And which wasn't exactly what Elena had planned on when she'd set the event up. Elena had been hoping people would stay on and have some afternoon tea. In anticipation of this she had cooked a huge batch of scones. But today it looked as though nobody was interested in hanging on after they'd had their palms read.

What on earth is she telling them, Elinor wondered to herself. She watched Jennifer going in to have her palms read and decided she'd ask her how it went afterwards. As Jennifer walked back into the café after her session, Elinor hurried up to her.

'Jennifer, did everything go OK?'

Jennifer looked at Elinor implacably.

'No, it didn't go well. I'm sorry if it hurts you but your mother is a first-class bitch, if you want to know the truth. Nobody in their right mind would say the things she said to me just now.'

Jennifer strode angrily to the entrance of the café and walked out without a backward glance.

With a sense of impending doom, Elinor looked around the room. She decided she was going to have to take control of the situation. Thinking spontaneously wasn't an asset of hers, but she decided desperate times demanded desperate measures.

She pretended to look at her phone for a minute and then stood up.

'Right, everyone!' she yelled, above the babble of voices. 'I'm afraid my mother's had an urgent call from home. We'll have to reschedule the palm reading for another day. I'm so sorry, everyone.'

There was a collective groan from everyone gathered and then Elinor was pelted with questions. What was wrong? Was her mother going to be OK? Could they help at all?

Elinor managed to put her amateur acting skills to work and within a short space of time had cleared out the café, promising they would do it again soon.

She then sat down on a chair and sank her head down into her hands. A little while later Morwenna appeared in the doorway, looking absurdly incongruous in her floor-length silk ball gown.

'Elinor, where is everyone? I've been waiting for ages.'

Elinor lifted her head and gazed at her mother, too emotionally exhausted to say anything.

Her mother looked around the empty room.

'Did you say something to them?'

'No, Mum, you did. Congratulations. You probably lost me a good few friends this afternoon.'

'Oh, honey. Don't be so silly. It's only a little harmless fun.'

Elinor smiled sceptically.

'Really? "A little harmless fun?" Is that what you call this week from hell?'

Morwenna opened her mouth to speak but Elinor lifted up her hand.

'No, don't say anything more, Mum. I'm tired of your lies.'

'But...'

'No, I don't want to hear it.'

She saw Elena standing in the doorway looking confused.

'Elena, I'm really, really sorry. I had to cancel the palm reading. My mother was upsetting everyone with the things she was foretelling. I saw a few people leaving in tears and I decided we had to stop.'

'Who gave you the right to cancel my palm reading event, Elinor?' asked Morwenna in a furious voice.

'You did!' yelled Elinor, unable to tolerate her mother's misbehaviour any more. 'You've bloody well been causing havoc since you got here! I just wish you'd go home and leave me! I've had enough of your idiotic behaviour!'

Elinor glanced apprehensively for a moment at Elena but she didn't seem to be remotely shocked. In fact, she seemed totally unfazed. Maybe her Spanish upbringing helped in this respect.

'Elinor, why would you speak to me like that?' asked Morwenna, bursting into tears. She sobbed loudly, with fat tears streaming down her face and her shoulders shaking, but Elinor remained stony-faced.

'Mum, I've had enough of your disgraceful behaviour. You'd better tell me what's going on or there's a good chance our relationship will never be the same again.'

Morwenna collapsed onto a chair and sobbed her heart out. Elena, soft-hearted as always, went up to Morwenna and patted her heaving shoulders awkwardly.

'There, there,' she said consolingly. 'Elinor doesn't mean the things she say. All will be better in the morning.'

'I bloody well do mean the things I say, Elena. You've no idea what a nightmare she's been.'

Elinor waited with her arms folded at the other side of the room. Morwenna's sobs slowly but surely died down and within a few minutes Elinor caught her mother peeking hopefully at her. Elinor stayed where she was and stared angrily back at her. She saw her mother blench as the realisation that she'd seriously incensed her daughter hit home.

Morwenna looked down at her hands, her upper lip quivering.

'I'm sorry,' she whispered.

'What did you just say, Mum?' asked Elinor impatiently.

'I said I'm sorry, OK? I'm sorry I screwed everything up for you. I couldn't help myself. I was so utterly distraught when I heard you had no intention of returning to Glasgow. And yet you didn't seem to spare any thought as to how *I* would feel. You were too busy swanning around with your new Cornish friends and your new boyfriend.'

The venom in Morwenna's voice seemed to shock even Elena.

'I've nothing left,' continued Morwenna, in a milder tone of voice. 'You're the only one who makes my life worth living. My life's just empty without you. And I so wish I'd never sent you to stay with Leo. At the time, I just didn't know how to snap you out of your issues.'

There was a silence in the room while all of them remained lost in thought.

Morwenna reached up and grabbed Elena's hand.

'I'm sorry I made a mess of your event, Elena. I wasn't planning to, at all. I promise you. I don't know what came over me.' She turned to face Elinor. 'All I wanted to do was hurt you, Elinor, the way you hurt me so callously when you told me you didn't want to come back to Glasgow.'

A thought popped into Elinor's head. She stood up angrily.

'Mum, was it you that cracked the top of my surfboard?'

Morwenna looked at her daughter aghast. She didn't say anything but she didn't need to. Her face said it all.

'Ahhh! Mum! I can't believe you!' shouted Elinor, making her mother flinch and cower in the corner.

'I never realised how controlling you were until today,' continued Elinor, shaking her head in bemusement. 'If you'd loved me at all you'd have let me cut myself loose from you. You'd have set me free. You can't live your life through me. That's what went wrong with you and Dad.'

'Listen, you keep your dad out of this,' spat Morwenna, looking thoroughly ruffled.

Elinor bit her tongue, rolled her eyes and looked across at her dejected mother.

'What do we do now?' she asked.

Morwenna looked at her pleadingly.

'Are you sure you won't come back?'

Elinor shook her head firmly.

Morwenna bent her head down sadly.

'Listen, Mum, you get loads of time off with your job. We

could do more stuff together. Like weekends away, that kind of thing. It's true I hadn't really thought about the repercussions for you when I decided to stay. You see, my stay in Cornwall's healed me. When you find that kind of relief you never ever want to go back.'

Morwenna nodded resignedly.

'I can see that, Elinor. I always did see it. I'm just sad I wasn't the one to help you. But you're right. You're stronger down here. As I said, I'm sorry for being so unreasonable.'

Elinor went and wrapped her arms around her repentant mother, who started to sob again. She didn't know if her mother was ever going to get used to the idea of her living permanently in Cornwall, but she hoped she would.

Elena, who'd been watching their interchange with all the intense fascination of a soap opera addict, clapped her hands happily and announced she would make them all some tea and scones.

61

'She'll be fine. Don't you worry about her,' said Leo, handing Elinor a cup of tea after dropping Morwenna off at Newquay Airport.

'I know, I think she'll be fine,' agreed Elinor. 'I'll make sure I keep in regular contact with her.'

They both drank their tea in companionable silence as they sat in the living room at Trenouth. Elinor couldn't help feeling guilty about it but she'd felt a deep and profound relief when she saw her volatile mother making her way through security. Hopefully, over time they'd be able to patch things up but for now she needed the calm of a normal, run-of-the-mill day.

Occasionally, the rustle and cawing of a jackdaw that had built its nest on top of the chimney echoed down. Elinor hoped it wouldn't take it into its head to explore further down the chimney as had happened already a few times, according to Leo. He'd become an expert at trapping the birds and releasing them back to the outdoors.

Elinor shut her eyes briefly, enjoying the peace. But something was niggling inside of her, refusing to let her relax.

'Tony's asked me to move in with him,' Elinor said suddenly, voicing her concerns at last.

Leo nodded.

'I thought the day would come,' he said sagely.

'But this place feels like home to me. I love it so, so much. I'm feeling torn in two, to be honest with you, Leo.'

'I've been thinking about you moving in with Tony for a little while. I think it's the right decision for you both. But I was also thinking how you're sharing studio space with Barbara at the moment. Come the summer, that woman has so many visitors it'll be like Clapham Junction over there. I know you'll hate it.'

Leo stood up stiffly and walked over to his desk to pick up a folder. He returned with it to the coffee table. Opening it up, he pulled out a large chart and smoothed it carefully on the table.

'I've had an architect out to look at converting the garage into a studio space. It would mean inserting a door on the side-wall and a large window right across the area where the garage door is, which is south-facing. He's also suggesting putting a skylight in the roof. Both would have blinds, of course, so if it became too sunny you could dim the light.'

'You can't do that!' exclaimed Elinor, aghast. 'You love that garage! Seriously, this would be a very bad idea. You'd regret it.'

Leo who'd been studying the building plan, looked up at Elinor.

'I have never in my life bothered to waste any time on regrets. You should know that by now. I've thought it all through and made up my mind. You're not going to be able to change it now. To be honest with you, I've enjoyed having you around and it would be lovely for me to see you paint here.'

He leaned back onto the armchair.

'This way you can use Trenouth as your work space and you don't have to separate yourself from everything you love around here,' he said calmly. 'I know I couldn't do it. But it's also true you and Tony need your own space together. This would be the best of both worlds.'

Elinor swallowed the lump in her throat.

'What can I say, but thank you? Thank you so much. You've made things so much easier for me. It would've broken my heart to leave Trenouth for good.'

Leo looked pleased with himself. He crossed his legs and folded his arms, beaming back at Elinor.

'There's only one small problem left,' he said.

'Oh? And what's that?'

'You're going to need to get yourself a car to run around in.'

Later that day as the sun was setting, Elinor jumped over their Cornish hedge and made her way along the coast path until she reached the path bypassing Fox Cove. She climbed over the rough wooden stile and breathed in the heady scent of the gorse flowers. Walking along the dusty path, she listened to the waves gently murmuring far, far beneath her.

The tide was in.

The ocean was looking docile and welcoming today. Only the dark streaks of the ocean's currents, out of land's reach, hinted at its more dangerous intentions.

Elinor sat down on the bench, enjoying the peacefulness of the scene before her. It was half past eight so most people were probably away preparing, or having, their dinner. The sky was turning a vibrant orange just above the horizon, with bright pink clouds arching around the dying sun in homage to its beauty and power.

She must have been sitting there for around twenty minutes when someone suddenly cupped her face with their hand and kissed the side of her cheek. She turned around smiling happily, knowing intuitively who it was.

Tony settled himself down on the bench next to her and stretched an arm behind her. Starting to feel a little chilly now the sun was sinking further she huddled into him, shielding herself from the gentle breeze that was lightly puffing from the west.

'How's your day been?' he asked.

'Good. I've had an eventful week but things are calming down nicely.'

Tony nodded, staring out to the far horizon.

'Have you given any more thought to moving in with me?' he asked casually, still gazing fixedly into the distance.

Elinor could tell he was making himself very vulnerable asking her for a second time. She wrapped her arms around him, trying to reassure him.

'Yes. Let's do it, Tony. To be honest with you, the thought of leaving all of this was killing me,' she said, nodding at the view. 'Leo, and Trenouth too, they mean so much to me. I'm not sure I can really explain why. It could be the security and stability, or maybe I'm simply hooked to the ocean. But Leo told me today that he's decided to convert the garage into a studio for me, so I can paint there. Which means I can be with both you and Trenouth.'

Tony dipped his head and kissed her softly on the lips. She could feel his happiness vibrating through him. She put her hands up to his face, brushing away his thick, fair hair and studying his kind brown eyes as they looked down at her. She smiled at him tenderly as he pulled her even closer to him. Then they turned to face the ocean and watched the molten sun melt into the water as it disappeared quickly over the horizon.

She knew she'd never really be free of her anxiety but for the first time in a very long time she looked forward to the future with hope in her heart. She already had two commissions to work on, she had a solid relationship with Tony and Trenouth was now a permanent fixture in her life. It was a far cry from the days when she used to lie curled up on her bedroom floor in Glasgow, the tears dripping down her face and onto the floor as she wished she could join Mark in the afterlife.

As she and Tony walked back along the cliff edge, breathing in the elixir of oxygenated air with its salty tang, she silently sent a prayer heavenwards, asking that the bubble of happiness that surrounded her now would last for years into the future. She'd suffered for long enough and now was the moment for the sea to erode and smooth the scars left in her soul from the past.

62

The wind blowing offshore combined with the groundswell had created near-perfect conditions for surfing.

These waves were six-foot grinders, powerful breaking waves that were hammering down onto the restless surface of the sea. Rolling in from the left hand side were beautiful barrel waves with their foaming lips curling over delicately.

As she lay on her front, two of the guys started gesturing manically and calling out to her in their surfer dialect.

'Akaw! Akaw!'

Elinor turned to look behind her and raised her thumb to them.

A huge, perfectly shaped wave was making its way rapidly towards her. She started to paddle fast with her arms, moving with precise, almost mechanical actions, trying to keep up with the wave's momentum.

As though it was a living creature she suddenly felt the wave nudge her surfboard upwards. Once she felt it take hold of her, she lifted herself quickly up onto the waxed surface of the surfboard, only to find herself sliding down rapidly on the vast glassy face of the wave.

Instinctively she let her surfboard slide horizontally to the right, desperately trying to build speed so as to outrun the white tail of spray forming on her left hand side.

There was no fear involved any more. She'd let go of that a long time ago.

Time suddenly slowed as she stood on the surfboard, with every sense on alert and her instinct guiding her every move. She was living in the moment and for a short time she felt free, soaring and hovering on the harnessed power of the ocean.

Almost in a hypnotic state, she savoured the taste of salt in her mouth as the spray stung the skin of her face. She could hear the deep boom of the rollers crashing down ahead of her onto the shallow shelf of sand. The wind was howling loudly in her ears, taunting her with defeat.

She sped downwards across the long length of the wave, feeling the power of it fading as it came closer to shore. Bit by bit she urged her surfboard on, trying to keep its speed flowing. Finally when the wave was spent, she skated briefly across the flat surface at the very edge of the ocean, before letting herself fall gracefully into the foamy embrace of the broken water.

In that brief moment when she had been flying high on the wave her habitual anxiety had disappeared, almost as though the ocean itself had decided to take the burden of her anxiety off her. It was those brief moments of mental freedom that made her present life bearable.

The ocean had saved her. Literally.

ACKNOWLEDGEMENTS

I feel enormous gratitude for Cathy Tingle, my literary guardian angel, who has watched over my writing like a hawk.

Thanks are also due to Stephen, my wonderful husband and biggest fan, for his faithful encouragement even though he has no interest in reading novels.

My appreciation also goes to Charlotte Mouncey for her patience, wonderful cover work and all the hard graft in putting the book together.

Finally, thanks to James Essinger for his insightful, caustic and often humorous commentary, and his willingness to take on my books.